"…a dramatic and tension-filled tale of
her memory of a perfect father with the
he was… Recommended for readers who enjoy sports-themed novels with complex family dynamics."

—**LIBRARY JOURNAL**

"Clarice James is a sensitive and deft writer who has not only an authentic relationship with the Lord but a powerful relationship with language. You can enjoy both in *Double Header*."

—**DAPHNE SIMPKINS**, author of *Nat King Cole: An Unforgettable Life of Music* and The Adventures of Mildred Budge series.

"The loving sibling rivalry between Casey and her brother in *Double Header* is a hoot! I loved the honest portrait of Casey and was oh-so-able to identify with many of her foibles."

—**STEPHANIE PRICHARD**, co-Author of *Stranded.*

"*Double Header* gripped me from its opening sentence. I couldn't stop until I'd laughed every last laugh the book elicits and solved each mystery weaving its way through the story with tentacles that grabbed my heart and wouldn't let go."

—**TERRIE TODD**, author of *The Silver Suitcase*

"*Double Header* knocks it out of the park. The characters became instant friends and caught me wanting to resolve their predicament. Honest relationships, real dialogue, and vivid color attend this mystery of the heart."

—**SANDRA LOVELACE**, co-author of *Children in Church: Nurturing Hearts in Worship*

"*Double Header* is sketched with excellent character development and dialogue that will make you feel like you're sitting on the sidelines watching this story unfold."

—**STACEY THUREEN**, writer, speaker, and patient advocate

"James pits hyper-organized Casey Gallagher against her brother laid-back Griffin McGee for laughs and smart dialogue. But the story turns into an exploration of loss, regrets and reconciliation, as Casey learns that there are aspects of her life that she can't—and shouldn't—control."

—KATHLEEN D. BAILEY, journalist at Nutfield Publishing of New Hampshire.

"Clarice's clear, energetic style moves at a comfortable pace through multiple subplots that she has cleverly interwoven to surprise and entertain us at just the right moments to keep you turning pages. The deeper you get into this Boston-based story, the more you're drawn into the emotional journey that shines a divine light onto very likable, everyday familiar folks."

—REV. TOBY QUIRK, Army retired Lt. Colonel, author of *Letters from a Country Pastor* and *A Squirrel in a Bottle*

"Issues of faith, a father's infidelity, a surprise half-sibling, are all handled with grace."

—SOPHIE CUFFE, co-author of *Arrow That Flies*, Blood Brothers in Christ series, Book One

"The characters Clarice dreams up are so real you wonder if they are people from her own life, or whether you'll run into them at the mall or your next trip to a Red Sox game. The plot of the book moved along at a good pace, keeping me engaged and interested until the very end."

—JEREMIAH PETERS, author of *A Message to Deliver*

Double Header

DOUBLE HEADER

Clarice G. James

Mountainview Books, LLC

Double Header

Edited by Carol Kurtz Darlington

Cover photograph of Boston © Sean Pavone | Dreamstime
Cover photograph of woman © Stanjoman | Dreamstime
Cover photograph of field © Maunger | Dreamstime
Cover photograph of hat © lokisurina| istockphoto
Cover photograph of old paper © Avalon_Studio| istockphoto

ISBN: 978-1-941291-24-5 (paperback)
ISBN: 978-1-94129-25-2 (ebook)

To my father, Leo Gregoire, for showing me the power of dreams, and to my mother, Yvette Gregoire, for teaching me the value of working for them.

Acknowledgments

This novel—and any others I write—is all my husband's fault. When I first met [Ralph] David James in 2005, I was in the midst of writing a memoir about my past seven years as a widow. When I expressed concern to him about people recognizing themselves in my story, David suggested I turn it into fiction. A logical solution to my emotional dilemma. And there you go—that's the perfect tagline for our marriage. David's been making my life simpler and less confusing since the day I met him. I am thankful every day for his love, patience, kindness, tech support, and quirky sense of humor.

My protagonist, Casey Gallagher, has many of the good qualities of my daughter, Erin Hennessey. Thanks, Erin, for your knowledge of running, Fenway, and close mother/daughter relationships. Mostly, thanks for letting me help decorate your house when my creative juices needed time away from the computer.

Thanks to my two sons, Christopher and Darby MacEacheron, mainly for their sports knowledge and humorous bantering. You gave me plenty of material for Casey and Griffin, my bickering-sibling characters. I believe Darby came up with the name Double Header. But I'll let you two argue that point.

Thanks also to two of my grandsons, Michael Hennessey and Darin Flynn MacEacheron, who inspired key characters—Boston Red Sox pitcher Mike Hennessey and catcher Darin Flynn. First you lent me your names; then I incorporated some of your physical and personality traits. Whenever I pictured you two while developing these characters, it always made me smile.

I am grateful for my fellow writers and critiquers who helped me in various ways. Here are only a few of them: Mike Anderson dug for the spiritual lessons; Ellen Davison taught me how to show not tell; Lisa Lawmaster Hess corrected my tenses; Cricket Lomicka pushed me to use all five senses;

Steven Moore deleted needless blabbering; Jeremiah Peters taught me about tension; Teresa Santoski inspired me with her flawless passages; Terrie Todd uncovered my inconsistencies; and my husband David let me use many of his funniest lines.

Thanks to my family and friends for not running away every time I brought up my writing. Thanks as well to my advance readers. Your encouragement and suggestions made my book better.

A big thank you to my professional team: my agent Joyce Hart of Hartline Literary Agency for her wisdom and experience; Shaun Kuhn of Suzy-Q Author Coaching for his marketing expertise and sense of humor; and publisher C. J. Darlington and the staff of Mountainview Books, LLC for a job done well. Above all, thank you to Jerry B. Jenkins. Without his generosity and desire to give back, there would be no Operation First Novel contest to enter.

One last thank you to Mr. James Ruberti, my English teacher at Barnstable High School (Cape Cod, MA) decades ago. He made putting words together fascinating and fun. I had a chance to thank him some years back, but it's worth doing again. Excellent teachers deserve extra credit.

Finally and for always, thank you, Lord Jesus.

1

I met my half brother the week I turned thirty. I knew it was him; he was wearing my late father's boots.

Six months earlier, my younger brother Griffin and I were escaping the cold for four days of sun and research in Ft. Myers, Florida. With our SUV running outside Terminal C at Logan International in Boston, my husband Sam jumped out to help Griffin and me with our luggage. "Listen up, Casey," he started.

"I know, be vigilant." I took my bag from him. "Wish you were coming with us."

"To watch you work? No way. Besides, when we go away," Sam said loud enough for Griffin to hear, "it will be *alone*."

"Cramp your style, do I, Lieutenant Gallagher?" Griffin faked a body check on Sam. "This coming from a guy who spends all his nights with cops and robbers."

I pushed on the car's lift gate to make sure it was latched. "Stop yakking, you two, before we get a ticket."

The biting winds nipped at my resolve to leave my wool coat behind, but I held fast, thinking back on the heat of southwest

Florida. Sam, my cop in shining armor, finished his condensed version of his hyper vigilance speech, kissed me good-bye, and drove away.

Our annual trek with Dad to the Boston Red Sox training camp had been a tradition since we were kids. After his death three and a half years ago, it became more about our memories and new material for Double Header, our sports column. Our purpose this trip was to observe the subject of all the chatter, pitcher Mike Hennessey. Against all odds, we hoped to score an interview with this local boy from South Boston.

I stood on the platform shivering, not sure if it was due to the temperature or from laughing at Griffin, whose prized, autographed baseball cap had taken flight in the wind tunnel that is Logan Airport. His frantic pursuit between cabs and cars across the concrete dividers ended when the hat came in for a smooth landing on a pristine, errant snow drift under the porte-cochère.

Unbelievable. If that had been my hat, it would have skipped across the top of every oily puddle like a flat stone on a still lake. Then a bus would have run over it.

"I can't believe you're still wearing that stinky hat," I said. "Didn't you get that in junior high?"

Pointing to my bag, he said, "Ha! Coming from someone who carries her stuff around in an old carpet bag."

"How dare you talk about Hildegard that way! She's a vintage, leather-trimmed tapestry train case, barely broken in, made by a German artisan."

"Big whoop. Looks like a Mary Poppins hand-me-down. Who names their luggage anyway?"

"Excuse me, wasn't it your wife who replaced your Scooby-Doo backpack a few years ago? What were you, maybe twenty-five?"

"Heads up." He elbowed me. "Security checkpoint ahead. But I think it's safe to say I won this round."

"Remember, little brother, whenever you think you've won, it only means it's not over."

I was first in line at security. The agent tilted his head back a few degrees before he ran his ultraviolet LED flashlight over my driver's license. He checked my face against my photo. "Casey M. Gallagher, blonde hair, blue eyes, pretty smile. How 'bout that? Looks just like you. Have a good flight, Ms. Gallagher."

"Thanks." I paused for Griffin to catch up. He was involved in a verbal volley between a man he'd never met and a woman he'd never see again. My brother attracts people like an ice cream truck on a dusty, back road in an Alabama August.

Frowning, the TSA agent signaled to Griffin to keep moving. He examined his license and face with the same degree of scrutiny he had mine. "Griffin McGee? Why do I know that name? Hey, you the one who writes Double Header?"

"That would be me."

"I've seen you on TV too." The agent did a double-take back at me. "Wait a second—Casey? That's why you looked familiar. You the other half of the team?"

My brother answered for me. "Yes, Casey is the older half."

It was too late to stop my reflex eye roll. "He means wiser half."

The agent smiled. "You two remind me of me and my sista."

"Always pleased to meet a fan." Griffin flashed a smile our orthodontist was thrilled to claim.

"Fort Myers, huh? Spring training?"

People knew instinctively that it was okay to talk to Griffin. The constant grin playing around his eyes was an open invitation.

"Yeah," Griffin said, settling in for a long story. "It's a tough job, but someone's gotta do it. We hope the weather—"

Noticing an impatient frown on an elderly woman behind us, I interrupted. "Come along, hotshot. We're keeping this man from doing his job."

I slipped off my linen blazer and tried not to think about the possibility that I might be placing it in the same scuffed-up gray plastic bin where previous passengers might have dumped stinky sneakers. Traveling. Why did it always make me think of germs? I wrote a mental Post-it to stop at a newsstand to buy some hand sanitizer.

Griffin crammed his shoes, fleece pullover, and backpack in a single bin. Once past the scanner, he continued his conversation with the man behind him. I sighed when he shook hands with the guy with no thought as to what that stranger might have touched. I shook off the creeps, reminding myself that no matter how hard I tried to avoid unnecessary handling of people and matter, it was Griffin who never got sick.

We had enough time to make it through the line at Dunkin' Donuts before our boarding call. Once we reached our row, we squished our carry-ons in the overhead compartment and jammed our laptops under the seats. As I sidestepped to the window seat, my cell phone rang.

Griffin nudged me. "Ten bucks says it's our esteemed literary agent, Roberta 'Bulldog' Herzog."

"I won't take that bet." I checked my phone and sighed. "Morning, Roberta."

"Boarded yet?" Without bothering to wait for my answer, she continued. "I'm being sincere here—try to dig up some news while you're there. No reason you can't mix business with more business. Don't forget, I need your column by two o'clock Wednesday."

"Have we ever been late?"

"Oh, wait, I almost forgot. A piece of fan mail came pouring in for you today."

"Such a comedienne, you are. Email it to me."

"No, I mean a real letter, light blue fancy stationary, handwritten address and all. Says 'Confidential' in the bottom left corner."

"Are you sure it's not for Griffin?"

"Nope, it's addressed to Ms. Casey McGee. Sent to the *Lowell Sun.* The newspapers forward all your mail to me, remember? I'll send it to you."

"Okay, but to my home, not my office."

"What's the address of your hotel? If I mail it this morning, you'll get it before you leave."

Give Roberta the address of my hotel for a piece of fan mail? I don't think so. She's liable to deliver it in person—from her home in New York.

She started to speak again, but I cut her off. "Gotta go. Flight attendant's orders."

Griffin said, "What's 'not for Griffin'?"

"A letter marked 'Confidential.'"

He tilted his head. "You sure? It might be another one of those scented envelopes from a woman dying to be interviewed by me."

"Sorry to disappoint you, Lothario. It's addressed to me."

"Ah, perhaps a second note from that old gent with the shaky handwriting, asking why the Celtics don't play Larry Bird anymore."

My eyes misted at the memory of that sweet man lost in dementia to whom I'd taken the time to respond.

Griffin buckled his seatbelt. "The real reason she called was to harass us about the column, right?"

"Yup, that and to tell us to dig up a new story. And you thought I used to nag."

"Used to?"

I ignored him. "Roberta's good at her job for the same reason she drives us nuts—she's relentless."

"Yeah, she's got the perfect traits for an agent. Frank, not insulting. Truthful, not mean. Bossy, not overbearing."

Our eyes cut to each other and we chimed in unison, "Maybe a little overbearing."

The thing was, Griffin and I hadn't even talked about getting an agent before Roberta contacted us. I'd figured we needed to have at least one book underway before a professional would give us a shot. I remembered her sales pitch: "I'm visiting family in Boston and saw you on a local cable show. The sister-brother angle intrigues me. Let's meet."

It was unlikely any other agents would come knocking, so we accepted her offer to represent us.

Pre-Roberta, Griffin and I had been writing our Double Header blog-turned-syndicated column for three years. Only a handful of local papers had picked us up.

Now, five months post-Roberta, our syndication count was up to twenty-plus midsized papers and our blog got close to a thousand hits a week. She'd booked us on numerous regional radio and television sports talk shows, increasing our industry recognition.

We had Roberta to thank for that. And she reminded us as often as she felt necessary.

Once the plane cleared the clouds, we settled in and relaxed.

Griffin faced me. "Hey, did you find much we can use in Dad's stash?"

Five months ago, Mom had remarried and moved to her new husband's house. While getting our old home ready for sale, she'd discovered Dad's boxes of sports memorabilia hidden in the attic. The vision of my father sneaking up the pull-down staircase so his valuables wouldn't fall victim to one of Mom's decluttering frenzies always made me smile.

"You're kidding, right?" I said. "It's a treasure trove that spans forty years. It'll take some time to go through."

I dreamed of one day collaborating with Griffin on a series of full-length sports biographies. With my fulltime career as an account executive at Kincade Marketing Solutions in Boston and his teaching and coaching positions at Plymouth North High, we'd have to wait until our schedules made a way. Until that day, we researched, collected, and filed.

"How do you plan to organize it all?"

"Well, first, by not giving it to you." I spiked an imaginary football. "Pretty weak defense, McGee."

"Enjoy your minor victory. It will be short lived."

"To answer your question, I'm sorting alphabetically by player name and cross-referencing to the year and team. After I get through Dad's boxes, we can each add our contributions."

His eyes widened. "Am I supposed to be collecting stuff too?"

My shoulders sagged in disbelief, my frustration making me sputter.

He smirked. "Don't struggle so much, sis, and the hook won't leave a scar."

2

The flight to Ft. Myers had some rough edges, the main one being a four-year-old kicking the back of my seat for three hours while I tried to work. I strongly suspected my brother had egged him on.

When I stepped outside the airport, the heat wrapped me up like a hot, moist towel, bone-soothing and therapeutic. Since the only green I'd seen all winter was the shamrock shock of the Boston Celtics' uniforms, I found the verdant shades of manicured lawns and palm fronds calming.

I took a few seconds to text Sam: *Safe flight. Talk later. Love, C. P.S. Do your dishes!*

We picked up our rental and drove straight to JetBlue Park at Fenway South, home of the training camp. Within an hour of landing we were in the stands waiting for the start of the exhibition game.

The park was like a miniature Fenway minus the iconic Citgo sign in the distance. Instead, tall palm trees lined both the city block and the perimeter of the field. Even though the fans there always seemed loyal—booing and cheering like they would in Beantown—the atmosphere was less intense.

Not once did we ever hear a bunch of drunks yelling "Yankees suck!"

We chose seats in the sun that first day, but all the seats, even those in the shade, had good sight lines toward the field. Our eyes, of course, would be on the mound and pitcher Mike Hennessey.

This was our third time back since Dad died. Griffin started humming the old familiar seventh-inning-stretch song which Dad used to sing loud and off-key to embarrass us. I'd asked Griffin not to sing it the first few years because it hurt too much.

When I started humming along, Griffin responded by singing as loud as he could.

Take me out to the ball game,
Take me out with the crowd.
Buy me some peanuts and Cracker Jack,
I don't care if I never get back.

I held it together until he reached into his backpack and pulled out Dad's 1971 Rawlings glove and beat-up Red Sox hat. "I'll use the glove to catch fly balls, and you wear the hat for luck."

Before I could protest, Griffin switched out my pink ball cap for Dad's old navy one. In that brief exchange, I caught a slight scent of my father. In an instant, the soul shelter I'd cobbled together for my private grief collapsed. My tears went public, but the private memories that came with them were sweet.

It was good to be back. Despite my tears, I felt stronger this year. Like nothing could stop me now.

"Stee-rike three!"

Griffin jumped up and down, fists flying, his voice hoarse from hollering for nine innings. "Yes! Hennessey! Show 'em how it's done!"

While my brother always plays the fan, I'm usually scribing to meet a deadline. After Hennessey's performance, even I couldn't hold back a shout-out. "Doing Southie proud, Mike!"

Before Hennessey left the mound, he removed his hat, wiped his brow with his sleeve, and ran his hand through his thick, sandy-colored hair. He took long, slow strides to the dugout, keeping his head down the whole way. This twenty-four-year-old kid had just made his professional training camp debut by pitching a one-hitter, yet he seemed embarrassed by the fans' attention.

Not a braggart, Mike Hennessey. Refreshing.

For some reason, the lanky six-foot-five pitcher reminded me of the fast-growing Leyland cypress trees planted alongside our condo. He'd grown as fast in the major league as those evergreens had grown in our yard. This particular cypress flourishes in acidic soil and is rarely affected by the winds. I hoped Hennessey fit the analogy when it came to pro ball.

"Hey, Griff, he might be worth the price they paid for that golden arm after all—if only for his fastball."

"Yeah, but the problem is getting a golden glove to catch it. The catcher they paired him with today had to scramble hard for more than a few of his pitches. The front office won't have a choice—they'll sign Flynn before opening day at Fenway. I'll bet on it."

The successful battery of pitcher Mike Hennessey and catcher Darin Flynn had played together from Little League through the minors. It was uncanny how they read each other's moves and minds. Hennessey seldom shook off a signal from Flynn. Like their every game was rehearsed in Heaven.

Since both pitcher and catcher were the same age, from the same South Boston Irish stock, Griffin and I had been mulling over monikers for the pair.

"How about the Boston Battery? Or the SoBo Sox?" Griffin said.

"Maybe. I was thinking the Irish Twins. They're like brothers and the same age. We'd definitely get some spin off it in Boston, especially Southie."

"Irish Twins? Yeah, I like it. Let's use it in our next column—before someone steals it. For a girl, you're pretty smart."

"Gee, thanks." I landed a punch on his arm and made sure it stung. He was my brother and it was expected, even if I was pushing thirty.

"About the column," I continued. "I've got the next six weeks of general topics lined up, but we have to work on adding a personal dimension. Up until now, we've written about the players' performances and stats. We're missing that insider's feel. It'll be good practice for our biographies too. What do you think?"

"Yeah, you're right. Don't worry, we'll get there."

Why I had actually expected any well thought out or practical input from my brother is beyond me. I wanted to make things happen; he wanted to see what happened. I had a plan; he had a dream. I played life by the rules; he played life by ear.

3

On our second day, I rose at six so I could get my run in before Griffin bugged me about the all-you-can-eat breakfast bar. He called as I was two-stepping the stairs up to the hotel.

"You're breathing hard. Don't you ever take a day off?" he said. "This is supposed to be a fun trip."

"Running *is* fun."

"Yeah, right. More like a competition between you and your alter ego."

Griffin was right. I had a tough time letting go of my habits, good and bad. But I wasn't going to admit it to him. "Interesting concept, slacker. We can discuss it in the dining room after you belly up to the buffet with your big, fat paws. Meet you there in twenty."

On my way to meet Griffin, I got a call from Nora Ingersson, my administrative assistant at Kincade. Truth is, Nora wasn't solely mine. She was a twenty-two-year veteran who handled the workload for five account executives.

"Sorry to bother you, Casey, but something weird is going on here. A trio of suits from the New York office showed up this morning, all stern and all business. The main floor receptionist was in a tizzy because they walked right by her without signing in, ignoring protocol."

For security reasons, everyone who entered the building was required to sign in at the large mahogany desk, positioned directly in front of the elevator doors. I doubted the receptionist was part of the security firm's first response team—unless perusing an Avon catalogue was part of her cover.

"The New York higher-ups never stoop to come to Boston," I said. "Why now?"

"No idea. But when they reached our floor, they marched into Gordy's office without knocking as if he wasn't a VP himself. Before long, they all filed into a conference room and didn't come out for almost two hours."

"Gordy never said anything after they left?"

"Not to me. But I wanted to give you a heads-up."

"Thanks. I'll check with him when I get back."

If I'd heard this from anyone but Nora, I would have deleted it from my playlist. But I trusted Nora's intuition. She was right; this was weird.

Even with my brother's appetite, breakfast was quick. We made it to the ballpark by ten, in time to watch four hours of practice. Once Mike Hennessey was through for the day, we skipped out.

On the way back to the hotel, Griffin suggested we squeeze in nine holes of golf before dinner. "Remember the course we played with Dad that last trip? We go right by it."

"You're kidding, right? It's two forty-five in Florida on a sunny, not-so-humid day in March. Fat chance we'll have with that. Besides, we didn't bring our clubs."

"Come on, we can rent them."

With no real reason not to try, I agreed. We found the course easily enough, but when we passed a full overflow lot, I knew our chances were zilch. On our first approach, Griffin found an empty space right near the clubhouse.

Figures.

"Now all you have to do is put that charm of yours in gear and finagle us a tee time. I'll be in the car working on my half of the column. It's due tomorrow, remember?"

Not the least dissuaded by my skepticism, he said, "Will do, Ms. Used-to-Nag."

I smiled when he wasn't looking.

Ten minutes later he walked out with a bag of clubs over each shoulder, swinging a pair of pink golf shoes in one hand. I couldn't believe it.

"Just your size. In the rental inventory."

I examined the shoes. "Rentals? They look brand new." I pulled tissue paper from the toes. "Hey, they *are* new."

"That's the good news. Now for the bad news. Are you game for a foursome?"

I sighed. "Are we gonna be playing after dark waiting for a pair of old geezers to catch up?"

"Trust me, it'll be fine. They'll be out in a minute."

I changed shoes and headed to the practice green. Before I could get the putter out of the bag, Griffin hailed me over. "Case! Let's go!"

He was shaking hands with a couple of guys—young guys. Hmm. A positive sign.

The shorter of the two was stocky but muscular, not fat. Red hair stuck out of his visor, and his baby face made it hard to tell his age. The other was well over six feet and slim, maybe early twenties. His deep-set eyes and narrow jaw looked familiar.

Walking toward them, I could have sworn I heard Griffin say, "Watch this."

I slowed my pace and gawked. There, flanking Griffin, were Mike Hennessey and Darin Flynn, the Irish Twins themselves.

How did my brother do it?

I sauntered the last few steps, trying to act like my hanging out with sports celebrities happened all the time. The smirks on their faces confirmed my suspicion about my performance—I'm a lousy actress.

After handshakes all around and a few laughs at my expense, we proceeded to the first hole. My thoughts alternated between getting material for our next column and wondering if these pros were jocks-of-all-trades. I wanted healthy competition, but I didn't want to lose.

Darin said, "A-yo, Griffin, what's your handicap?"

"You mean besides having Casey for a sister?"

I snapped back, "And being dyslexic at reading the greens."

Darin laughed and turned to Mike. "This is gonna be fun, I can tell."

They offered me a "ladies first" pass, so I teed up. I was pleased when I hit it long and straight down the middle. Darin's ball fell about ten feet beyond mine, while both Mike and Griffin's fell short, one to the left, the other to the right. They lagged behind us to the green. Darin and I made par while Mike and Griffin bogeyed.

When Mike shanked his ball on the second hole, he thumped the ground with the head of his club. "Aagh! What's up with that?"

"Calm yourself, Hennessey," Darin said. "It's simple physics. It happens when the path the club takes toward the ball at impact is further out than it was at address. Try to keep your weight back toward your heels in your downswing. It'll help the swing plane."

Mike shook his head. "Give it to me in English, Flynn, not in physics."

Griffin caught Mike's eye and aimed a thumb in Darin's direction. "He always talk like that?"

Mike said, "Yup, but only in sports. Otherwise he'd scare the girls away."

Darin switched clubs. "And you, Hennessey? The only curve I've seen you with lately is your pitch."

"Ya know, Flynn," Mike said, "if and when the Sox offer you a deal, I suggest you take some of your signing bonus and buy yourself some words the rest of us can understand."

Walking the fairway on the second hole, Griffin used his chin to point in Mike and Darin's direction. "Is it me, Case, or does this bickering sound familiar?"

I whispered back. "Hey, let's not miss this chance. You work Hennessey, and I'll take Flynn. Dig deep."

After a couple more holes of us razzing each other, I felt comfortable enough to ask Darin about his status with the Sox. "Since Mike brought the subject up, got any news fit to print in our next column? Something that would give the fans in Southie something huge to be happy about?"

His smile was anchored by deep dimples set in his chubby cheeks, which any self-respecting great aunt would pinch, or at least want to.

"Not much of a poker face there, Flynn," I said, sure I had my answer.

Mike laughed. "Haven't you figured it out by now? That *is* his poker face."

I let that putt sink in before I realized what he meant. Darin smiled when he made par, smiled when he bogeyed, and smiled when his ball scuttled to a premature stop on a wet green.

"A smile that's so contagious," Mike said, "the CDC even threatened to quarantine his face if it continues."

Darin shot back. "Hennessey, with a nickname like Gampy, I wouldn't talk. What's your dad always saying? 'Son, wipe that *grim* off your face.'"

I two-putted for a birdie and picked up my ball. "Hey, can we get back to my question? About the Sox. Got anything for us, Darin?"

Griffin cautioned, "Watch her. She's a sneaky one. Trying to distract us for the win."

I gave Griffin a look which I hoped would say "No, bonehead, I'm trying to get the scoop, and you're not helping!" Too bad he read my face as poorly as he read the greens. I reminded myself to swat him at the end of the round. A round I planned to win.

"We don't mind the questions," Mike said. "You've supported us from the start. We appreciate it."

I was surprised to learn that while we'd been following their careers on the field, they'd been following ours in print.

Darin winked at me. "Did I mention that Mike and I plan

to go in on a townhouse together in Southie within the next few weeks?"

It was the inside tip I'd hoped for. "Keep us posted?"

"After my family and Mike's, you'll be the first to know."

The stress-free round was fun—not a sore loser in the bunch. Okay, maybe one, but since I beat the closest player by five strokes, it didn't factor into the match. To top that, before I could bring it up, Darin suggested we exchange phone numbers.

As soon as Griffin and I were alone in our car, I turned to him. "How in the whole Baseball Hall of Fame did you convince Mike and Darin to join us?"

He tapped his watch. "Wow! You waited three whole seconds to ask."

"Give!"

"It was simple. They asked me."

"They asked *you*?"

"Yup. They heard me begging the guy at the counter for a tee time. I think the part about me having to face my mean old sister is what sealed the deal. Then one thing led to another."

"One thing led to another. You know, if there is such a thing as the luck of the Irish, you got your full share and mine too."

"Luck? I'll have you know it took pure salesmanship to convince that pro shop clerk to rent me those brand-new, size eight FootJoys. I figured you'd go for the foursome—but never for used shoes."

4

Our flight back to Boston was on time. I knew Griffin's wife Jillian would circle around rather than park in the dark at Logan. She'd heard my husband's beware-of-your-surroundings speech often enough to heed his warnings like the sensible second-grade teacher she was. We watched her drive through the arrivals area—and by us—twice. We finally connected on her third pass.

It was almost eleven when they dropped me off. I schlepped my body and my luggage over the threshold and noticed the messy stack of mail on the hall console. Shuffling through it, I saw a manila envelope from Roberta.

Probably the fan letter she'd mentioned.

Thinking of Roberta prompted a half-laugh. As promised, Griffin and I had emailed her our column on time. In a convulsion of restraint, we both agreed it was worth the wait to tell her about our new golfing buddies in person. We didn't want to miss our agent's zero-to-manic-in-two-seconds-flat reaction.

The mail could wait, especially considering what we'd received in the past, like the letter from a stage mother touting her son's skills during his first year of tee-ball.

I unpacked and started a load of laundry while pondering our new relationship with Hennessey and Flynn. I was pleased with what it might mean for our future—professionally and personally. The Irish Twins (a term which they instantly took to) had promised us an exclusive interview when—not if—Darin signed with the Sox.

While maneuvering my empty suitcase to the back of our walk-in closet, I noticed my father's black leather state police boots, the ones he wore in his early years on the force. I had retrieved them from a pile my mother had set aside for Goodwill. For the past few years, like honor guards protecting his memory, they stood on duty in the shadows of my wardrobe.

To avert an onset of melancholy, I turned away and closed the door.

Wanting to feel fresh and rejuvenated to greet Sam after his shift, I ran a bath and soaked in bubbles for almost an hour. Time away made me appreciate him more. How good it would feel to be all wrapped up in each other.

Sam had been with the Massachusetts State Police for over nine years. He'd been assigned to four-to-midnights with the Norfolk Detective Unit a year ago. Although he never admitted it, I knew he preferred that shift because it held more potential for action, action I preferred not to think about.

I climbed into bed with a book but never cracked it. I was relaxed, the kind of relaxed when your mind wanders here and there as if it had no say in the matter—from the scent of my sheets to a client's advertising slogan, from my broken can opener to needing a pedicure, from Thai food to missing my dad and back to Sam again.

I turned my head toward the clock. Twelve forty-five. He would be home soon.

I awoke in his arms at 6 a.m. We lingered in bed until my breakfast menu changed from turkey bacon and eggs to coffee and juice and Sam had fallen back asleep.

Later, sitting at our table for two in the alcove off the

kitchen, I sipped my coffee and did a mental walk-through of the day that lay before me. Sam surprised me when he rounded the corner, filled a cup, and joined me.

"You didn't have to get up," I said, looking at his puffy eyes.

He shrugged. "I know. I wanted to."

"Missed me, did you?"

"What do you think?" He jiggled his eyebrows.

I reached across the table and rapped his hand. "Those dirty dishes crawling out of the sink tell me you did."

"Oh. Sorry." Sam stirred the milk in his coffee. "I couldn't sleep in this morning anyway. Meeting Coletti at the gym."

"Oh, yes, Coletti, the wannabe-Lieutenant-Sam-Gallagher recruit. What's his first name again?"

"Tommy. Since he passed the exam and made it through six months of training, he's no longer a recruit but a probationary officer. Probie for short."

"You're still his hero, right?"

It was easy to see Sam as a mentor, even if it meant spending extra time outside of working hours. No one who knew my husband could ever lump him in with grumpers and bellyachers. He was all about loyalty, integrity, and service. Excellent qualities in a cop, even better in a spouse.

Sam ignored my teasing. "Listen up, this kid's gonna be an excellent cop one day. I can tell by the questions he asks. Even I wasn't that focused so soon out of college."

"That's 'cause you had me." I kissed the top of his head on my way to the sink.

He followed me with his cup. "You can be distracting," he said, wrapping his arms around my waist.

Together we rinsed the dishes and put them in the dishwasher.

After a kiss good-bye that made it hard to leave, I picked up my train case Hildegard and headed for the door, stopping long enough to flip through the mail again. I grabbed the only piece of mail that looked personal and opened Roberta's manila packet. I removed the pale blue parchment envelope, tucking it in my bag along with the newspaper and a few other envelopes. My plan was to read them on the T.

I parked in my usual spot in the MBTA lot in Braintree to catch the Red Line into the city. Driving may have been quicker, but I found it less productive. Taking the T gave me time to catch up on the news on the way in and catch up on my work on the way out.

I'd been on staff at Kincade Marketing Solutions for almost eight years. I'd interned for two years in college, working directly for Gordy Ackerman, VP of the middle market division. It gave me the head start I needed. When Gordy offered me a position after I graduated from Simmons College, I accepted.

Between my marriage, my job at Kincade, and writing the column with Griffin, life couldn't get much better.

Once aboard the train, I joined my fellow commuters on our way to various destinations, swaying together in syncopated rhythm like full-bodied bobblehead dolls. I'd figured out long ago that the unspoken urban rule of no talking and no eye contact is what allowed public transportation to become private.

I skimmed the business section of the *Herald,* not surprised to find yet another photo of my best friend Vanessa Vance. This time it was alongside an article on a whistleblower she'd recently defended—successfully, of course. I'd seen her client on the news. Newspaper people weren't dumb. They knew a photo of Vanessa with her long legs and polished looks would draw more readers than that of a disgruntled, middle-aged, balding man.

Since our years together at Simmons, Vanessa had always known what she wanted to be when she grew up—an attorney in a prestigious law firm. She'd become that and a lot more—a partner in a deep-pocket Boston firm before the age of thirty. She'd even found the perfect husband in Bryson, a pilot with a major airline whose schedule didn't interfere with her career.

It'd been too long between visits, a by-product of our grown-up lives. I reminded myself to call her.

I finished reading the newspaper, ending with an article on the Red Sox's new pitching coach. I made a note to get the Irish Twins' opinion. I took a breather and switched to my favorite pastime, making up lives for my fellow passengers. I labeled it "sharpening observation skills," a useful tool for the biographies I would write someday.

Seated across from me was a mid-fiftyish man with clean, thinning brown hair in a brown polyester suit, beige shirt, and brown tie. I pegged him as an honest accountant, maybe for a small distributor housed in a back-alley building somewhere in Allston. Definitely not the Financial District or Beacon Hill. I nicknamed him J.P. for Morgan.

Next, the young Asian male wearing black slacks and a white shirt. The red tie stuffed in his pocket screamed uniform. Perhaps a talented cellist waiting tables to repay his fare to America? I named him Shang, for his dreams had been shanghaied by this forced conscription.

Okay, perhaps a bit melodramatic.

The college-aged girl with the perfect nose and $300 Coach book bag was easy. A spoiled yet intelligent daughter of a plastic surgeon from Milton whose parents' idea of teaching her responsibility was making her ride the T to her classes at Smith. Her name? Tippy. Yes, Tippy Montrose. I liked it.

Did any of my traveling companions make up things about me? If so, what? Maybe they recognized me from a TV appearance or from my Double Header headshot posted with Griffin's in one of the print or online newspapers. Would they tell me if they did?

That reminded me, our fan mail.

With only minutes to go before my stop, I reached in my bag and found the letters. The first linen envelope turned out to be an invitation to a financial planning seminar presented by a man I remembered from a cheesy infomercial.

No thanks. Next.

The letter Roberta forwarded had been sent to a newspaper that carried our column. Was it from fan or foe? Between the feel of fine blue stationery and the neat cursive on the envelope, I guessed fan.

It took only seconds of reading to prove how wrong I could be.

5

Eyes straight ahead, I plowed down the sidewalk through the white noise in my head until I reached Columbus Ave. I entered the building that housed Kincade. If I passed anyone on my way to the elevator, I never saw them.

Thankful to have the elevator to myself, I rode it to the third floor in a daze. I shouldered my way out the half-opened doors, took a hard right, and slammed right into Nora, knocking her up against the wainscoting. The file she was carrying flew out of her hand, and papers floated down around us.

Nora chuckled. "Been watching a lot of hockey lately, Casey?"

"Sorry, so sorry." Averting my eyes, I bent to help her pick up the mess I'd made.

If this fifty-five-year-old woman wore makeup, it was hard to tell. Nature gave her the color she needed through gardening, hiking, swimming, and skiing. I don't know when her short, Norwegian blonde hair had turned white, but the colors were so close it took me a while to notice.

"Never mind," she said. "I can get these. Besides, Gordy said to send you to his office as soon as you came in."

Gordy wasn't usually a problem, but I couldn't deal with him right now. "Nora, please, could you cover for me? I need some time."

She rested her hand on my arm. "Sure thing, sweetie. You come along when you're ready."

I hurried down the hall to my office. Once inside, I pressed the door behind me until it latched. After a split-second reflection, I turned the lock for good measure. Trembling, I placed Hildegard on the credenza and reached inside for the letter. When my fingertips grazed the parchment, my hand recoiled like a skittish animal expecting a trap to snap. I backed away.

Pacing the room, around and around, I rubbed my temples in a soothing counter-clockwise motion. It was futile; I was not soothed. I stared out the window at nothing, past the hand-picked furnishings of my well-appointed office, furnishings which now looked like insignificant, blurred shapes in muted shades of gray.

I still couldn't make sense of the woman's letter. Her claims seemed outrageous, yet her reason for making them perplexed me. What could she possibly hope to gain?

My mind scrambled for a way to deal with this, a way that did not involve going to my mother. I cut back to the credenza, opened my bag, and pulled out the envelope. Searching for clues, I checked the postmark: Brookline, MA. Not much help. I read the letter again.

Dear Ms. McGee,

I've had to make some tough decisions in my life, and writing this letter is one of the toughest. I'll continue as gently as I can, even knowing it will not make things easier for anyone.

I chose to write you because, from reading your column and seeing you on TV, I believe you may have the strength needed in this situation.

Let me start by telling you that I worked with your father Ned almost twenty-five years ago. We were partners on the police force for almost three years. I was so sorry to hear of his death.

Knowing the man your dad was and how much he loved his family, I imagine that what I'm about to tell you is something you would not expect to hear. Even as I write this, I still have a difficult time understanding how or why it happened.

Yet here it is: I confess to having a one-time sexual encounter with your father while we were on the force.

I won't lessen the gravity of my behavior by making excuses. The only explanation I can offer is that it happened in the aftermath of a particularly frightening close call while working a high stress case together. As wrong as it was, it was not premeditated and our mutual remorse was immediate.

Knowing we could not undo what we had done, I believed the only recourse I had was to put distance between us. Within a week, I resigned and moved out of the area. I had no communication with your father after I left.

Even after I learned I was carrying his child.

During my pregnancy, I met an amazing man who loved me as I was and wanted to care for both my child and me. We married before my son was born so he could have his father's name. Ironically, my greatest shame resulted in our greatest blessing.

Our son has always known that his dad was not his biological father. We were as honest as we could be with him about the circumstances under which he was conceived without revealing anything about your family.

When he grew up, a longing to learn all he could about the father he never knew surfaced. Even knowing the sad fact that his biological father is deceased has not lessened his desire.

He wants to find peace, not cause turmoil. I was able to convince him to give me time to contact someone who might help him in his search.

Casey, for better or worse, that someone is you.

I know singling you out to tell you this news is not fair. But I did not want to write your mother and compound her grief. If she has to hear this from anyone, I thought it would be better to hear it from family.

Though I sympathize with my son's need for resolution, he agrees with me that a meeting with any biological relatives should not be forced. I will leave that decision up to you. I know it's not much of a consolation, but it is all I have to offer.

Sincerely,
Lisa Erickson

PS: I know you'll need time to broach this matter with your mother and brother. If and when you feel ready, you may write to me at PO Box 115341, Boston, MA 02116. Again, neither I nor my son will do anything more without your invitation.

I stuffed the letter back in its envelope.

My father, unfaithful? An illegitimate child? Not likely. What are they after? What's their scam?

I sat down at my desk, slumped forward in my chair, and buried my face in my hands. The question that had been lurking in the back of my mind stole the advantage and crept out to taunt me.

What if it's true?

Despite my full-court press against this woman's allegations, I had to consider some unpleasant options. One, it could be true, and two, if it wasn't she was a lunatic, maybe dangerous. If her son believed her story, could I trust him to keep his word and not snoop around? If he started asking questions, it would be too late for damage control.

Above all, I didn't want my father's memory sullied by innuendo and doubt.

Was I overreacting? Perhaps. I wasn't naïve; I knew this stuff happened in families all the time. I never thought it would happen in mine. True or not, I didn't have a choice. I had to speak to my mother before someone else did.

When I called Mom that night to see when we could get together, she told me she had the next day off.

"After putting twenty-six years in at JB & Son Marketing, I finally cut back to part-time."

"Good for you, Mom. You deserve it."

When she mentioned that her husband, Webster, had a meeting at a client's office the next morning, I invited myself over. It would be hard enough to tell my mother that her late husband might have had an affair without doing it in front of her new husband.

The only thing I could see at the end of this long, dark tunnel was hurt.

How could the eighteen-mile drive from my condo in Kingston to Mom's house in Sandwich seem agonizingly long yet pass by in a flash? I arrived as Webster was pulling out of the driveway.

He stopped and rolled down his window. "Looks like winter didn't get the memo about the vernal equinox. Got a fire going for you and your mom."

That was Webster-speak. He couldn't just say, "It's still cold out." I thanked him for the fire.

He waved and called out, "Have fun!"

Putting my game face on, I waved back. Fun? Yeah. Like catching a puck in the chest.

Sitting for a moment before I got out of the car, I tried one last time to put the brakes on my spinning thoughts. I still hadn't come up with a good way to tell her.

What was I thinking? There was no good way.

I walked around back. Through the French doors, I caught a glimpse of my mother in the kitchen. She was smiling to herself as she turned the flame down under the teakettle. I was willing to bet she was humming. She used to do that with Dad.

Only five months had passed since Mom and Webster's marriage, a marriage that had brought love and contentment back into her life as well as humming. Now here I was, like a sour note to spoil her song.

After knocking, I let myself in. "Hi, Mom."

"Hi! Oh, you just missed Web."

"Nah, we got a chance to say hello in the driveway."

"I wanted you to see how far he's come on your website design. You and Griffin will be impressed."

"I'm sure we will." We'd hired Webster, a professional web designer and developer, because he was talented, not because he was married to Mom. (Okay, so the family discount of FREE might have helped.)

Mom picked up her kettle. "Want some tea?"

"Sure."

"English breakfast okay?"

"That's fine."

"Milk and honey?"

"Okay." The small tea talk was killing me, but I was sure there was something in some etiquette handbook that said you had to chat before you told your mother you had a new brother and she should set an extra place for Sunday dinner.

Mom lifted the serving tray and led the way. "Let's sit in the sunroom. It lives up to its name quite nicely this time of day. And you can thank Web for the scones. He picked them up at Beth's Tea Shoppe this morning. Apricot, your favorite."

Eating was the last thing on my mind, yet I responded politely as Mom had taught me. "Sounds delicious. That was thoughtful. Tell him thanks."

I looked around on my way to the sunroom. Even more things had changed in the month since Mom had sold the home I'd grown up in. Initially, it had surprised me that she had decided to live in Webster's home instead of ours. "Web's home hasn't been touched by marriage and children," she'd said. "My home, our home, has. I don't want him bumping into our family memories around every corner."

I noted that Mom and Webster had blended their tastes and furnishings seamlessly, right down to the collage of photos of both their families. "You've done an excellent job with the house, Mom."

"Thanks. I can't say combining households was easy, but we're happy now that it's done. Since you and your brother wanted some of the furniture, culling was less painful."

We got settled on the sofa with our tea.

"Everything okay, sweetie?"

Leave it to my mother to get straight to the point. Before the last word of her question was out, I rushed to take a bite of scone and lifted my cup to my lips, my feeble effort to slow the pace. It didn't help that the hot tea dissolved my scone morsel in seconds, giving me nothing to chew on but angst.

"Is Sam okay?" she asked.

"Sam? He's fine, actually. More than fine." My weak attempt at stalling had devolved to lame.

"That's good." She studied my face.

I took a deep breath and expelled my fear. I opened my mouth to speak but heard a voice other than my own.

"Hey, Mom! You home?"

Grr. Griffin. What was he doing here?

6

Mom put her teacup down and cocked her head. "Griffin? Is that you? We're in the sunroom."

Both Griffin and Jillian walked around the corner.

Mom smiled. "And you're with your lovely wife!"

"Hi, Case. Saw your car outside," Griffin said. "What're you doing here?"

"I was about to ask you guys the same thing. Don't you two have school today?"

"Hey, you missed your calling," he said. "You should've been a truant officer. Even us lowly public school teachers get personal days."

"You three took a personal day to come see me?" Mom looked from Jillian to Griffin to me, her brow beginning to furrow.

"You mean us *four*," Griffin said.

"Four?" Mom peered around Jillian to see if someone else was with them. "Is Sam here too?"

Jillian followed with a soft laugh then leaned into Griffin who put his arm around her and patted her stomach with his free hand.

"This little one makes four!" His face was one big burst of joy.

"Are you saying what I think you're saying? Is it true? I'm going to be a grandmother?"

"How'd you figure it out so fast, Mom?" Griffin looked as if he would fly away if Jillian wasn't holding on to him. "Pretty cool, huh?"

Mom and I jumped up and took turns hugging them then went back around for seconds. In the midst of smiles and happy wishes, Mom turned to me and said, "Is this why you were acting so mysterious, Casey?"

Clearly puzzled, Griffin started to say something. I threw him a look like a knuckleball. Thankfully, he caught it. Although I was thrilled for my brother and his wife, I'd always assumed I'd be the first to get pregnant, being the oldest and married the longest.

However, Sam and I had a long-term plan, which meant another promotion for him and me staying at Kincade for at least five more years before we started our family. While we were on schedule, Griffin and Jillian seemed to prefer a life of surprises.

A question whizzed by my mind in a blur. Would this little surprise affect our working together?

I pushed my concern away, refusing to spoil this moment for them or my mother. I spent the next half hour asking all the right questions: "What's your due date? Are you going to find out the sex? Any names picked out?"

Griffin said, "I kinda like Polly for a girl. What do you think, hon?"

"Hmm." Jillian tilted her head from side to side. "Polly? It is kinda cute."

"Yeah, and if you want, we could use your grandmother's name for her middle name."

"That's so sweet, Griff. She'd be honored."

His sappy smile told me he was up to something. "Jillian, what is your grandmother's name?"

Her eyes brightened. "Esther."

I held my tongue. It took a few seconds before Jillian

smacked Griffin on his arm. "Polly Esther? I should have known! Mom, can't you tell him to behave?"

Mom laughed. "Sorry, he's all yours now. And I've got papers to prove it!"

Alone in the car on my way home, the story I never got to tell my mother overshadowed the baby announcement. How much time had to pass between receiving good news and receiving bad to be considered socially acceptable? Days? Weeks? Months? I wondered how long I would be able to eat, sleep and breathe anxiety until I could find the right time to tell Mom… and Griffin.

My phone chirped. At the first stop sign, I read Griffin's text: *what r u hiding from mom? she will find out. confess u sinner!* I tossed the phone on the passenger seat. Knowing my brother, I figured he'd forget and I wouldn't have to respond. Gripping the steering wheel, I headed home.

My intention had been to handle this matter on my own. The fewer people who knew, the better. Why hadn't I told Sam? He was my husband, for Pete's sake.

This was my father, that's why. And I was embarrassed.

Since my first attempt at talking it through with Mom had failed, I decided to get Sam's input. With hours to go before the start of his shift, we'd have time to talk.

Sam called right as I stuck the key in the front door. "Hi, Case. Special training was scheduled for today, and the chief suggested—and I use that word loosely—that I help out."

"So you won't be home until after your shift?"

"No. Uh-oh, break's over. Gotta go. Love ya."

My dismal saga would have to roil in the pit of my stomach until tomorrow or the day after, depending on our schedules. Our crazy work hours didn't always pose a problem, mainly because they were mutually bad so neither of us dared to complain. Today was an exception. This wasn't the kind of conversation I wanted to have at one in the morning at the end of Sam's shift.

Thinking a run might improve my mood, I went to my bedroom to change. Ignoring my running shoes, I flumped to the floor of the closet and held Dad's boots in my lap. My mind went back to the little girl I used to be, the one who sat on the floor night after night, so proud to help her daddy polish his high black boots until we achieved "the black mirror effect." I learned how to spit shine like a seasoned trooper and knew every seam and crease in the soft leather.

Brightly-lit memories came rushing back in no particular order: Mom and Dad dancing in the kitchen to '80s music while Griffin and I mimicked their old-fashioned moves. Our family vacationing at Disney, Dad, Griffin, and me shaming Mom into riding Space Mountain. Best of all, Dad, Griffin, and me cheering the Patriots on to their Super Bowl victory in 2002 while Mom kept us in snacks.

How could I have missed an affair in all this?

Since the day I'd rescued Dad's boots from the Goodwill pile, I'd kept the leather conditioned as a private memorial to him. I reached for the Kiwi polish and rag and turned the tiny metal lever to remove the cover from the tin. The pungent oil and wax incited memories. Putting one hand inside the left boot to hold it steady, I pressed the rag into the black paste with the other. I began to rub slowly, making small circles just as my father had taught me.

Turning the boot sole up, near the heel I saw the tiny red Magic Marker heart I'd drawn as a child. The initials inside, *NM + CM*, were faded but still visible. I had even marked this special duty with our imprint.

I couldn't let the ugliness of this accusation threaten our idyllic past.

Tears fell, mixing with the polish. I kept rubbing, not so gently. Anger welled from my swollen soul, and my precious memories were soon mottled with betrayal and uncertainty.

Dad, is it true? Why? What else don't I know about you?

After shoving the boots aside, I wiped my tears with the cuffs of my sweatshirt and put my running shoes on. I stepped outside, inhaled deeply, and took off. But no matter how fast or how far I ran, the pain kept pace with each stride.

7

Despite a fitful night's sleep, I went in early on Friday. To keep my emotions in check and my mind sharp, work was the distraction I needed.

Nora greeted me as I stepped off the elevator. "Morning, sunshine. You're here earlier than usual. Anything I should know about?"

"No. Since I was out yesterday, I need to catch up on some things, that's all." I wasn't lying, really.

"By the way, if you want to get reimbursed, bookkeeping needs your expense report for last month."

"Thanks for the heads-up. I'll get to it soon."

She stepped closer and put her hand on my arm. "Let me know if I can help, Casey."

I sensed she wasn't talking about my expense report.

Not much got by Nora Ingersson. She fulfilled her role as an administrative assistant with the same precision and instinct as an Olympic coach. She knew what each of us needed to perform our best—no easy task since we all had different strengths, shortcomings, and preferences. She was so efficient that I often suspected an opposite universe was in play, one where we were all working for her but not smart enough to figure it out.

Before I could decide how to respond, Gordy, always the first one at work, shouted, "Is that you, Casey? I need a favor."

Our whole division knew doing favors for Gordy was a no-brainer. We got theater tickets he didn't want due to the "ungodly noise level" and seats to sporting events he didn't understand. The biggest favor I'd ever done for Gordy was to take the VP's corner office off his hands because he "couldn't stand the glare from all that glass."

When I entered his office, Gordy was rustling through a messy stack of papers on his desk. My nickname for him was Macarena Man because, more often than not, he was patting his back pocket for his wallet, his front jacket pocket for his glasses, his belt for his phone, or his wrist for his watch.

"Put that to music, Gordy," I'd teased once, "and you've got a wedding dance."

Combating years of her husband's dishevelment, Gordy's wife finally discovered TravelSmith, a catalogue filled with clothes guaranteed not to wrinkle. After one express delivery, Gordy went from Colombo to Bond. Okay, that might be a stretch. If not smooth, he looked smooth*er* in his taupe herringbone sport coat, no-iron twill shirt, and black microfiber slacks. If only he could keep his tie straight and his shirt tucked and his hair from looking like he'd just woken up from a nap.

One of my dad's expressions slipped out. "What can I do you for?"

"A couple of potential clients are coming in from Rhode Island today . . ." He patted his shirt pocket then reached inside his jacket. "Oh, here it is." He handed me a business card. "Joe and Lisa Ianella. They want to do dinner in the North End. I reserved a table at Pomodoro's, but Italian doesn't agree with me. I know it's short notice, but any chance of you taking them for me?"

"Sure, I've been wanting to try that place."

"Thanks, kid. I can always count on you."

"Any time, Gordy."

Halfway to my office, I heard him cry out, "Nora! Are my glasses out there?"

Even a hectic day followed by a late yet pleasant night out with potential clients couldn't distract me for long. Only a few days had passed since my visit to Mom's, but I'd waited as long as I could stand. I called ahead the next day and stressed the need for privacy. I knew my tone would ensure that Webster would be out. This time I'd have no reason to balk. In the meantime, I refused to imagine what this half brother was like until I was sure he existed.

When Mom didn't respond to my knock, I let myself in and found her in the den reading, curled up on the sofa.

"Must be a good book. You didn't hear me knock."

She smiled. "You might say that." Setting the book on the end table, she patted the cushion beside her. "Sit. Now tell me, Casey, what's this all about?"

My words broke in pieces on the way out of my mouth. I cleared my throat and began again. "Do you remember Lisa Erickson?"

"Lisa Erickson? Your dad's old partner?"

"Yes. I got a letter from her."

"Wait, how would you know Lisa? You were just a little girl when they worked together. Why on earth would she write you?"

"She says it all in here." I handed her the envelope.

She opened it slowly, eyeing me, then the letter before she started reading. She hadn't gotten through the first page before she said, "Oh, Casey, I'm so sorry you had to find this out."

"Find this out? You mean it's true? Why would Dad . . . I mean, it can't be." I started to stand, but she took my arm and eased me back down.

She held both my hands. "I'm afraid it is. It's as Lisa said. It happened once and it was over."

I looked hard at my mother. "I can't believe you knew."

"I knew your father well enough to know when something wasn't right. I suspected what had happened when Lisa quit the force without giving much notice. Dad told me after she moved away."

"You believed him, about the one time?" I felt like I was reciting dialogue from a daytime soap opera.

"Yes, I believed him. Your dad wasn't silly enough to think the cure for our marital ills could be found in jewelry or a trip to Hawaii. He knew telling me the truth was the only chance we had."

She held the letter up. "Why would Lisa write to tell you about something that happened so long ago? Why be so hurtful to you, to me, after all these years? Why?"

"Keep reading." I folded my arms across my chest, my anger searching hard to place blame.

Mom looked at me, a question in her eyes. When I said nothing more, she returned to the letter. Adjusting her glasses, she began where she'd left off. It wouldn't be long.

She stopped and raised her head, staring straight ahead. Still holding the letter, her hand dropped to her lap as she whispered, "Oh, Lord, help me. She had a child, Ned's child."

"So you didn't know?"

"No. It's not like we were on each other's Christmas card lists. If we'd known, you and Griffin would've known, because Dad would have taken responsibility."

"You would have let Dad help her? After what they did?" I couldn't grasp it.

Mom acted more concerned about this woman and her son than about the fact that Dad had cheated on her. I stood up and paced. "If Sam cheated on me and got some woman pregnant, I don't think I could be so blasé about the whole thing. He'd be out the door!"

Mom smiled a sad smile, the same one she'd used when I was eight and refused to believe there was no Santa Claus. "I assure you, at the time I was anything but blasé. If your Dad were here, he'd attest to it."

"This doesn't sound like something Dad would do, I mean, unless he had a reason."

She peered at me over the rim of her readers. "Casey Nicole, what are you suggesting?"

The fact that she'd used my middle name told me to tread lightly.

"I mean, did you ever . . . I mean, have you ever . . . ?"

Mom's tone deepened and her cadence slowed. "I know you idolized your father, but if you're asking me if I cheated on him first or ever, the answer is no. If you are asking me if I ever did anything to push him in that direction, I might have to give you a qualified not sure."

"What do you mean by a qualified not sure?"

"Sit down, Casey. Let me tell you a little about how it was back then. Maybe it's time you heard about your imperfect parents."

I sat, not sure I wanted to hear any of it but knowing I had no choice.

"In the early years of our marriage, your Dad and I were happy and in love. He was excited about his job as a cop and excelled at it, so the promotions came fast. With each promotion came more responsibility, more stress, more danger—a way of life I was not prepared to accept—especially once you and Griffin were born.

"At the time I was equally pleased with my job as a stay-at-home mom with two beautiful, healthy children. His chaotic, dirty world on the police force collided with my clean, organized one. The real-life stories he brought home intruded on my fairytale. I asked him to leave the job at the office, so to speak. Ironically, I was afraid his work would affect our marriage. In the end, it did, but not as I'd expected."

I sat up straight. "How did you . . ."

She put her hand on my forearm. "Let me finish. One night, while working a tough case that blew up in their faces, Dad and Lisa almost got killed. Simply put, with no release valve and no one to turn to at home, they turned to each other. So in that way, I might have been guilty of not being the wife he needed. I was selfish, overprotective, and wrong."

"You're kidding, right? That was their excuse? No release valve? No one to turn to?"

"It's true. It happens. The professionals have more than a few terms for it. I'm not trying to whitewash it. It's infidelity, nonetheless."

"How did you forgive him? I don't know if I'd have that in me."

She stood up and walked across the room. She lifted the familiar framed cross-stitched pattern off the wall, one that had hung in our house forever. "Your grandmother gave me this cross-stitch kit a short time after Dad confessed his affair with Lisa."

"*You* did this? I remember it hanging on the wall in the hallway, but I never knew you did cross-stitch."

She returned to the couch and handed it to me. "Read it out loud, please, for me."

I took the frame from her. "Love is patient, love is kind. It does not envy, it does not boast, it is not proud. It is not rude, it is not self-seeking, it is not easily angered, it keeps no record of wrongs. Love does not delight in evil but rejoices with the truth. It always protects, always trusts, always hopes, always perseveres."

When I finished, I noticed Mom was holding the book she'd been reading when I first came in. It was a Bible. She flipped through the pages until she found what she was searching for.

"Those verses are found in First Corinthians. I used to think they sounded so romantic when I heard them recited at weddings. Putting them into practice is anything but romantic. It's plain hard work. Listen to them again when I replace the word *love* with my name.

"Annie is patient, Annie is kind. She does not envy, she does not boast, she is not proud. She is not rude, she is not self-seeking, she is not easily angered, she keeps no record of wrongs. Annie does not delight in evil but rejoices with the truth. She always protects, always trusts, always hopes, always perseveres."

I noted how personal the verses had become. "Is that even possible?"

Mom put the Bible down and turned to me. "You know what the funny thing was?"

"Funny? I can't imagine anything funny about this at all."

"The time it took me to complete this cross-stitch is the same length of time it took me to begin to forgive your father. It wasn't a one-time thing either. For a long time, I had to forgive him multiple times a day."

Any resentment toward my mother melted like a ragged cloud in the final rays of the afternoon sun. "It must have been hard."

"It was. It took months of me burning with jealousy and months of your father sleeping on the couch, trying to earn my trust back. I was a slow learner." She paused for a moment; then a wry smile appeared. "Never did enjoy cross-stitch after that either."

"Understandable." I hung the framed verse back on the wall.

"Reading those verses day after day reminded me that loving your father for better or worse was a choice I'd made on our wedding day. Going through that horrible time made our commitment to each other stronger, and we didn't dare take it for granted. If you love someone, truly love them, you do all you can to protect their reputation in life and their memory after death. I didn't want to dishonor your father or our vows by telling anyone about his indiscretion. I couldn't."

"It looks like someone else wants to do that for you."

"Perhaps. Have you told your brother yet?"

"No. I wanted to speak with you first."

She touched my cheek. "Because you were hoping I could make it all go away?"

"I guess . . . yes."

She leaned over and wrapped her arms around me. "I wish I could fix it, but I can't. Until the Lord showed me in His Word, I didn't completely forgive Lisa myself until a year or so ago—after I wrestled with God for a time."

I let her comment go by like a low, inside slider.

"Have you thought about what you're going to do next?" she asked.

"I guess I'll decide, or rather we'll decide, after I tell Griffin."

"I'll support whatever decision you two make. I know it will be the right one."

"What *is* the right decision, Mom?"
"You'll know, honey, you'll know."

8

Two days passed before I had the opportunity to tell Sam the whole story, replete with my frustration and shame. By the time I finished, my face was a tear-stained, mascara-smudged mess.

Holding me in his arms, Sam tried to soothe me. "Listen up, Case. Your father made a mistake. A big one, yes, but you've got to let it go."

"Let it go? What exactly does that mean? Maybe I should invite this so called half brother 'mistake' over for a cup of tea or, better yet, a beer?"

"Hey, that's not a bad idea. Have a beer summit and invite Griffin too."

I pulled away at his attempt to lighten the mood. "Don't marginalize my feelings, Sam."

He took a step toward me. "Casey, this whole thing is not the kid's fault. Meeting with him might help you to accept things."

"I don't want to accept things." Arms crossed, I sat down hard on the couch.

Sam sat next to me and spoke firmly. "Maybe it's time

you did. You've had your father up on a pedestal your whole life."

I snapped my head around to face him. "He was a good man and the best in his field. I was proud of him."

"Yes, and he was human. Grief has stages, Case, and I think you're stuck in stage one."

"So I'm supposed to forget he existed?"

"I never said that." Sam put his hands on his knees and pushed himself up. He walked over to the bookcase and picked up a photo of Dad and me taken at an awards ceremony. "Between photos, plaques, and awards, our home office seems more like the Ned McGee Memorial Library than my sanctuary. It's tough living in the shadow of another man."

"That's not fair." Anger turned my tears hot. "I don't know why you feel that way."

Sam plonked the framed photo down. "Really? You limit my talk about the force to the mundane and routine—the stuff you can handle comfortably. Yet you recount your dad's acts of bravery and heroism with pride. When I'm recognized for an achievement at work, you counter with a greater one of your father's like it's some sort of morbid competition."

"I do not!"

"Yes . . . you do. Answer me this, Casey. At night, when I'm at work and you're home alone, whose boots do you polish?"

I was stunned. This private act of love for my father was one of those sacred places where those who loved me, those I trusted, were not supposed to go . . . maybe even pretend did not exist. I felt betrayed.

He closed his eyes and shook his head. "I'm gonna go before I make things worse." He rushed out the front door, letting it slam shut behind him.

I waited for some time, expecting him to return, maybe to apologize or to talk it out. When he didn't, I went to the office to figure out what Sam felt and why.

I previewed the gallery of photos of Dad in his uniform, shaking hands with selectmen, governors, and senators. His citations and awards had been numerous, spanning decades of service. Removing one of my favorites from the wall, I touched the image of his face with my fingertips. That moment in time stood still. It was the day the superintendent presented Dad with the Medal of Honor for "acts of extraordinary heroism above and beyond the call of duty."

When Mom remarried, she'd given me most of Dad's career memorabilia. At the time, I thought I had the perfect place to display it. Apparently not. I had to concede, Sam was right. It looked like an exhibit in a museum.

And I was the chief curator.

Why couldn't Sam understand that it was all I had left of my father?

Griffin phoned me at work the next morning. "Wanna play scout this afternoon? I see some good, raw talent in some of my new varsity players this season."

"Sure," I said, thinking about the conversation I had to have with my brother sooner rather than later. I wanted to wait until the pregnancy glow wore off, but with Griffin that might mean waiting until he was doing 2 a.m. feedings.

I arrived in time to watch the final four innings of his high school varsity baseball team who were 4 and 0 for the season. As we left the field, my mind replayed the news I had to convey.

"Casey, wake up! Your mind was wandering three light years to the right. You almost trampled that little kid."

"Sorry. Thinking about the column," I lied.

"Forget the column for a minute. What do you think of my team?" Griffin was tough but fair. He recognized natural ability but believed in hard work. He wasn't one of those coaches who gave out awards hand over fist to make everyone feel special until no one felt special.

"You're right. There was some sharp play out there. Your shortstop and first baseman have agility and speed. The kid built like a redwood tree—number nine—he can hit. What's his average?"

"It's excellent, .310. We can talk more about it at the house. Jillian told me to ask you for dinner since Sam's on duty."

"Works for me."

I was relieved the opportunity to get together in private had presented itself in a natural way, because I didn't have the strength to make something up. Yet as soon as I knew what lay ahead, my hands started to sweat and continued sweating the full five miles to his house.

Since Jillian's morning sickness had plagued her until evening, Griffin offered to go for takeout. While he was gone, it gave us time for baby talk. Jillian spread out her new baby scrapbooking supplies, which I oohed and aahed over while admitting to myself that scrapbooking was something I'd never do. I was not surprised that she already had four sonogram-themed pages completed.

She showed me the quilt she was working on and the gender-neutral items she'd bought since they didn't know the sex of the baby and didn't want to find out. "It'll be fun to be surprised, don't you think?"

"Either way will be fun, I'm sure." Personally, I couldn't imagine why someone wouldn't want to know. How else could they plan? "I do have one secret wish though." I leaned in toward her. I was a sucker for making Jillian feel good; she made it easy by being so sweet.

"What is it?" Jillian, wide-eyed, asked in a whisper.

"Girl or boy, I hope it has your auburn hair and green eyes. What a beauty he or she will be!"

She put a protective hand over her stomach. "What if the baby has Griffin's dark brown hair and hazel eyes?"

"Then ditto! But don't tell my brother I said so."

She smiled a new-mother smile. "Thanks. My secret wish is that our baby doesn't have an appetite like his daddy. Griffin eats like he has a wooden leg."

Coming through the door with brown sacks of Chinese, Griffin laughed and said, "That's *hollow* leg."

"Oh, it is? I didn't know wooden legs were hollow," Jillian said, sounding like someone who's been teaching seven-year-olds a little too long.

Griffin kissed the top of her head. "Come along quietly, Jilly, before your white rice gets cold."

After dinner was over I helped clean up, not exactly stalling, but close. When Griffin and Jillian led the way to the living room, I knew it was time. Before we got sidetracked by another topic, I blurted, "Griffin, I have something important to tell you."

He leaned forward in his recliner. "Oh yeah, what?"

"Do you want me to leave?" Jillian asked, already pushing herself up off the couch.

I motioned for her to sit back down. "No, you're family."

Griffin repositioned himself on the edge of his chair. "What's got you so serious?"

I took a deep breath and let the words fall out on exhale. "I got a letter from a woman who used to work with Dad about twenty-five years ago. In it she confessed to having an affair with him." I inhaled and waited for their reaction.

Jillian and Griffin looked at each other then down at their laps. Something was off. Neither spoke for a long few seconds until Griffin said, "Is her name Lisa?"

"How did you know? Did Mom tell you?"

"No. I overheard Mom and Dad talking one night when I was a kid."

"You knew?" I was stunned by his confession. "How come you never told me?"

"I didn't want them to know I knew." Griffin shrugged. "I thought if I told you, you'd bring it up."

I could feel the heat rising and suspected they both could see it. "You should have told me!"

He protested louder than I expected. "Why? From what I could see they'd worked things out." He looked pretty sure of his reasoning. "Besides, even if I had told you, you wouldn't have believed anything bad about Dad."

Here it was again. First from Mom, then Sam, and now Griffin.

"What else do you know?" I asked.

"Nothing. That's all." He looked at me sideways. "Why?"

Something in me wanted to punish him for keeping this secret from me. "What would you say if I told you we have a half brother no one knew about until now?"

Griffin jerked forward. "What?" He bobbed his head and blinked twice as if to clear his mind like an Etch a Sketch. "Say again."

"Lisa had Dad's son. According to Lisa, he's twenty-four years old and wants to meet us."

"A brother? Wow. What's his name? What does he . . . where does he live?" Griffin stumbled over his questions.

"She didn't say, and I haven't asked. I wanted to talk to Mom first to make sure this Lisa person wasn't some kind of con artist. But I guess you would've known that already."

"Give me a break. I was a scared kid. What else did she say?"

I reached for Hildegard and pulled out the letter. "Here. Read it yourself."

Griffin got up, took the letter from my hand, and sat on the couch near Jillian. When they finished reading it, he went to his office and made a copy before handing it back to me. "So when do you want to meet him?"

"I don't," I said flatly, hiding my disbelief at his question.

"What do you mean?" Griffin asked. "You don't want to meet him now . . . or ever?"

At the end of the night, we'd reached a stalemate. We agreed to table the matter for a while and that I'd relay that much to Lisa. I made Griffin and Jillian promise not to tell another human being, including her parents. Before leaving, I sort of apologized to Griffin, admitting to myself that none of this was his fault.

I was being irrational and knew it. Either I didn't care or couldn't help it. This one stupid act between so-called mature adults had had repercussions no one had ever imagined. I was angry at everyone involved—Mom and Griffin for not telling me, Lisa Erickson for the affair, and her son for having the audacity to be born.

On my drive back home, like a dowsing rod my anger found its true source. I raised my eyes to the heavens and cried out, "Thanks, Dad, for taking the easy way out and leaving us with your mess to clean up."

9

Three days before Opening Day at Fenway, I got a call from Darin Flynn. "A-yo, told you I'd let you know as soon as it was official."

"About time! Have they announced it?"

"Not yet. Contract's been signed, sealed, and delivered, but the Sox front office wants to wait seventy-two hours before they hold a press conference."

"Mike must be relieved."

"Yeah, we'll celebrate when he gets back. The team's in Cleveland for a couple more days. Now, what do you want to know about me for that column of yours?"

"Everything! Wait. Are you free for dinner tonight?"

"Sure, what do you have in mind?"

"Why don't you meet Griffin and me at my house in Kingston? I'll cook, you can talk, and Griffin can take notes. On second thought, we'll order in, Griffin will get you to talk, and I'll take notes."

Darin laughed. "Not your standard issue interview."

"It's more like passing secrets between friends. It won't hurt a bit."

That night, Griffin and I learned that Darin Flynn had been born and raised in South Boston, his father was a senior software engineer with a reputable company in the city, and his mother was a stay-at-home mom with eight children.

Griffin gave me a noogie as he passed by my chair. "Yikes! I have all I can handle with one sibling."

I batted Griffin off like I would a pesky fly. "A stay-at-home mom? Like the kind who works harder than a lot of 'working' women?"

"That's Mom. And with Hennessey at our house most of the time, it's like she had nine kids. We're not a run-of-the-mill blended family. Dad was widowed when he met Mom. He had a daughter, and she had a son. They had three together and adopted three more. When my parents tell people some of their kids are adopted, it's always fun watching them try to guess which ones."

Darin ran his hand through his thick, curly hair. If possible, he smiled more when he talked about his family than he did about baseball.

"Any more Irish redheads like you?" I asked.

"Only me and my brother Andrew. How about you guys? Do you have a large family?"

I answered before Griffin could. "Mom and Dad, me, then Griffin."

Griffin took a swig of his Pepsi. "Going on four years since Dad passed away."

"I'm so sorry to hear that," Darin said. "That must have been rough."

"Yeah, it was," Griffin said. "Mom's happy, recently remarried, so we don't have to worry about her being alone." His face brightened. "And, as an unexpected turn of events, we'll be meeting another family member soon."

Why on earth was Griffin telling Darin about Lisa's son when we hadn't even decided to meet him? I was seething . . . until Griffin said, "Yup, my wife Jillian and I are expecting our first child in October."

What is wrong with you, Casey? You forgot about your brother's baby?

Darin congratulated Griffin then teased him about all the changes a baby would bring.

After a few minutes, I steered the topic back to our interview. "So I take it Mike lived nearby growing up?"

"A few streets over. Our parents met at church and became friends. That's how Mike and I ended up at the same parochial school." He laughed. "It took him years to forgive my parents for suggesting it."

Later, Mike and Darin had moved to public high school and applied to various colleges. Even though Darin was accepted by a couple of Ivy League schools, he chose to join Mike at UMass.

"Was Mike the main reason you chose UMass?" I took a bite of my salad while waiting for his answer.

"Mike was one of the reasons. But UMass is an excellent school, and it was less of a financial strain for my family."

Griffin asked, "When did you both start playing ball?"

"You know how it is. We always played ball—in the backyard, in the street, in the park."

"How about Little League?" Griffin asked. "Man, I loved Little League!"

Darin grinned. "That came later, but it wasn't until we were in high school that Mike started to make a name for himself."

I finished jotting down a note. "You were part of the Cape Cod Baseball League during summers in your college years, right?"

"Right, but my first summer was with the Defenders out of Holman Stadium in Nashua, New Hampshire." Darin popped the last bit of his vegetarian pocket into his mouth. "The following summer I joined Mike on the Cape, both of us playing for the Orleans Firebirds. That's when the MLB scouts took notice. Mike went to the Pawtucket Red Sox straight out of college."

"You didn't have to wait long to reconnect with him." Griffin nabbed another piece of pizza. "I think the Sox scouts were afraid they'd lose you."

"Maybe. After years of reading each other's moves, it seems to work."

I smiled at his understatement. "Yes it does, doesn't it?"

"Almost as well as it works for Casey and me." Griffin wiped his hands on a napkin and leaned back. "Except you catch fast balls from Mike, and I catch flak from Casey."

Roberta called to arrange a late lunch meeting for the following day. "I'm flying in to Boston tomorrow. I've got a couple of PR ideas to bounce off you two."

Finding a balance between Roberta's ideas and our principles could be tricky. Some of the lines we wouldn't cross. While visible to us, they were blurry to Roberta. When that occurred, I could count on Griffin to crack his standard response to make things clear: "Nope. Not gonna do it, don't have to, can't make us."

She knew not to argue.

Since Roberta was staying with family in Boston, she asked if we wanted to meet in the city. Craving seafood, I suggested my favorite place, the Union Oyster House, only a few quick turns from Faneuil Hall.

When I'd first heard of this place, I found it hard to believe the doors of any establishment had been open to diners since 1826. It only took one visit for the tin ceilings, original brick walls, and worn dark wood to convince me.

Enjoying a first-class menu against a historic backdrop could go a long way to soften Roberta's brusqueness.

"What's the earliest you can make it?" she asked. "If we get there before four, we'll have a better chance at a quiet booth."

"I can leave work early, but Griffin might be late."

When I arrived, Roberta was standing outside the restaurant talking on her iPhone, smoking a cigarette. Her signature bouclé suit in vibrant shades of red and orange, a half size too small, matched the color and condition of her over-treated hair.

She segued from her phone conversation to talking to me,

exhaling simultaneously. "The Sox are in town for a long stretch at the end of this month and into May. I'm waiting for a callback from your boys' agent. Thought they might be more agreeable if you asked them personally. It's a guest spot with you two on the brand-y new TV show, *Red Sox Nation*."

I pointed to her cigarette with my chin. "Thought you quit."

"I did. I'm on the patch."

Managing to keep a straight face, I asked, "How's it working?"

"Actually, pretty well." She took a final drag before she flicked the butt into a storm drain.

"Ah, denial, a handy tool in an agent's kit. Does it make it easier to overcome editors' objections?"

Roberta looked at me like I was speaking Punjabi. "What objections?" Then she pulled the door open and walked into the restaurant.

Following in her steps, it took my eyes a moment to adjust from the light of day to the darkness of centuries past.

Once we were seated, Roberta resumed her pitch. "So about your boys . . ."

"I wouldn't say one golf match and a few phone conversations qualify Mike and Darin as 'our boys,' but I can ask." I knew if I gave Roberta a hint that we were friends, she'd use it to her advantage, not theirs. "When's the taping? Don't you want to know if Griffin and I are available first?"

"The show will be taped in the late afternoon on April 29 and aired later in the evening. I'll get a time for you, but I'm sure they'll do whatever they can to accommodate the Irish Twins. Remember, it's a new show."

About forty-five minutes passed before Griffin joined us. "Your suit matches your hair to a tee, Roberta."

I covered my mouth with my napkin.

Roberta raised her glass to him. "Good eye, Griffin. I'm surprised you noticed."

I interrupted Griffin's fashion commentary to bring him up to speed on our meeting. Then we ordered dinner and talked about my list of topics for our upcoming column installments.

"You said there were a couple of things you wanted to talk over, Roberta," I said. "What's the second?"

"Oh, yes. There's a fundraising event coming up I think you both should participate in. I want you to convince your Irish Twins to do a couple of Double Header interviews in conjunction."

"What kind of event?" I asked, starting with the basics.

"It's a 9K run which starts at Yawkey Way and ends at Fenway Park. The runners finish the race when they cross home plate. The entries are limited, so you have to sign up soon."

"I've heard about that," I said. "What's the cause again?"

Griffin cracked himself up. "'Cause you want us to use Hennessey and Flynn to get free publicity?"

Roberta answered, "I don't know what you're talking about, Mr. Wise Guy."

He threw his head back and laughed. "Yeah, I bet you don't!"

"I'm being sincere here. It's a worthy cause. The money raised helps provide services to local veterans. If you had your eyes peeled, McGee, you'd already know about it."

"Isn't that what super agents are for?" Griffin took a sip of his drink.

"I see you've been reading fairytales again." Roberta took her napkin from her lap to dab at the corners of her mouth. "I've told you this before, but I'll tell you again. You are in charge of your careers, not me."

"What's your connection to the race?" I asked, getting the conversation back on track.

"My nephew's serving a tour overseas." She reached into her briefcase and pulled out some papers. "Here's the information. The Red Sox are involved, and so is Mass General Hospital. It's all legit."

I took the papers from her. "If the Red Sox are already involved, wouldn't that include Hennessey and Flynn? Why would they need us?"

"You found me out. They don't, but I do. I promised my sister. Your boys will boost awareness and raise more money for the vets. If that's a selfish reason, then I confess I'm guilty. In turn, if it gives you and your column some publicity, there's nothing wrong with that. Besides, you two socialites got something better to do the third week in May?"

She had us there. Griffin scanned my face. I gave him the go-ahead signal.

He leaned back and tucked his thumbs into his front pockets. "Okay, we're in, but you know what this means?"

Roberta bit. "What?"

He grinned. "I'll need to build myself a bigger trophy case."

"In your dreams," I said. "You'll be eating my dust, McGee."

10

After four years as my college roommate, Vanessa Vance knew everything about me. Except the fact that I had a half brother. I needed an objective ear, so I asked her to meet me for lunch.

"Mind if we meet at three instead?" she said. "I've got a noon meeting with a new client. Of course, I can reschedule if that doesn't work for you."

I knew if I asked her, she would have. "Three o'clock is perfect—the quiet space between the lunch rush and early evening specials."

Vanessa had known me in my idealistic years, when I'd initially chosen psychology as my major with a goal to heal the world. However, as I learned how the human mind worked, I realized I didn't want to listen to other peoples' problems for the rest of my life.

She is the one who pointed out to me that my reluctance to change my major to marketing had less to do with it being a poor choice and more to do with my not wanting to follow in my mother's footsteps. She wouldn't buy my whiney argument "But it's so unoriginal."

As if my choice of career wasn't prosaic enough, a few years later I married a cop like my father. I forgave myself the clichéd choices because I loved my husband and liked my work.

Instead of waiting for Vanessa in the foyer of the restaurant, I took a table by the window. I would know when she arrived. Everyone would. With her silky mocha skin, cropped bronze hair, and gazelle-like, six-foot-one-inch frame atop her usual four-inch Jimmy Choo pumps, she looked more like a fashion model than a litigator. She had impeccable taste and a budget to match. I knew her suit—a jacket paired with a skirt, never slacks—would be tailored to fit her every curve and would show enough leg to be professional yet distracting.

"There you are!" Vanessa's greeting wafted above the din.

Like a line of synchronized swimmers, a wave of heads followed her as she crossed the room. Did she even notice anymore? Or was she immune to the admiration?

We kissed cheeks like European friends, keeping our vow never to use fake air kisses like housewives from New York.

"It's been too long, hasn't it? How's Bryson? Still with United?" She'd met her pilot husband on one of her many trips to her firm's office in Los Angeles.

"Yes, he managed to fly above the layoffs. As long as he's in the cockpit, he's happy. And Sam? That cop still being sweet to you?"

"As always." We got our catch-up questions and anecdotes out of the way over lunch. By the time dessert and coffee arrived, Vanessa got serious. "Now that we know your mama is fine and my mama is fine, tell me, what are we here for? And don't tell me you missed me. You're too busy to miss me."

"The pot calling the kettle black."

"I *am* black. What's your excuse?"

We both knew that whoever initiated the get-together was the one with "the situation," as we referred to it. "You're right. There is something I want to run by you."

"Let's hear it." She pushed her dessert plate aside and rested her arms on the table.

With Vanessa, I didn't have to justify my feelings. I simply had to be truthful. And because none of this affected her personally like it did Griffin, I wouldn't be on the defensive. She'd be candid but not brutal.

I told her the whole story, including my reaction to it.

She slapped her cheeks with her hands. "Oy vey! Let me summarize the case as I see it. First, I know how much you adored your father, so I understand why this is a shocker. Second, you're a freak about planning, and you couldn't plan for this. Third, frankly, I think you'll want to meet your half brother one day. Until then, you're entitled to your feelings, so take as much time as you need and don't accept the guilt."

"So I'm not crazy?"

She laughed. "Oh, you're crazy all right. But that's what I love about you. That and the fact you'll be turning thirty way before I do."

I slumped in my chair. "And we were having such a pleasant time."

Vanessa tapped her fingers on the table. "So, do you think this kid will keep his word about waiting for you to respond? Or do you think he's already searching?"

I straightened. "I hadn't thought about that."

Until now.

"Has anyone fitting his description phoned you or Griffin or approached either of you in person?"

"How would we know since we don't have a description?" My mind started walking backward over the past few weeks. Had anyone new approached me?

"Well, if you need a lawyer, you've got my number."

"Why would I need a lawyer? Why do you legalese types always run to the worst case scenario?"

Vanessa presented a litany of horror stories about families losing entire estates for back child support. When it was time for her to go, she left me choking on a heaping portion of reasonable doubt.

11

Almost two weeks had passed since I received Lisa Erickson's letter. Since I told Griffin I would respond soon, I rummaged through my drawer of note cards. Discarding the hearts and flowers and puppies, I chose an impersonal geometric design.

Dear Ms. Erickson,

As you can imagine, your letter came as a shock to our family and it's taken some time to assimilate this news.

I've discussed the matter with both my mother and brother. My mother revealed that my father had told her about the affair shortly after it occurred. They were able to work through it and come out a stronger couple.

Even though we can sympathize with your son's desire to meet with his biological father's family, we are not agreeable to that at this time. Perhaps someday, but we are not there yet.

Sincerely,
Casey McGee Gallagher

I didn't feel the need to elaborate or make promises I couldn't keep. I licked the flap and pounded it shut with my fist like a six-year-old boy.

Even though her letter was postmarked "Brookline, MA" the reply-to address she'd given me was a post office box in Boston, the Clarenden Street branch I passed every day on my walk from the Back Bay T station to my office. Coincidence? I didn't know.

I dropped it off right where she would pick it up, and that gave me goose bumps. I surveyed the people milling around the boxes and counters. Was she here? Or was he? How would I know? What would I do if I did?

I got outta there fast.

Now that my response to Lisa was in the mail and off my mind, I needed to make things right with Sam before the Red Sox opener at Fenway.

During the days following his walkout and my subsequent emotional lockout, silence had been the buffer between us the few times we'd been home together and awake. While some say the silent treatment is unhealthy, I believe at times it's more viral to open your mouth. The quiet had helped us sort through our feelings without inflicting additional pain.

That didn't stop me from making the occasional face behind Sam's back. I half hoped he wouldn't see me, half hoped I would get caught. Does that even make sense? What was maddening was my knowing that he wasn't doing the same. Leave it to Sam to show me up by taking the high road.

We were clumsy in our efforts to avoid all physical contact while simultaneously yearning for it. The only exception was a few perfunctory peck-on-the-cheek good-bye kisses when it would have been too confrontational not to do so.

In the face of what my mother, husband, and brother had intimated or outright said, I realized my relationship with Dad was at the core of my dysfunction. I didn't understand how Dad loving me and me loving him could be wrong. I loved my husband; I was certain of that. So why did I put Dad first? Had I done that when he was alive too? Or was I doing that now because he was gone? Was it grief or guilt preventing me from letting go?

Ironically, finding out that my father was not the sinless saint I thought he was is what drove me to take this honest inventory of my feelings. Admitting the problem was a start. But it didn't mean I'd be free overnight.

After a work week of grunt-and-mumble breakfasts and sleepless nights each on our own refrigerated side of the bed, I was ready to talk. I rolled over in bed to face him.

"Sam?"

"Yes."

"Remember our marriage vows, when we promised to hold hands in the hard places? I'm sorry I let go."

"I'm sorry too, Case. Getting married months before you lost your dad wasn't the most ideal situation. I should have been more understanding."

I snuggled up closer. "I think I underestimated grief."

He put his arm around me. "We both did. From our honeymoon to grief in six months. I don't know if we ever let ourselves experience either fully."

"There's something else. Mom told me that long before Dad's affair she'd asked him not to talk about work at home because she couldn't handle the stress. I've done the same thing with you, and I want that to change. I want you to be able to tell me anything, anything at all, whenever you want."

We spent an hour talking, sharing feelings we'd never admitted. Determined to improve communication, we agreed to deal with pet peeves and misunderstandings before they took root. When it came to my dad, we both knew I could use some more time.

Without my bringing it up, Sam said, "And don't worry about me sharing this news with anyone else. When and if that happens will be your decision."

Our talk cleared the air almost as much as our lovemaking did.

Going to Opening Day at Fenway was a longstanding family tradition years before I began my career at Kincade Marketing Solutions. So when Gordy, no sports fan himself, offered me two tickets for exclusive club seating with the condition that I babysit clients, I had to decline, but it was tough.

"Gordy, you know this is one of the few personal days I take every year for family. We've had our tickets since the first day they went on sale."

"Yeah, but I thought as long as you were going anyway..."

Gordy Ackerman had never been to Fenway Park or any baseball game, ever.

"It won't work. Our seats are nowhere near Kincade's."

"Oh." He paced behind his desk. "Is there any way you can find someone else to take them, as a favor to me? These clients are avid football fans."

"Baseball, Gordy, baseball. I'll handle it, no problem."

"Thanks, Casey. I owe you one."

"Someone will owe me, but it won't be you, Gordy."

To be fair, Kincade supported me in my side venture when other employers might not. My perks included occasional free tickets to home games—something to cheer about since an average Red Sox game for two can run well over $200. They also gave me flex time for interviews and media appearances. It wasn't strictly philanthropic—they know good PR when they see it—although the little my humble sports column provided them was like a drop in the ocean for a company that spanned the Northeast region. Yet when so many other companies used booze to entice clients, I was grateful Kincade preferred sports.

Opening Day arrived. After a few hours of work, I left to meet Sam, Griffin, and Jillian at Park Street, where we'd take the T to Kenmore Square and walk the short distance to the park. As I did twice every weekday on my way to work, I passed the post office where I'd mailed the letter to Lisa Erickson. Although the constant reminder of this kid and his mother chafed like a tight wool turtleneck, I wasn't about to let it change my routine.

Even as I determined not to, I studied the people coming and going, speculating whether she or he was among them. I had no idea what Lisa or her son looked like, yet somehow I knew none of these people were them. I made snap judgments based on split second glances. Not him—too young, too jovial, too sloppy, nothing like Dad. Not her—too gray, too ethnic, too highbrow for a cop.

I shook it off and refocused on Opening Day. When I reached Park Street, Sam and Griffin were there but no Jillian. "Where's your wife?"

Griffin said, "To be ballpark frank, the mere thought of a whiff of a hotdog brought the nausea back. When I left her, she was practicing the art of cradling by hugging the porcelain bowl."

I stared at Griffin. How could he have left her alone?

"Don't give me that look. Her mother's with her. What kind of person do you think I am?"

Before I could reply, I was distracted by a young man standing near them.

"Eh, eh," Sam interrupted. "Before your sister answers, let me say I think you're a generous person since you offered Jillian's ticket to me. Casey, meet Tommy Coletti."

I extended my hand. "We finally get to meet. I'd tell you that Sam has been boasting about you, but he probably doesn't want me to blow his bad cop cover."

"Yeah, that would be him. I'd be lying if I told you Sam hasn't bragged about you more than a few times."

Griffin laughed. "Good answer! Not one, count 'em, two smart cops."

I had pictured Coletti as having a muscular build, olive skin, and thick, dark wavy hair—my stereotypical version of Italian handsome. Instead, he was built a lot like Sam, about six feet, wiry with a medium-brown buzz cut. Still handsome, though.

If you could be this wrong about Coletti, could you be wrong about the people you see at the post office? I wondered.

Oh, shut-up, Casey.

Gate C at Fenway opened at noon. Die-hard fans crowded Lansdowne Street, hoping to score one of the tickets held back by the Sox for the home opener. Although the first pitch wouldn't be thrown out until 2:05, we'd come early for the complete experience. As I walked up the ramp to the concourse overlooking the field, a chill rippled through me. It happened every year at my first Fenway game.

Sam and Tommy went to get some cold drinks while Griffin and I found our seats. No sooner had we reached our row when Roberta called to gloat over our exclusive story of the Sox signing Darin Flynn. I switched to speaker so Griffin could hear.

"Bravo! Your story was online before the mighty cavalcade of sports reporters could clamp their chewed-down pencil nubs between their sweaty little fingers and start scribbling."

"Pencil? What's a pencil?" Griffin asked. "Is that an app for a smart phone?"

"Casey, give your brother a head-slap for me, will you?"

Griffin and I had written the article the same night Darin had dinner with us. When they made the announcement, all we had to do was hit Send.

Roberta continued, "Minor league columnists don't often scoop major league journalists, so this will go a long way to help me get you more TV time."

Griffin leaned in closer to the phone. "Let me get this straight. Are you admitting we did something right?"

"Second that head-slap, Casey," Roberta said. "I'll call you later."

That she would.

When Sam and Tommy returned with the drinks, we talked hockey while waiting for the ball game to start.

Being a local himself, Tommy was a Boston Bruins fan too. He'd played hockey as a kid—still did, we discovered—so he'd followed the Bs faithfully even in the years when many forgot they existed.

"They're having a fantastic year," Griffin said. "What do you think their chances are of bringing the Stanley Cup back to Boston?"

"They'll clinch it," Tommy said. "I feel it in my bones."

I chuckled. "What are you, twenty-four, twenty-five? A little young to be feeling things in your bones, don't you think?"

"Age has nothing to do with it. Think about it. I'm a cop. Sore bones come with the profession."

"Yes, I've heard that lament from my husband."

"Besides, I don't know why you're asking me what I think," Tommy said. "I read your column. You know your stuff."

Griffin high-fived me. "Fooled another one!"

Tommy said, "For real, how do you decide what to write about every week?"

I answered, "I keep a running list of topics. Some we schedule in advance, but most depend on what's going on in the news. It's more like we each write a column on the same topic then email them to each other to review."

Griffin said, "Then Casey smoothes out the transitions before we turn them in. Sometimes she even keeps a few of my words."

I ignored him. "It works better when we don't collaborate prior to deadline. It has a more honest feel to it, unrehearsed."

Griffin chuckled. "Yeah, at first the editors asked us to fake tension and drama whenever we could. Then they discovered we did that naturally."

"Who came up with the column name?" Tommy asked.

"I don't remember exactly," Griffin said. "We went back and forth between that one and Sibling Rivalry. We finally tossed a coin, and Double Header won."

"Easy to remember. That's what counts." Tommy's cell phone rang. "Hi, Pop. What? Calm down, go slow . . . She said what?"

We didn't mean to eavesdrop, but it was hard not to since the game hadn't started.

He listened for a minute and massaged his forehead before switching his phone from one ear to the other. "This is important how? Geez, Pop, don't worry about the meatballs. I'll talk to her."

Once he hung up, Sam repeated, "Don't worry about the meatballs?"

"Yeah, meatballs. This morning my sister Ali announced she was a vegetarian. When Pop asked her if that meant not eating his meatballs, she said yes. To a Coletti this constitutes a catastrophe."

"Wow. Wish we had your family," I said. "Meatballs are nothing."

"Be careful what you wish for," Tommy said. "If my family gets that upset over food, how do you think they deal with real problems? I assure you, we've got more going on than meatballs right now." He turned toward the field and hung a Closed sign on his face.

None of us asked what those problems might be.

Turning around a zero-to-six start for the season, the Sox won the Fenway opener in part due to the Hennessey-Flynn battery. Before meeting Mike and Darin, I might have gone on one of my annual rampages about the obscene salaries and signing bonuses of pro athletes, but I skipped that tirade this year, deciding to be glad for the local boys. Besides, I got paid to write about them.

Unfortunately, not nearly as much as they did.

On our way out of the park, Sam initiated a couples' get-together with Tommy and his girlfriend. I was pleased. My husband was no Griffin—his social interaction was limited and usually handled by me. Their tentative plan was to meet in the middle geographically at a local pub known for its "killer buffalo wings."

Of course, being the smart cops they were, they opted to leave the details to the women.

12

Nora rapped on my open door. "Do you have a minute, Casey?"

"For you? Sure."

She looked behind her, stepped in, and closed the door. In a voice one level above a whisper she said, "Something fishy is definitely going on."

"Like what?"

"Not sure, but after you left for the game yesterday, the suits from New York paid us another unannounced visit. This time they weren't alone. A whole entourage burst in on Gordy."

"He didn't say anything to me when I came in. Are you sure they weren't contractors or potential clients?"

"No, I recognized a few faces but not all. If office gossip is reliable, after they left Gordy's office they went through every space on all three floors like they were taking inventory."

"That is curious. I'll talk to Gordy as soon as I can, but it'll have to wait. I have clients waiting for callbacks, a presentation to make in an hour, and monthly expense receipts to gather before bookkeeping sics human resources on me."

"If you have those receipts," Nora said, "I can take care of that report for you."

Oops. Human resources must have sicced Nora.

By happenstance, I found myself alone in the elevator with Gordy the next morning. "What's with all the New York big-leaguers coming to town again?"

His lips curled down and he shrugged. "Who knows? I felt like they were taking my temperature. And the thermometer wasn't under my tongue, if you get my drift."

"Besides the Kincade execs, who were the others with them?

"I'm not sure. Maybe investors or bankers. All very hush-hush. Our recent forecasts have been stellar, so maybe all that talk of expanding to Los Angeles is turning to action. But you didn't hear that from me, got it?"

"Got it."

Gordy leaned back against the elevator wall and crossed one foot over the other. "The wife and I sure wouldn't mind a long stint in sunny California, though."

"Nice place to visit, but I could never live in the home of the Lakers."

"I've heard the smog is bad, but the lakes, polluted, are they?"

I had to cut back on the sports talk with Gordy. "Tell you what, Gordy, if you get transferred to LA, I promise to visit."

Roberta called around noon with the news that we'd been granted a last minute guest spot on the Boston sports talk show *From the Bleachers*. "The show's host is Peter Maddox, a former baseball player from the '70s. The other panel regulars are Linda Briggs, a local sports journalist, and Danny Pace, a farm team coach. They want you at the studio by three."

"Roberta, even if I could leave work early today, there's no way Griffin can make it in time."

"Go it alone."

"Alone? Uh, I guess . . ."

"Be there by three."

Click.

I held the cool cell phone against my forehead. "Why do I let that woman bully me?"

Resigned to the reluctant commitment I'd made, I skipped lunch so I could leave work early.

On my way to the studio, as I did before every interview, I practiced taking Rs off words that didn't need them, like *Linder*, and putting them back on others, like *Peta*. My mantra went something like this: "Lindaaa, Peterrr, Lindaaa, Peterrr, pitcherrr, catcherrr, batterrr, parrrk." Even though my Massachusetts accent wasn't as pronounced as the generations before me, it was apt to rear its ugly mother tongue when I got nervous.

If the opportunity arose, I decided to use the term *strong throwing arm* instead of the slang *bazooka*. That word begged for an R at the end. I didn't know Peter or Linda, but I liked Danny already, simply for having a first name that ended in Y.

I was sent to makeup as soon as I arrived then briefed on the show's theme: the Irish Twins. Their use of the nickname Griffin and I had coined jacked up my confidence. Still, I knew Griffin and I played well off each other; I didn't know how I would play with others. And they had the home advantage. *Oh, grow up, Casey.*

"Here's our girl," Peter said as I walked onto the set. "Welcome!"

Danny stood and rolled a chair out for me. The wide semicircular desk gave us something to lean on or hide behind—in my case, both. Linda smiled as I scooted in next to her. At least I think it was a smile. After folding and unfolding my hands several times, I finally found a pose that felt natural.

A few minutes into the show after some opening banter, Peter turned to me. "Casey, you and Griffin came up with Irish Twins nickname, didn't you?"

"Yes, it seemed to fit."

"And stick," he said. "I know you told me before, but tell the rest of our audience how you and your brother met them. That story's a hoot."

Telling the tale of our golf outing gave the audience a clear snapshot of Griffin. My self-deprecating style was enough to make me, the doubting Thomas of the duo, seem sympathetic. In a brief encounter with humility, I left out the five-stroke drubbing I'd given them.

Peter laughed even after hearing it again, and Danny marveled at how it had all turned out.

But Linda's question dropped like a dying quail, "What do you think happened to your boy Hennessey between Opening Day and yesterday's game? The only thing he pitched was a fit when he was pulled in the fourth after giving up six runs."

Whoa. So much for the warm welcome.

"Linder-a. I've seen that look before. Hennessey wasn't mad at being pulled. He was mad at himself. Flynn talked to him. I'm sure he'll rebound his next time out."

Peter leaned forward. "Speaking of Flynn, he's like a crouching animatronic robot behind the plate. He doesn't struggle with mechanics at all."

Linda snapped, "No, lack of speed on the bases is his problem."

Danny said, "Give the kid a break, Linda. It's not like he kept his slow wheels a secret."

Thank you, Danny.

On my way home I debriefed myself, admitting I'd been defensive when Linda talked trash about the Twins. I'd defended Mike, when truthfully his game and attitude had been way off the day before. From confidence and razzle-dazzle against the Yankees to dissidence and lackluster against the Rays, it didn't make sense. When the manager went to the mound with the catcher, it was obvious it was Darin who talked Mike down.

What could have gone wrong in four days?

Later that night, Roberta called to tell me that our scheduled guest appearance with the Irish Twins on the new show *Red Sox Nation* had been postponed due to a change in the station's programming. "I had a few choice words for that station manager."

I cringed and wondered if our names were forever expunged from their guest roster. "I'm sure the hosts are more bummed than you are."

"I hope they saw your solo appearance on *From the Bleachers*," she said. "That will make them sorry they canceled. You were terrific!"

"Think so, Roberta, even with the extra Rs I let slip?"

"I would have called her Linder too, if not worse. She has a point though. Find out what's wrong with your boy, and I bet you find a story."

Roberta rarely said good-bye, so I hung up without a reply before I was caught talking to dead air again.

Darin and Mike had gone the distance to make room in their schedules to appear with us on the *Red Sox Nation* debut. I was embarrassed to tell them it was a no-go, so I asked Griffin to do the dirty work. "You're better at this. People find it easier to open up to you, so ask if everything's okay with Mike."

Griffin called me after he spoke with them. "Nothing's wrong. They're working out some personal stuff, that's all."

"That's all? Did you ask what personal stuff?"

"Nope. Besides, they didn't have time to talk because they were late for baseball chapel."

"Baseball chapel?"

"Yup."

"Did you ask what that meant?"

"Why would I? It was clear. They were late for baseball chapel."

Agh! Griffin could be so frustrating.

13

Since I promised myself I'd take a proactive interest in Sam's work life, I reminded him about the get-together he'd suggested with Tommy and his girlfriend and offered to call her. Per usual for Sam, it took him a few days to get her number, then another day to get her name, Gina Zicaro.

When I called Gina, we agreed to meet at the "killer buffalo wings" place Sam and Tommy had drooled over and then follow with a round of miniature golf at the new indoor center. I would have chosen the driving range but Gina said, "The putt-putt course is totally more in line with my athletic abilities." I decided to be a good sport since she seemed like onc too.

I was wrong. What a surprise.

Sam and I were waiting for Tommy and Gina at the bar when they made their entrance.

"I should've known. OMG, this place is a dump!" Gina shrieked above the noise of the full bar.

Heads turned, and not just ours.

"Shh," said Tommy. "Keep it down, Gi."

Even if Gina hadn't uttered a word, her five-inch red stilettos, tight black pencil skirt, and leopard-print halter top were loud enough to gain attention.

"Don't shush me and don't call me Gi! Find your friends, and let's get outta here!"

"Gina, give it a chance, huh? The wings are fantastic, you'll see."

She shimmied her shoulders and got in his face. "Don't care about your fantastic wings. We shoulda gone to the new French beef-stro in town. That place totally has class."

Wow. A memorable introduction. And we still had the whole evening ahead of us. I choked on "nice to meet you" when Tommy introduced us and settled for "hi." My poor husband. His maiden voyage into the sea of social event planning had run aground.

In the end, Gina agreed to stay but refused to order anything from "that filthy kitchen." She spent the whole forty minutes we were there pouting, pressing the wrinkles out of her skirt, admiring her nails, and flipping her long black hair extensions over her bare shoulders. Tommy tried his best to placate her, but his best didn't cut it. The minute our feet touched the sidewalk, Gina announced she had a headache and would take a cab home.

Phew. We'd been granted a reprieve. Now what to do with it?

The peculiar thing was Tommy didn't seem to be bothered or embarrassed by her behavior, like it was a usual occurrence. I didn't know what to say without making him feel bad or without lying, so I said nothing. I didn't expect Sam to comment. Still, as a precaution, I flashed him my warning eyes with a subtle headshake.

Tommy waved bye to the cab then asked, "Hey, how about the indoor batting cages instead of mini golf? Okay by you, Casey?"

Without hesitation, Sam and I agreed.

The place was crowded with only one spot free. In a sympathetic move, we let Tommy bat first. Once in the cage, he said, "I've developed a simple system that helps clear my head. Watch and learn."

As the first pitch came toward him he yelled, "Vancouver Canucks!" *Thwack!* After the second, "Beef-stros!" *Thwack!* After the third, "Secrets!" *Thwack!* His bat connected with every ball he yelled at. "Try it, you'll see."

Sam was next in line and followed suit getting hits off cries of "repeat offenders," "drug dealers," and "the Yankees."

Sam cheered me on. "Okay, show us what you've got, Case!"

I gripped the bat, feeling silly even after watching them go before me. When the pitching machine started, I said, "Housework" loud enough for the guys to hear me. Swing and a miss.

Tommy called over, "You can do better than that. I heard you at Fenway, remember? Besides, you've got to let it all out for it to work."

I repositioned my feet and changed my grip. This time I took a deep breath and howled, "Lies!" *Thwack!* "Trust!" *Thwack!* "Betrayal!" *Thwack!* In seven-second intervals, I smacked my emotions into the air and emptied myself in the process. Cathartic batting, who knew? Too bad the relief was only temporary.

After our time in the cages, I made an effort to get to know Tommy better. Since both my grandfather and father had been staties and I had married one too, I knew it was common for cop families to beget cops. I asked Tommy if he had other relatives in law enforcement.

"Not a one. My father's a postmaster in Boston. My mother's a nurse at the new Spaulding Rehab facility in Charlestown. My sister Ali is a student who wants to be a chef for 'fat rich people' when she gets her degree in ecogastronomy, whatever that is. And my brother Nick is a Marine." He chuckled. "Hey, maybe my family just has a weird thing for uniforms."

He paused and turned to Sam. "That reminds me, what do you think my chances are of getting May 22 off? It's a Sunday."

"Why? What does that have to do with uniforms?" Sam asked.

"It's The Run to Home Base 9K Race. Proceeds go to returning vets."

"If it's for the military, I'm sure the commander will do

his best to make it happen. Hey, Case, isn't that the race you and Griffin signed up for?"

"Yeah. Our agent told us about it. Her nephew's serving overseas."

"So's my brother. In Afghanistan almost eight months now."

"You never mentioned it," Sam replied. "It must be tough."

"It is," he said then changed the subject. "You know, my aunt is some sort of agent or publicist. I hope your agent isn't as controlling as she is. Drives my mother crazy with her interfering."

"If it makes you feel better," I offered, "I'm pretty sure those character traits come with the job—especially if she does it well."

We said goodnight to Tommy and climbed in our car. Sam leaned over and kissed me. "Have I told you how much I love you today?"

I kissed him back then flipped an imaginary hair extension over my shoulder. "I take it you didn't think much of Gina?"

Between college and career, I'd spent eleven-plus years in the city. I was used to the sounds and smells of Boston: the T rumbling, the voices soft and loud in a variety of tongues, and the traffic clatter with its random toots, blatts, and sirens droning on like an orchestra warming up. Each instrument rehearsing a different tune. The smell of freshly ground coffee and bread right from the oven mingled with the fragrance of flowers and perfumed women along with the stench of trash bins, diesel fuel, and perspiration, as if they were always meant to meld.

True, I didn't hear the sounds as loudly or smell the smells as sharply as I had in my newbie years. But the people-watching still had me hooked. So it was not easy to stop obsessing about the faces I saw near the post office on my daily walk to work. The closer I got to the building, the harder I trained my eyes to ignore my peripheral vision. Then I heard my name.

"A-yo, Casey!"

It was Darin and Mike.

"What are you guys doing here? Don't you have a game today?"

Darin answered, "Yep, but we don't have to be at the park for a couple of hours. We're going by to see Mike's mom. Seems like ever since my sister Tess started interning at the company where Mrs. Hennessey works, Mike's had this urge to visit his mother every time we're in town."

Mike blushed then steered the conversation in another direction. "Hey, thanks for sticking up for us on that *From the Bleachers* show. I don't know what we did to tick off that reporter, Linda. She doesn't like us much."

"Yeah, we're not allowed bad days?" Darin said. "Tell me she's never gone through a time when things came a little loose."

"Shake it off. Tomorrow she'll be taking her nasty out on someone else. Besides, she might have been mad at me for scooping the story on Darin." I hesitated for a second before asking, "Now, when you say bad days, was there something particular bothering either of you?"

Uh-oh. Even I could hear that I'd switched to reporter mode.

Mike slipped a look at Darin before he answered maybe a little too quickly, "Just a crummy day, ya know. Hey, tell Griffin we're sorry we couldn't talk the other day. We were running late."

"Yeah, he mentioned that." I winked at them. "Tell me, what does the expression 'baseball chapel' mean?"

Darin smiled wider than usual. "It's not a euphemism, Casey. It's baseball chapel. We get together at the team chaplain's house and read the Bible, pray, and talk about stuff."

"Oh, I had no idea." I lowered my head and squinted at Darin in mock accusation. "Mr. Flynn, you neglected to tell me that in our interview. Holding out on me, were you?"

"Nah, it's just that some of the players like Mike here like to keep it private, that's all."

Mike glanced sideways at Darin and dropped his chin. "And there goes my privacy."

"I didn't hear a thing," I said, which wasn't true. I heard my conscience whisper, "Wouldn't your mother love to hear this bit of news?" Even though my mother doesn't preach per se, one of her I-told-you-so looks can go places words can't reach.

"What about you, Casey?" Darin asked. "Do you know the Lord?" His smile sat there waiting for an answer.

I shifted my bag from one shoulder to the other. "Uh, not as well as you do, I'm sure."

Darin continued. "Talking about God can be awkward, I know. But if I honestly believe what I say I believe about God and *don't* talk about Him, my faith would be pretty selfish, wouldn't it?"

"Uh, suppose." Mercifully my cell phone beeped. "Sorry, gotta go. Our weekly staff meeting starts in a few minutes." Bad enough I had to worry about an unknown brother unsettling my life. Did I have to worry about an unknown god too?

Do you know the Lord? Oh, God . . .

The building that housed Kincade Marketing Solutions was built in the 1940s. With its substantial footprint and painted brick façade, it imposed upon the glitzier glass highrises built in the late '80s and attracted clients who related to tradition, solid principles, and dependability.

The ground floor was home to a florist, a small art gallery, a real estate firm, and a café. The Carrara marble floors, white with gray-blue veins, gleamed in the sunlight filtering through the floor-to-ceiling windows. The oversized crown molding and Venetian plaster walls made a formidable, though not ostentatious, impression.

With offices in Boston, Hartford, and New York, Kincade was at the top of its field in the region. Getting a position or even an internship there was coveted by top students and graduates from prestigious colleges around the country. Now, I recognize the extent of my good fortune. But ten years ago, being young and full of myself, I simply thought such a position was due me for maintaining a 4.0 GPA at the right school.

I arrived a minute before the start of the meeting. There was a new face at the table. Female, young, doe eyes, perfect nose, long hair. She looked vaguely familiar, but I wasn't sure why.

Gordy stood and called the meeting to order then turned in the young woman's direction. "I'm pleased to introduce Poppy Brandeis, our newest marketing associate."

A chorus of unrehearsed greetings followed until the door opened and a guy about my age sauntered in.

Gordy, still standing, announced, "Oh, and this is Lyle Wexler, a middle market VP like me from our New York office."

Wexler wore dark-washed straight leg jeans, a plaid shirt with the sleeves rolled up and tail out except for the few inches tucked in near his belt buckle. Sporting overpriced Salvatore Ferragamo sneakers, he looked like he'd just swaggered out of a Nordstrom catalog, slick hair product and all. I was surprised at his casual dress. I expected more from New York.

Wexler took a seat to the right of Gordy near the head of the table. Throughout the meeting he leaned back in his chair, bounced his fingertips together, and yawned. He didn't say a single word.

But Poppy made up for it.

Suffering from a mild case of real-business-people envy, she raised her hand until she was called on, injecting a zombie noun into every question. "How does Kincade harmonize strategic ideation with tactical execution?" "What are our remarketing stats?" "Do we newsjack to leverage our sales message?"

By the end of the meeting, I longed for old familiar words like *paradigm shift*, *synergy*, and *seamless integration.*

Who are you fooling, Casey? You used to spit out buzz words faster than a pitching machine just like this fresh-out-of-college enthusiast. The only difference is the verbiage. She can't help the fact that she's only twenty-two, so hold off on your opinion.

When the hour-long meeting adjourned, I challenged myself to give the New Yorker a personal welcome despite my assumption that he would not care. The worst that could happen is that I'd be wrong . . . or right. Mostly, I wanted to know how long he'd be in Boston and why. By the time I got to the other end of the table, Wexler was gone.

Poppy Brandeis wasn't. I benched my cynicism and extended my hand to Poppy. She said she was "honored to meet me" like I was a venerable fixture in the industry. I wasn't sure if I felt honored or insulted.

During our brief discussion I stuck to simple terms, hoping she'd get the hint. She did not.

When Poppy uttered the word *sox*, I got a little excited until I realized she was using the abbreviation for the Sarbanes-Oxley Act, which had nothing to do with sports but everything to do with corporate accountability. I hated the fact that I was stumbling for my professional foothold in her presence.

As Poppy picked up a Coach book bag, the tumblers in my mind fell into place, unlocking a memory. Poppy Brandeis was my made-up Tippy Montrose from the T! The one I'd pegged as "the intelligent-yet-spoiled daughter of a plastic surgeon from Milton." Wow. My guess wasn't far off.

"You know, Poppy, I think we may ride the T into the city together."

"We may have, but that horror's over since my parents gave me the BMW I wanted for graduation."

"A BMW?"

"Just a 1 Series. More like a starter car."

The half-carat diamond studs Mom and Dad had given me came to mind. One person's extravagance was another's economy.

Backing away from the conference table to make my escape, I tripped on Hildegard and felt old.

I skipped the elevator and took the stairs to the third floor, hoping to avoid another Poppy encounter. On my way to my office, I saw Wexler slouched in the chair opposite Gordy's desk. He punctuated each word he spoke by alternately pointing his steepled fingers at Gordy then at the ceiling.

Gordy noticed me in the hallway and waved me over. Before I could reach the threshold, Lyle got up, gave me a curt nod, and closed the door.

So much for my welcome.

Nora came up behind me and whispered, "Who's that with the boss?"

"Lyle Wexler. He's a VP from the New York office. It appears he doesn't want his meeting with Gordy to be disturbed." Little snit.

"He was one of them."

"One of them?"

"The corporate suits I told you about, the ones snooping around three weeks back."

"You sure?"

"Yes. I'd recognize that hair anywhere."

14

Webster suggested that Griffin, Jillian, Sam, and I come for brunch at their house to celebrate Mother's Day. Our intention was for Mom not to work. Her intention was to pay no attention to our intentions. She cleaned the house and shopped for extras even after we told her not to. With the food we brought, we could have invited the Patriots' defensive line.

"Whoa, Mom, what a spread!" Griffin said. "We didn't have anything like this growing up."

"What are you talking about?" She slapped his hand away from a platter.

Griffin winked at me. "Casey, don't you remember those old TV dinners Mom used to feed us?"

"You mean the ones with the four or five items in a tin tray? With a smudge of some sort of cobbler or other that always had a few dried-up green beans stuck to it?"

He snagged a pickle when she wasn't looking. "Yup, those are the ones. You've gotten kinda chichi since you married Webster."

Mom fought back. "May I remind you that you both begged me for those frozen dinners?"

"Whatever makes you feel better," Griffin said, escaping another swat.

Before Mom could prompt me, I remembered to thank Webster for all the work he'd done on our website and blog. "We've had so many compliments on the site, and the blog hits are increasing daily."

"That's no surprise with you two writing it," he said. "Content is king, as they say, right, Annie?"

Mom smiled at her husband like she liked him—a lot. "That's true, but without technology no one can find the content, and without aesthetics no one will want to read it."

"Mom's right. There's no way Griffin and I could have tackled those aspects."

While waiting for the grill to heat up, I snatched a few chips. One soggy bite made me ask, "Who brought the chips?"

"I did," Griffin said. "Why?"

"They're stale. You've been shopping at Odds & Ends Lots again, haven't you?"

Jillian looked at him and sighed. "Not again, Griffin."

He protested. "Hey! They've got some neat stuff there."

Webster laughed. "That's the chance you take when you buy your comestibles within reach of concrete frogs and all-purpose tarps."

"Comestibles? Mo-om," Griffin whined. "Your husband's using big words again."

"Hence the nickname Webster, which he's had since third grade." Mom winked at her husband. "Web, what have I told you about using that kind of language in front of the children? Try not to obfuscate matters, especially around Griffin."

Sam choked on his drink. "Looks like Webster's turned Annie to the dark side! We might have to start calling your mom Merriam now."

I gave him a fist-bump for that one.

Jillian sighed. "My husband, always looking for a deal. And, as you can see by the holes in the pants he's wearing, he never throws anything out."

Griffin countered, "Don't be silly, Jilly. The day I pull these pants up and all I've got is a waistband, out they go!"

Sam had pulled a Sunday shift, so he had to leave early. Since I'd driven myself, I hung back prepared to enjoy another picking-on-Griffin holiday.

Until Mom drew me aside and asked, "Have you and your brother made any decisions about meeting Lisa's son?"

"Mom, I know you've talked to Griffin, so what you're really asking me is if I've changed my mind, and my answer is no."

Griffin came over. "Geez, you're acting the same way you did when Mom started dating Webster. It's not all about you, Casey. All this guy wants to do is meet his father's kids. Don't you feel guilty at all?"

"I thought about it and decided I'd rather feel guilty than meet him." I sounded like a freshman at Smart Mouth Prep. I didn't usually talk that way in front of my mother, and it didn't make me proud.

Griffin's eyes flashed. "For once, Casey, can't you put your playbook aside and just punt?"

Before he could say anymore, Mom calmed him with a touch to his forearm. "Your sister needs more time. Moving ahead from a position of pain is never recommended."

He shook his head and walked off.

Mom brushed my face with the back of her hand. "Casey, as water reflects the face, so one's life reflects the heart. I see misery whenever this subject comes up. It might help if you tried to consider this situation a blessing rather than a curse. Please try."

I mumbled, "I'll think about it."

How can a person change the way they feel simply on someone else's say so? As for considering this a blessing rather than a curse, that would take an act of a god I strongly suspected did not exist.

I was awake when Sam tiptoed across the bedroom floor and climbed into bed. Another time check—one-thirty—told me I'd been wrestling with my thoughts for over two hours. When

I stirred, Sam kissed me hello and goodnight then whispered, "Go back to sleep."

He drifted off with no effort while I rolled and unrolled the blankets around me like a malfunctioning window shade. Fed up with my restlessness, I thought maybe a do-over of my normal bedtime routine would clear my head and relax my body.

I got up. Not wanting to awaken the night, I navigated through the house by the red, blue, and green lights of the various appliances and electronic components. I did a double-take passing the office. Our blinking computer stations spooked me with their eerie resemblance to a UFO landing in Roswell.

The digital clocks in the kitchen fought over the correct time. About five minutes passed—or was it seven?—before it occurred to me to heat some milk. While the microwave's ninety seconds hummed by, I wrote *milk* on the lopsided shopping list clinging to the refrigerator by its weak magnetic strip.

After lighting a candle more for mood than light, I eased myself into my cushy reading chair and stretched my legs across the ottoman. With a twirl of my spoon I skimmed the film off the top of my warm milk before I took a sip. The new issue of *Runner's World* caught my eye. I picked it up and flipped through the pages at a quick clip, racing past words and pictures without seeing a thing.

I tossed it aside.

With both hands, I held my mug to my lips, reviewing my compartmented life.

My marriage: Sam and I were committed to marital strength training, built up through transparent communication and a greater degree of trust. My job: I could easily give Kincade another five years if things stayed the same. Double Header: Griffin and I were skating by for now. To avoid thin ice, we'd need more time to devote to this second career, but I was sure we could find it.

Then why was I so restless?

My thoughts zigzagged to Mom and Webster. When they first started seeing each other two years after Dad died, I acted

like a spoiled pre-teen. Webster's a good guy, but it t while to accept him, mainly because I hadn't totally Dad's death. Seeing Mom over-the-moon in love lonely made it easier. Thinking back on my selfish beha embarrassed me.

The whole "spiritual renewal" thing seemed to wo Mom too. I had the same theory on that as I did on ball p and their silly superstitions—If they believed something wo then on some level it did, for them.

I was excited for Griffin and Jillian, maybe a little envic Not about the baby, per se. More so that they were content a less complicated lifestyle.

And probably sleeping.

Resting my head on the back of the chair, I closed my eyes. The sounds of silence were comforting: the freezer moaning like it had intestinal distress, a cell phone bleating for a re-charge, and the furnace groaning over each degree. What amazed me most was the circuitry and programming of my wireless printer which allowed it to wipe its nose and clear its throat when nothing else was going on.

I lifted my head and opened my eyes. The flame from the candle was flickering on a picture of Mom, Dad, Griffin, and me, all smiling in the foreground of Cinderella's castle. Griffin and I were about eight and ten. Holding the photo for a closer look, I ran my fingertips over the glass. The subject that plagued me resurfaced, Dad's son by Lisa.

What was that four-year-old boy doing while his father was at Walt Disney World with us?

I tried to imagine what he looked like, if he was anything like Dad or Griffin or me. Did he have the McGee sense of humor? Did he like sports? Did he have Dad's eyes? Mom used to say they were like "midnight blue marbles splashing through an icy sea."

For the first time, I was thinking about this kid without anger. Yet when I asked myself why I was being so hardheaded about meeting him, I had no answer. My wee-hour reveries didn't resolve my issues, but it got everything out on the table. When I slipped back into bed, it took only minutes for sleep to find me.

Still, morning came early. It wasn't the aroma of coffee that woke me but the bull-moose call of our Keurig.

15

After a hat trick of victories against the Yankees in New York, the Sox were back in town for a week. Credited with one of the wins, Mike's spirits were high when I called.

"So, Hennessey, now that you've pretty much figured out baseball, how about you and Darin joining Griffin and his wife and Sam and me to watch a Bruins game?"

"I can't speak for Flynn, but it sounds good to me."

"Sam will probably invite his cop friend, Tommy Coletti, too. He's one of those diehard hockey fans who's certain the Bs will bring the Stanley Cup home this year."

"He might be right, ya know," Mike said. "I hope we do as well."

A few days later, the Red Sox game against the Orioles was rained out on the same day as the Bruins home game. Mike invited us to a neighborhood pub in Southie. Griffin, Tommy, and I could make it, but Sam was scheduled to work and Jillian took a pregnancy pass.

It was a long shot, but I asked anyway. "Mike, Griffin and I are scheduled to tape a spot on the *Red Sox Nation* show late this afternoon. Do you and Darin want to make a surprise appearance at the studio since they postponed the show's original debut?"

"Would they mind?" Mike asked. "It's kind of last minute."

I laughed. "You're kidding, right? They'd wet their pants!"

"I'll get there as soon as I can," Mike said, "but Darin has a promise to keep."

"Oh? Be ready, Mike. You know I'll want details."

"Details? He's helping one of his sisters study for a calculus exam. Not a groundbreaking story."

"Guess not."

Or was it? A story on Flynn and his family might be the perfect change-up to surprise our readers. I added it to my list of column topics.

The *Red Sox Nation* cohosts were prepared for Griffin and me but not for Mike. When the lanky pitcher, dressed in jeans and an orange V-neck, walked onto the set their mouths fell open like a couple of wooden dummies who'd lost their ventriloquist. It took a few seconds for them to find their voices.

Finally, one of them spoke. "For those watching who might not know, we've just been surprised by Red Sox pitcher Mike Hennessey. We're glad to have you, Mike. Your recent outing against the Yankees showed us you're a true champion."

"Champion?" Mike smiled. "As far as I can figure, it only takes one lousy game to go from champ to chump. But since you're offering, I'll accept the compliment."

Griffin raised his hands, palms up. "See why it's easy to like this kid? Leave it to Mike to out-humble the bunch of us."

I jabbed Griffin like any bratty sister would if given the chance. "No reflection on your humility, Mike, but out-humbling Griffin isn't much of a feat, is it?"

Griffin clutched his midsection and leaned over in mock pain. "Again, Casey? Is there no end to your abuse?"

When one of the cohosts asked us how we'd met the Irish Twins, Griffin was more than willing to tell the whole golf outing story, again. He played up the part about my doubting his ability to find us a tee time and a suitable foursome.

Even Mike joined in. "Ya know, I only wish we'd captured the look on Casey's face!"

I allowed them to banter at my expense before I countered. "Have your laugh boys, but may I remind you who took that golf match?"

Griffin and I left the station with an open invitation to return. Of course, it might have had something to do with our showing up with Mike.

Tommy was waiting for us outside the pub. It was a street-corner hole in the wall, a *Cheers* sort of place "where everybody knows your name," most of them Celtic. Unless the four flat screens were made in Dublin, the only things Irish about the place were the faded green, white, and orange flag, the shamrock coasters, and the name Donegal's.

We sat at one of the communal tables, and Mike introduced us to his neighborhood cronies. With names like McGee and Gallagher, Griffin and I fit right in. Since Tommy was a solid Bruins fan, the locals forgave him the surname Coletti.

The crowd cheered like Boston Garden was within hearing distance. When Boston beat Tampa Bay, the room rumbled from the floor up. Even if the Bruins didn't hear us, they may have felt the quake.

When the victory cheers subsided, we heard a ruckus near the entrance. A tall, middle-aged man entered, swaying in the wake of spirits and bluster. He noticed Mike and pivoted to face our table. "If it isn't our ver-ry own Red Shox star pi-cher, Mike Hennes-shey."

Mike raised a hand in the direction of the drunken patron and turned back to us. "No worry. I'll handle it."

One of Mike's friends mumbled, "Here we go again."

Tommy's cop adrenaline kicked in. He stood, ready to act if he had to.

Mike approached the man and led him to a table near the

bar. After a few words no one could hear, Mike signaled to the bartender who brought over what looked like two mugs of coffee. The man pushed his away. Mike inched it back and rested his hand on the guy's forearm. Leaning in, the man picked up the cup with both hands and took a sip.

For the next ten minutes, Mike listened as his tablemate alternately growled and laughed at who knows what. When Mike got up to leave, he patted the man's shoulder and called over to the bartender. "Lou, can you see that he gets home safely?" The bartender nodded.

It occurred to me that it must be tough for a person as private as Mike to deal with the attention of fans, more so the unruly ones. When he got back to our table I said, "That had the potential for ugly. I'm impressed."

Tommy added, "Smooth job defusing the situation."

Mike shrugged it off. "People get confused when they drink. Then they start feeling bad about themselves. He needed some attention, that's all."

Griffin turned to Mike's buddies at the table. "A golden arm *and* people skills? I'm thinking his contract negotiations went well, wouldn't you say?"

Before anyone could respond, Mike stood and placed some money on the table. "We should probably get going. You guys have a bit of a ride ahead of you."

He waved to the locals as he led us outside into the fresh night air.

Under the ambient lighting of the city streets, he gave us a ten-cent walking tour of his old (and current) stomping grounds. "The Flynn's house is over there, third one on the right. My parents live a few streets over. We used to cut through the backyards to get to each other's place—mostly me going to Darin's."

"Sounds like my neighborhood," said Tommy. "Except mine's in the North End."

"The whole South versus North, Irish versus Italian thing is bunk," Griffin added. "We all know the real rivalry is between potato and pasta."

"Unh-uh, McGee," Tommy said, "you're not gonna drag us into that stale argument."

Like an old man reminiscing, Mike recounted stories about what it was like when he was a kid. "If you look up that street you can still see one of the fields where we played. Ya know, Darin and I go by there every once in a while and throw the ball around with the neighborhood kids. Some of them have no idea who we are. It's cool. You get to be yourself."

After listening to Mike, I understood why he and Darin had bought a townhouse here when they could have well afforded something much grander closer to Fenway. This was home.

"Sounds like you like kids," said Griffin. "Plan to have a family one day?"

Wow. Griffin was asking a personal question. I shut my mouth.

"Hope so. Being on the road so much, it's hard to maintain a relationship." Mike looked down and kicked at the lines in the sidewalk.

Unable to control my nosiness, I jumped in. "Maintain? Seeing anyone special?"

Mike stuck his hands in his front pockets. "Trying to."

"So Darin was right," I teased. "His sister, Tess?"

He raised his head. A smile escaped. "Yes. Tess. And you're right, she is special."

Tommy nudged Mike. "Hey, does Flynn have any more sisters worth chasing?"

I wasn't sure if he was serious, but I refused to spoil the moment by bringing up his voted-most-likely-to-be-disliked girlfriend, Gina Zicaro.

Whether it was the combination of the night's events or the fact that Mike was comfortable with us, he opened up. "It's tough not being able to spend more time with her. I envy you, Griffin, married with a baby on the way. I can't wait to be a father someday."

"I don't know how I got so lucky." Griffin's phone chirped and he stopped to read his text message. "Speaking of fatherhood, my baby's mother just reminded me to invite you to our Memorial Day cookout. Darin too. We're in Plymouth, only about an hour from Boston. I know the Sox have an early home game that day, but the party runs late."

"Thank your wife for us." Mike smiled. "I'll let Flynn know we have orders to keep the game short."

A niggling in the back of my mind made me ask, "Mike, that man back in the bar, the one who had too much to drink, did you know him?"

"Yeah, I know him." He turned and raised his chin. "He's my dad."

I found no solace in knowing that another family had tough stuff going on behind closed doors. Misery doesn't always love company.

Presented with another chance to shut my mouth, I took it. Twice in one night. Amazing.

16

With the Run to Home Base 9K opening ceremony scheduled to begin around 7 a.m., Griffin and I showed up around six. It was cold and drizzling, but the mood of the crowd wasn't dismal. The run through Boston would begin at Yawkey Way and end crossing home plate. I'd been to Fenway hundreds of times, but I'd never run across home plate. My chills had nothing to do with the weather.

Griffin bellowed, "Hey, Coletti! Over here!" Leave it to my brother to find the one runner we knew in the field of 2,500.

Tommy jogged toward us. "Swell day for a run, huh? Hope it stops raining and warms up a bit." He pointed to Griffin's racing bib. "I see by the stripe on your bib we've got the same start time. Get used to seeing my back, McGee."

"You mean seeing you *on* your back," Griffin said as he ran in place.

I found it typical that neither of these males considered the fact that they might be trying to catch *me*.

Tommy leaned forward on the long bench to stretch. "By the way, thanks for letting me tag along the other night. Mike's an okay guy."

I alternated legs for my calf stretches. "More than okay, I'd say."

Griffin added, "Sweet win for the Bruins too."

"Got that right!" Tommy high-fived Griffin.

After a few necessary-but-barely-audible speeches given by the event's sponsors, the sun came out and the race began. As it turned out, I did beat Griffin and Tommy's time, but it was anticlimactic because of the log jam rounding the bases. It was more of a photo op walk across home plate than a run. However, as it was with most fundraising events, the participants put their competitiveness aside, conceding that the charity was the main stake.

At least that's what we told ourselves.

I scanned the crowds as we cooled down. "Griff, have you seen Roberta? She told us she'd be here."

"Not yet, but I guarantee our fearless agent is here somewhere working the crowd of elites."

Tommy whistled and put one hand up like an NFL referee signaling a personal foul. "Whoa. Did you say your agent's name is Roberta?"

"Yes, Roberta Herzog," I said. "Why? Do you know her?"

"Know her? Aunt Bobbie's my mother's sister!"

"Aunt Bobbie?" I shot a glance at Griffin, trying to remember what we'd said about her in his presence.

"Yeah, I call her that to bug her. I didn't know she had clients in this area. I thought she stuck to New York."

Griffin elbowed me. "Uh-oh, we'd better be careful what we say."

Tommy said, "It's probably nothing I haven't said myself." He paused a moment. "Huh. Why didn't she mention you guys to me? She's up to something."

"Have you ever had reason to mention our names to her?" I asked.

Tommy scratched his head. "Guess not. And I've only known Sam since I joined his gym. Hasn't been that long."

"We signed with Roberta months before you met Sam or us," I said. "What reason would she have to tell you about us?"

Griffin faked shock. "You can't possibly suspect your poor, innocent aunt of ulterior motives?"

He laughed. "Suspect, no. Accuse, yes, because those are the only motives she knows. Now that she represents you, I'll bet her visits to our family are classified as tax deductions."

Even if on some level I agreed with Tommy's assessment of Roberta, I was grateful to have her. When she caught our appearance on a local television show six months ago, it was pure serendipity. Everything we'd heard about getting a literary agent told us it would be nearly impossible for no-names like us. Yet Roberta took us on. I had no problem being classified as a tax deduction.

I waited up for Sam that night. He didn't expect me to do that often, but I knew he liked it when I did. When he initially switched shifts and we'd figured out our schedules, it had all looked doable on paper. Not the same in real time. We hadn't talked for days—and I needed to.

"Hey, what are you still doing up? I figured after the 9K you'd be wiped. Got your text. How did it feel to beat your own record? "

"Feels even better since I beat Griffin's and Tommy's time too. And don't let those chowderheads tell you otherwise."

He hugged me. "That's my girl."

I walked over to the refrigerator. "Want to join me for some homemade lemonade? I bought it myself."

He smiled. "Why not? You worked hard to earn that money."

Sam was wired, so I let him ramble on about work, like the understanding wife I'd purposed to be. It was freeing to be more open with each other. When Tommy's name came up again I remembered to ask, "By the way, did you get my message about Roberta being Tommy's aunt?"

His wrinkled brow told me no. "Roberta? As in your agent? I don't know how I missed that text."

"Yup, he overheard Griffin and me talking about her at

the race. She hadn't told him about us either. He thinks she's up to something."

He drained his glass and stood to stretch. "Up to what?"

I shrugged. "I don't know. He doesn't seem to like her that much."

"Would you want her for your aunt?"

"Do you need me to answer that?" Slinking away from the thought of Roberta at all our family functions, I brought the empty glasses to the kitchen and stuck them in the dishwasher.

Sam headed down the hall and called over his shoulder, "How was your lunch with Vanessa?"

"I told her the whole sordid story, Lisa's son included." I put the soap in the dishwasher, closed the door until it clicked, and pushed Start.

He turned and waited for me to catch up. "What was her reaction?"

"You know Vanessa. She was her usual analytical self. I was doing fine until she suggested that the kid might already be searching for us. She asked me if anyone new had approached Griffin or me. I told her no. Can you think of anyone?"

"I don't know. How about on one of your runs or in the commuter lot?"

"Are you trying to give me the heebie-jeebies?"

"Sorry."

"How about you? Anyone strange come up to you lately?"

He grunted. "Everyone who comes up to me is strange. I'm a cop, remember?"

"Point taken. Lisa's letter did say he promised to wait for us to contact him."

"I may be putting myself in the line of fire by saying this, but if he's anything like his biological father, he'll keep his word."

I pretended I didn't hear him, reasoning it was better than one of my kneejerk remarks. Sam didn't push; he was learning. I trailed behind him to our bedroom and climbed into bed. Once he rolled over he was asleep in seconds, while I lay awake for an hour.

Despite Sam's reassurance, I felt compelled to go over my

interaction with unknown men in the past few months. No one on the T. No one at work except Wexler. No one at the gym—it was female only. No one at the post office. The only others were Mike, Darin, and Tommy. Griffin and I were the ones chasing Mike and Darin, so they were out. And Tommy had connected with Sam, not me.

My brain started churning. What else did I know about Roberta and Tommy? Not much. Maybe it was more than coincidence. How old is he? Had either of them ever mentioned his mother's name?

Stop swinging at outside pitches, Casey. It won't get you on base.

After driving myself crazy, I cruised toward dreamland.

But I made a U-turn when I remembered how my made-up "Tippy Montrose" turned out to be a lot like the real Poppy Brandeis. It was a long shot, but it wouldn't hurt to check into Tommy's background.

I got ahold of Roberta the next day. "We missed seeing you at the 9K yesterday. You were there, weren't you?"

"Of course I was. The real question is while I was hobnobbing with the bigwigs trying to make a name for you and Griffin, where were you two hiding?"

"We ran the race, remember? Then we milled around with the other runners. As long as we're asking questions, why didn't you tell me Tommy Coletti is your nephew?" I thought I'd catch her off balance.

"Why would I? How would I know you knew him?"

She was quick; I had to give her that. "Well, you know it now."

"I do. In fact, he's standing right next to me. I'm still at my sister's in Boston. Here, Tommy, say hi to Casey."

"Hi, Casey. What's up?"

"Nothing. Mostly, I was giving Roberta a hard time."

"Glad to hear that. Keep it up."

I heard voices in the near background. "Sounds like I'm interrupting something."

"Just my parents, my sister, and Aunt Bobbie all yapping at me at once."

"You the family utility player?"

"Yeah, but not by choice."

"Every team needs a go-to person. Your aunt thinks that's my role too." I chuckled. "The problem is who does the go-to person go to?"

"Exactly. For me, the one closest to that description is your husband. But don't tell him I told you."

"I won't. Cross my heart." Hearing how young cops looked up to Sam never got old.

Before I forgot my mission, I said, "Hey, mind my asking what your mother's name is?"

"Ramona. Why?"

"Uh, Griffin and Jillian are trying to come up with girl names. I thought I'd help." It was flimsy, but I don't think he saw through it.

After we hung up, I muttered, "Ramona, Roberta, no Lisa." Other than being a cop, Tommy was nothing like my father—in looks, voice, or mannerisms. Not one bit.

17

Sam and I showed up around nine to help Griffin and Jillian prepare for their annual Memorial Day cookout. The guys carried the patio furniture up from the basement, hosed off the cobwebs, and set it in the sun to dry.

I retrieved the outdoor cushions from the attic and spritzed them with fabric freshener. After lugging the gas grill out of the garage, Griffin fired it up and used a grill stone to get rid of the charred evidence leftover from their Labor Day cookout last year.

For every party they hosted, Jillian created themed tablescapes, never as simple as matching colored paper plates to balloons. This Memorial Day, each of the five tables was decorated to represent a different branch of the military. The seal of each was displayed in a two-sided acrylic frame and set in the center of the table. The linen and dinnerware were chosen to match their official colors: Army, black and gold; Navy, navy blue and gold; Air Force, ultramarine blue and yellow; Marines, gold and scarlet; and Coast Guard, red, white and ocean blue. To match those colors perfectly, she had a source I didn't know about.

She'd created centerpieces of freshly cut flowers, incorporating an item she'd found at the local Army Navy Surplus store. Tucked under the napkin at each place setting was a different list of quotes about the holiday and the military branch.

In a position of prominence on the deck, a tall round table stood at attention with a leather-bound book with the names and photos of friends and family who'd died serving their country. Next to it she had a journal for family and friends currently serving. She even included suggestions on how to support them.

That was Jillian. She thought of everything—and everyone. I was amazed at the setting and mood she'd created. I swirled my arm across the backyard like a game show model. "See, Jillian, this is why I can never host parties."

"Thanks, but I can't take all the credit. I got a lot of ideas online."

Griffin came over and kissed her cheek. "Proud of you, Jilly. You hit the mark with this one."

"I can only imagine the birthday parties your children will have!" I said. "They'll be the envy of every kid."

While awaiting the guests, Griffin and Sam got the bar and coolers stocked. Jillian and I sat on the brick patio in the Adirondack chairs Jillian's dad had built and her mom had painted cornflower blue. The sky was clear and the breeze mild and dry. Their Cape Cod style house had been reshingled a few weeks back; the scent of red cedar mixed well with the salt air. The spring chill melted under the strong sun.

I adjusted my sunglasses and put on my ball cap, pulling my ponytail through. Leaning over, I patted Jillian's belly. "How're you feeling?"

"Better, thanks. The morning sickness has subsided and—"

"Excuse me," I interrupted, "but I was addressing my niece or nephew."

She smiled and looked down at what was left of her lap. "We're coming up on the halfway mark."

Sam joined us. "Wow. That went by fast!"

"Yeah, can you believe it?" Griffin said. "Twenty weeks already."

I gave them an I-can't-believe-you-said-that look. "Maybe for you two it has. I doubt Jillian would agree."

"The baby's doing fine. I saw the doctor on Friday." She paused a moment then giggled. "Once we found her new office building."

"Yeah, it was a Three Stooges moment," Griffin said. "Her ob-gyn changed locations. In the meantime, the restaurant next door to her old office had expanded into their space. We walked in and it was like, 'Put your feet in the stirrups. Your waitress will be along shortly.' They even had those hypodermic needle disposal containers mounted on the wall for your dirty silverware."

Sam and I laughed. Jillian tried not to. "It scares me to think I could give birth to a child like his father."

An awkward half brother feeling crept up on us when we weren't paying attention.

I cracked the quiet. "So . . . who else is coming today besides our parental units?"

No sooner had I asked when Rich and Bernadette Bouchard, Jillian's parents, rounded the corner.

"Shh! They're here. Talk sports," said Griffin. He quick-handed the bag of rolls Rich lobbed at him.

Bernadette leaned over to kiss Jillian and me. "Don't get up, girls. We know where everything is. Rich, when you're finished horsing around could you give me a hand over here?" She stopped to take everything in. "Oh my, Jillian. You've outdone yourself!"

Moments later, Mom and Webster arrived with more food. A young couple walked up the driveway close behind them.

Griffin introduced them. "Meet Ethan Harte and Kate Kerrigan. Ethan's the one who helped put our kitchen back together after Rich and I made a mess of it. Kate's his bride-in-waiting."

Kate fake-fluttered her lashes at Ethan. "Only three more long weeks."

Rich stood up to shake Ethan's hand. "How's it going, son? I still say if those floors hadn't been so galley-west and crooked, we could have gotten those cabinets in ourselves."

"Give it up, Rich," said Griffin. "We were in over our heads and you know it. If it hadn't been for Mom recommending Ethan, Jillian and I would still be eating out. Which sounds way better than it tastes when you're on a fast food budget."

Mom reminded us that she and Webster knew Ethan and Kate from the dinner club Mom had started a few years back. "Before any of us became couples."

I turned to Kate. "Maybe you remember. We met at Mom and Webster's wedding?"

"Of course I remember," she said. "Hope we get a chance to talk this time. Annie—I mean your mom—tells me you two are close. Actually, what she says is she can't get away with anything without you knowing about it."

I chuckled. "Unfortunately, that works both ways. It was a curse when I was a teen."

Griffin called for everyone's attention. "Drinks are on the table over there. We have everything you might want, even have the hard stuff for Mom and Webster—Dunkin' Donuts decaf and Pepsi."

Knowing my brother, the party would go extra innings. "Who else are you expecting?" I asked.

"A few more teachers and coaches and their spouses. And if the Sox day game ends after nine innings, Darin and Mike said they'd drive down." He turned to Sam. "Hey, Gallagher, did you remind Coletti about the party?"

"Yes, but he worked the overnight shift, so they'll be late."

I yanked on Sam's shirtsleeve and spoke through clenched teeth. "They? Sam, tell me he's not bringing Gina."

His silence gave me the answer I didn't want to hear.

Tommy arrived around three—with Gina. She had on a zebra-print spandex dress with three-quarter-length sleeves that were longer than her hem. The strappy platform heels didn't help.

Sam razzed him. "Slept in, huh?"

"Not that late. It took Gina a while to decide which animal print was in season."

"Shut up," Gina snarked, "and get me a drink."

Charming.

On the way to the bar, Tommy spotted the memorial table. "What's this?" He fanned through the photos and read down the list of names. "Impressive. Are these all your relatives?" He turned to the second book. "Hey! You even have my brother's name here. Corp. Nicholas Coletti, USMC. Cool."

Gina folded her arms and struck a pose. "Didn't we totally do that whole Memorial Day thing with your family on Thursday?"

"What was Thursday?" I asked.

Tommy ignored Gina's comment. "The Garden of Flags at the Soldiers and Sailors Monument on Boston Common. Our family goes every year. Pretty moving tribute." He stole a peek at Gina. "At least it is to most people." He pulled a creased photo out of his wallet. "Hey, do you mind if I put this here for today? It's Nick with a few buddies from his platoon."

"We'd be honored," said Jillian, taking the photo from his hand. "Which one is Nick?"

He pointed. "He's the hotshot in the middle wearing the aviators."

One of Gina's over-plucked eyebrows twitched. She walked over and pinched his arm. "Tommy. My drink?"

After Griffin made another round of introductions, Mom excused herself from Webster and the Bouchards and approached Gina. They conversed for at least ten minutes, about what I could not imagine.

An hour passed and Gina announced they had to leave because she had another party to attend. "Come. Tommy. Now."

"What? You never said anything about another party."

"Do you totally think I would dress this way for a cookout?"

"Can't we skip it? Flynn and Hennessey—the Red Sox players I told you about—are gonna stop by."

"No, we can't. And since it's my car, you're either with me or you're not."

Tommy herded Gina toward the driveway out of our hearing range. They spoke for a few seconds, she more animated than he. Then she stalked off without a thank you or good-bye. He rejoined Sam and Griffin near the grill. Once again, his acquiescent manner indicated he was used to the abuse.

Why would anyone want to get used to it?

I asked Mom how she'd managed to carry on a conversation with the eye-rolling Olympian for as long as she had.

"We had a similar person join our dinner club for a long few weeks. I could have tried harder with her, and I've been at the mercy of my regrets since. Gina gave me a second chance."

"So how'd it go?"

"No noticeable breakthrough, if that's what you mean. But I'm only responsible for changing myself, not others."

Was that a veiled message for me? I searched Mom's face and determined it wasn't.

18

When the evening brought lower temps, Griffin lit the fire pit and we moved our chairs into a tight circle around it. In spite of his effort to warm everyone up, Mom and Webster and the Bouchards retreated indoors.

Sam, at thirty-two the old man of the fire pit crew, regaled us with some of his "dumbest criminals ever" tales.

"Listen, did I ever tell you about the perp who took a cab to rob a convenience store? He had the cabbie wait so he could get a ride home. Gave him a hefty tip too."

"What happened to him?" Jillian asked Sam.

"Doing three to five in Plymouth County Correctional."

"Still, my all-time favorite," Sam continued, "is the genius who robbed a bank and when the dye pack exploded, he tried to wash the bills at the local Wash 'N Suds. They got him on unarmed robbery."

Straight-faced, Griffin said, "And attempted money laundering."

My husband liked to keep his stories light even though his job was serious. However, that didn't hinder others from asking serious questions.

"What made you decide to become a cop?" Ethan asked.

Sam threw a log on the fire. "Not sure. My family always assumed I'd go into law, just not criminal law. When I got my master's in criminal justice from BU, they were not pleased when I chose law enforcement." He laughed. "To quote my mother, 'I never should have let that boy watch that NYPD Blue!' Still not sure if she was serious."

Tommy broke in. "Did you hear about the time Sam jumped the MBTA tracks—with a train in sight—to catch a druggie who'd snatched a baby? And if you read the story last month about the unnamed state cop who talked a woman out of jumping, it was Gallagher right here."

Sam squirmed in his seat. "That's old news. Ethan, how about you? Griffin tells me you're a woodworker by trade."

Griffin huffed. "Woodworker's a fancy word for a carpenter who takes twice as long and charges twice as much."

Jillian swatted Griffin's knee.

"It's true," Ethan said. "Some renovations move at a geologic pace, especially historical restorations." He reached for Kate's hand. "We've been working on my grandfather's old house for over a year now."

"Sure way to get to know your prospective spouse." Kate smiled at him. "Now, finished or not, we move in after the wedding."

Jillian asked, "Why so long, Ethan? It only took you two weeks to do our kitchen remodel."

"Yes, but the cabinets were new, and . . . a-hem . . . I had your dad and Griffin's help." The tongue in his cheek was so thick he couldn't swallow.

"Thanks to your recommendation," Jillian added, "we found the hand-scraped floors we wanted at Liquid Lumberdators."

Griffin winked at us and gave Jillian's shoulder a squeeze. "*Lumber Liquidators* had just what we wanted, didn't they, Jilly?"

When I got up to get a drink, Kate followed me to the cooler.

"I don't know if you know how much of an impact your mom and Webster have had on Ethan and me."

"Really? How so?" I expected to hear that Mom had helped her with some marketing tips and that Webster had done a website for Ethan.

"To be honest, we wanted what they had."

That was reassuring to hear. "Yes, they do have a wonderful relationship."

"Actually, it was their faith which led us to question our lack thereof."

Ethan had gotten up and come alongside Kate.

She continued. "One evening in their home, they introduced us to Jesus."

He put his arm around Kate's waist. "That's what was missing all along."

I don't remember what I mumbled, something like "good for you both" or "glad it worked out." To avoid getting in any deeper I excused myself, pretending I was needed in the house.

Something gnawed at me. Why had Mom shared something with virtual strangers before she shared it with me?

If she had, would I have listened?

Mike and Darin showed up around seven thirty accompanied by two young women.

After some handshakes and backslapping, Tommy asked, "Who might your lovely companions be?"

Darin motioned to the taller of the girls who had a flawless Hispanic complexion and long, wavy black-brown hair. "A-yo, this is my sister, Elena, the oldest of our magical mix of siblings." Then he turned toward the petite girl with the pretty Asian eyes. "And this is our sister, Tess. She's with Mike."

Mike and Tess dissolved into a puddle of self-consciousness.

"Speaking of magic,"—Griffin raised his glass to Mike and Darin—"that was a sweet win today. You pulled every rabbit out of the hat to do it too."

"Thanks," Mike said. "The clincher was when our new

pitcher notched six strikeouts in the last two innings. That southpaw has a backdoor slider that wails when it crosses the plate."

Studying Mike, Tommy said, "So you're not afraid he'll steal the limelight?"

"Steal it? Ha! I'd be glad to give him a share. It'll take the pressure off both of us." He grazed the back of Tess's hand with his. "Ya know, there's more to life than baseball." Somewhere in the midst of all the verbal jousting, I noticed Griffin, his usual comfortable self even in the presence of these celebrity guests. His confidence, not gained by any one achievement or award, was natural. While I strove for success and perfection, my brother accepted his lot in life with ease. It was ironic that the one thing I envied most about Griffin was that he never envied. I found that quality unique and attractive.

I liked my brother. Why didn't I tell him more often?

When I went inside to make some coffee, I overheard snippets of the conversation in the next room between Mom and Webster and Rich and Bernadette. Real estate taxes, squirrel-proof birdfeeders, and how many years before retirement were in the top ten. But the number one topic was their shared grandchild-to-be.

Walking by the doorway, I glimpsed Bernadette checking to see who else was around before she leaned in close to Mom. "Annie, the kids won't tell me a thing. Do you know what names they've picked out? Are they going to find out the sex? Did Griffin say anything about having the baby baptized?"

"That's the advantage to being grandparents. Jillian and Griffin have to make those decisions themselves."

Excellent sidestep, Mom. Sharp, yet graceful.

Bernadette wasn't mollified. "Since they were married in the Catholic Church, at the very least they should have the baby baptized there, don't you agree?"

I moved closer to the archway to hear Mom's reply. This could get sticky. Religion always did.

"I know how you feel, Bernadette. We want the best for our children and grandchildren. Sometimes I even think the

Lord needs my help. It's so hard to wait for Him to work in their lives in *His* time."

Go, Mom! What a diplomatic way to tell Bernadette to keep her nose out of Griffin and Jillian's business.

Hmm, was there anything in my life Mom found "hard to wait for?" Okay, so I knew there was. Didn't mean I had to think about it tonight.

When Bernadette started to speak again, Rich broke in. "Let it go, Bernadette. Whether it's a boy named Merton or a girl named Myrtle, baptized or not baptized, we'll love that baby."

They spent the next few minutes sorting out grandparent names like Nana and Papa and Grams and Gramps. Mom deferred to Bernadette. "As the maternal grandparents, you choose what you want to be called first."

I think there was an unwritten rule somewhere that the mother of the female in a marriage could pull rank on the mother of the male. Mom knew the rules and obeyed them.

It was hard not to think about the grandfather Dad would have been.

Mom turned to face Rich. "I was thinking, Rich, that if you don't claim 'Gramps,' maybe Web could have it."

Webster leaned forward. "You mean it? The kids wouldn't mind?"

Mom smiled and squeezed his hand. I could see it pleased her that Webster, who had no children of his own, was excited.

Later, when Mom and Webster and the Bouchards began their good-byes, Griffin teased, "Ah, yes, the old folks need their rest."

Mom laughed. "Ha! You repeat that to me in another twenty weeks. We'll see who needs their rest then."

"Rest? What rest?" Webster said. "Your mom and I got invited to Gina's other party."

Mom gave him a jab when Tommy wasn't looking, and Tommy wasn't looking because his eyes were on Elena Flynn.

As the night wore on, the men and women parted like water seeking its own level, gravitating toward topics that impressed one gender but bored the other. The women slipped inside for warmth; the men moved closer to the fire.

Elena and Tess gave us girls the lowdown on the Flynn siblings. In all, three girls and five boys. Three of the eight—Elena, Darin, and Andrew—had all been born in the same year.

Tess said, "Mom always said it was like having triplets without needing a tummy tuck."

The remaining kids were either adopted or born over a fifteen-year span. Since Kate and I each had one sibling and Jillian was an only child, we confessed it was hard to relate.

"Mike is an only child too," said Tess, finding yet another way to bring his name into the conversation.

Elena pushed at her sister's foot with hers. "He was always at our house, so we thought he was another brother. The day Tess realized he wasn't, things took a 180-degree turn."

"Oh, shush," said Tess. "He'll hear you."

"He already knows, Tess. Everyone does."

"I know, but until things settle down with . . ." Her words drifted away.

I could have finished her sentence—"with his father"—but didn't. I wanted to know the whole story. Instead I asked about the Flynn family's dynamics. "How did you older kids feel every time another brother or sister came along?"

"Like we didn't deserve it," said Elena, turning to Tess who nodded.

"It's quite normal for children to be resentful," I said, doing my best to validate their feelings.

"Resentful?" Elena looked confused. "Oh, no, what I meant was we couldn't believe God would keep blessing us!"

"I see," I said. But of course I didn't.

19

It had been nine weeks since the Sox had signed Darin and recharged the Hennessey-Flynn battery. Their stats reflected how well they worked together. Griffin and I wanted to interview them again for a fresh perspective. Even though we'd seen them on Memorial Day, we made it a habit never to mix business with pleasure. (Correction: Griffin made it a habit. I can't say the same for me.)

The Sox were off the next Monday, so Mike and Darin agreed to a late breakfast at a small diner in Southie. Since school wasn't out for Griffin, I had to go solo again. We met around eleven and opted for a booth in the back.

I slid in on one side and placed my bag on the seat near me for easy access to my laptop.

Darin pointed to my bag. "I see the ubiquitous Hildegard has joined us for the interview."

Mike responded, "Flynn, I thought you promised to spend some of your signing bonus on some words normal people can understand?"

Darin said, "Guess I never thought of you as normal, Hennessey."

Mike shoulder-butted him. "You're such a riot, Flynn." He turned to me. "Ya know, we enjoyed the cookout at Griffin's. We appreciated the invite."

His humility still surprised me. I refused to put a dent in his character by puffing him up, so all I said was, "Glad you could make it."

Darin added, "Elena and Tess said you made them feel right at home too."

"Gee, and we tried so hard to be nicer than that."

Mike grinned. "Now that sounds like something Griffin would say."

I shrugged. "Someone has to make up for the fact that he's not here."

Darin flagged down a waitress. "Sorry we have to make this short, Casey. It's the first day we've had off in a while, so my parents planned Tess's college graduation party for today."

"I understand. Your personal lives preempt Double Header. Let's get started."

While the waitress took our order, I reached for my laptop. I peppered them with questions when she left the table. "What's the biggest difference between playing for the pros and the minors?"

Darin answered first. "It feels more like business than a game."

Mike agreed.

I typed and fired off a followup question. "Does that spoil it for you?"

"No, it's still fun," Mike said. "Just on a different level."

"What's it like sharing a clubhouse with your heroes?"

"It's better," Mike said.

"What do you mean?" I asked, typing faster. Mike took his elbows off the table and leaned back. "Heroes aren't always real. The players are regular guys, ya know, like us."

"How are the Fenway faithful treating you?" I already knew the answer, but I wanted their take on it.

"No doubt about it," Darin said. "Boston fans are the best."

Mike added, "Being local sure doesn't hurt."

The waitress dropped our plates off. I bit into my cinnamon-raisin bagel while Mike flooded the nooks and crannies of his double order of English muffins. Darin tapped his soft-boiled egg with his spoon before he peeled it and sectioned off his grapefruit half into bite-sized triangles.

"So far, what's the most challenging part of being a pro?" I asked between bites.

Mike sighed. "For me, it's the long road trips."

"I'd have to say all the processed food," Darin said. "I can never be sure what preservatives and toxins I may be ingesting."

Darin's phone rang as we wrapped up the interview. "A-oh, Tess . . . Mike? He's with me." Darin turned to Mike, "My mom wants to know if your parents are coming."

"They said they'd be there." Mike's response didn't exude confidence.

"Did you hear that? We won't be long. We're having breakfast with Casey . . . Okay . . . Tess says hi."

"Tell her hi back and congratulations!"

After he hung up, Darin pulled an envelope out of his pocket. "Now, could I ask you a favor, Casey? My father asked me to read over the letter he wrote for Tess. He wants to give it to her at the party tonight. I'm not so good at writing. Your opinion would mean a lot."

"No problem."

Dear Tess,

I remember the day we brought you home. It was rainy and cold and, truth be told, with three children under four racing around already, we had no idea what we'd gotten ourselves into! It took only minutes for your little smile to warm our hearts and brighten our lives from that day forward. What we'd gotten ourselves into was a wonderful blessing!

There was much more about her childhood and the chicken pox, making the honor roll in high school, her mission trip, and her college achievements. I got through it all, amazed that I didn't choke up.

"Tell your dad I wouldn't change a word. It's perfect."

Darin's face brightened. "Why don't you come to the party? Tess would love it."

I declined. Not because I thought anyone would make me feel unwelcome. It was just that the Flynns and the Hennesseys were like one big family. My relationship with them wasn't the same. Part of me felt like I'd be intruding; the other part missed my dad.

With all the familial sentiments flying around, my memories of Dad's final weeks resurfaced on my drive home. I welcomed them, reliving every precious memory as if it had been yesterday . . .

"Mom, is it okay if I come by later to visit?"

"Sure, honey. Dad will love it."

I knew my visits gave Mom a break, even if it was only to run to the store, have her hair done, or take a long, hot bath.

If the hospice nurses didn't warn us often enough to care for ourselves, Dad did. "Don't make me feel like a burden, Annie. Get out and do something for yourself."

Griffin and I stopped by together one night. The three of us talked about great moments in sports and our all-time favorite players. That's when Dad told us about the sports memorabilia he'd hidden in the attic.

"I've been collecting for years. Got a lot of stuff on the Sox winning the pennant in '67. I say the sooner you get it the better. You know your mother. If she finds it after I'm gone, she'll throw it out faster than a fat man on his way to first."

Dad was so popular with his fellow officers that Mom had to limit their visits. One night, she mentioned a particular visit. "Gabe Reilly—he's the statie they call Deacon—came by today. He prayed with Dad. It seemed to help him."

I didn't begrudge Gabe Reilly that act. I thought it was one of those kind things people do that doesn't do any harm but doesn't do any good either. But I didn't say that to them.

Odd thing was, after that day Dad told me he was ready to go.

"Don't talk like that, Dad," I said, going against all that I'd read in the hospice material. "You have to keep fighting."

In a whisper, he said, "Casey, I've been fighting for the past five years. I want to surrender. It's freeing to know that in Heaven I won't be a burden to anyone."

"You're not a burden, Dad."

"Casey, promise me you'll let your Mom move on with her life. Don't give her a hard time. I haven't been a perfect man, but I loved Mom and you kids. I've had a good life. Not as long as I wanted it to be, but it's been a good one . . . "

I grieved hard for three years. Still do. But our family laughs more now than cries when we talk about Dad. The memories are less bitter—at least they were. The thought of Dad's indiscretion grabbed me by the throat and choked the peace out of me. Why, Dad, why? I thought you were stronger than that.

One day you were here, the next you were gone . . . leaving another child behind.

20

The melancholy lingered until morning and prompted me to invite Griffin and Jillian over for Saturday brunch. I thought it would be good medicine to go over Dad's collection together and talk about our first biography. "Come around ten. That'll give Sam plenty of time before he has to leave for his shift."

"Wait a minute. Are you gonna make this a working brunch?"

I laughed. "You don't trust me, do you? Can't a sister want to spend some quality time with her brother?"

"Why are you being so nice to me, Casey?"

"Get here around ten, brat."

I had a few of Dad's boxes out in the living room when they arrived. "I've been sorting through some of Dad's stuff." I held up a *Sports Illustrated* dated September 26, 1988. "Guess who was on the cover the day you were born?"

Griffin reached for the magazine, but I pulled it away.

"Right fielder and first baseman. Spent eighteen years in Boston. Only Yaz played more games for the Sox."

Griffin said, "Give me another clue."

"A mustache with eight Gold Glove Awards."

"Dwight Evans." Griffin pumped his fist.

"Right. Read the note Dad attached." I handed the SI to Griffin.

He read it out loud. "Born kicking and screaming on September 26, 1988, our son Griffin John weighed in at 7 lbs. 11 oz. He's a fighter!" He put his hand over Jillian's round belly. "We've got the kicking. All we need is the screaming."

We enjoyed the food and the laughs in between the childhood stories. I was finishing my last bite of quiche when Griffin changed the mood. "Casey, have you thought anymore about meeting our brother?"

His use of the phrase *our brother* still made my skin prickle.

I wiped my mouth with my napkin and crumpled it. "No, I haven't changed my mind. I'll let you know if I do."

"I was thinking—now don't get mad—that I would like to meet him, to get to know him. I've never had a brother."

"Well, I wouldn't like to. One *full* brother is enough. I don't want another half. Besides, brothers are overrated."

"Thanks, Casey. Love you too. I was also thinking—now don't get madder—that I don't need your permission, do I?"

I froze. It never occurred to me that Griffin would move forward without me.

"You would do that, knowing the way I feel?" I turned to Sam and Jillian for support. They slid their chairs back a few inches over the border into Switzerland.

My mind zigzagged. What if he reached out to Lisa? What if he met her son? How would I feel? I didn't know what else to say, so I blurted, "You're a big boy, Griffin. You can do what you want. Just leave me out of it."

So much for my nostalgic morning.

As was my habit, I wrote my half of our column early in the week. I gave it a quick once-over prior to emailing it to Griffin. Instead of the usual typos, I found frustration between the lines. My comments were antagonistic: "Perhaps if my brother knew the basics of the game . . ." My opinions were disagreeable, even on subjects upon which we normally agreed: "Yes, the Twins work well together, but tell us something we don't know, Griffin."

It was juvenile and unprofessional. I deleted it and started again.

Our headline for the week was "The Sox Are Winning! Why?" I knew Griffin would write about the hitting, so I focused on the catching, highlighting Darin's recent performance. When I reread it, I didn't find an ounce of conflict. It was as bland as plain yogurt. But I didn't want to risk another rewrite, so I let it slide.

With Darin on the brain, I thought about the question he'd asked me the day I spoke with Mike and him outside the post office. *Do you know the Lord?* I'd been asked by others if I went to church or what religion I was, but I'd never been asked that exact question before. He made it sound like God lived a couple houses up the street.

Sometimes Mom spoke about God in a personal way too. I could understand it coming from her since it was common for people to get more religious as they got older. But Darin and Mike? Their talent and salaries gave them more opportunities than their lives could use up, yet they didn't seem impressed. They could have lived anywhere in Boston but stayed put in Southie. They could have worked the press to their advantage but spent their time at baseball chapel instead. They didn't talk about themselves. They talked about God.

I liked my Irish Twins, so I decided to keep their religiosity out of my column. I didn't want to make them look bad.

Unless they got traded to the Yankees.

Foregoing a cordial hello, Roberta yammered into her phone, "Am I good or what? I've lined up two more TV appearances for you. The first one's in Watertown on Thursday, a four o'clock taping. I'm being sincere here—do you think Griffin can make it this time?"

"I don't know. Did you check with him? I'm his sister, not his mother." Every time Roberta used the phrase *I'm being sincere here* I wondered about all the times she didn't.

"A little touchy today, are we? You and Griffin fighting again? Might be a tool we could use. You know, inject some tension into the segment. Helps to fire things up sometimes."

"We're fine," I lied. "Why do I always have to be the responsible one?"

"Uh, because you *are* the responsible one."

I could hear Roberta chuckling over her comeback as I hung up.

Instead of dialing Griffin's cell, I called Jillian.

"According to the calendar, he doesn't have practice after school that day, so I'm sure he can make it."

I had no reason to doubt her. Jillian had everything on the calendar, and it was always up to date.

"Okay. Roberta wants us both there. Tell him to meet me at the TV station on Arsenal Street in Watertown. I'll catch a cab from work."

"Will do. Since he'll have his car, he can drop you off on the way home."

"Yes, well, we can confirm that before Thursday." I hesitated a few seconds before I spoke. "Jillian, the last time Griffin and I talked, he mentioned trying to contact Lisa's son. Do you know if he did?"

"No, he's been so busy he hasn't had the time."

Phew. Maybe he'd come to his senses. Then again, this was Griffin I was talking about.

After my introductory meeting with my clients Joe and Lisa Ianella, I felt sure they'd go with Kincade for their marketing. I made a few adjustments to their contract, faxed it to them for their signature, and promised to send a draft of their marketing plan the following week.

Even though I tailored every plan to each business, this was my first commercial maintenance company. Any ideas I came up with had to line up with the Ianellas' vision for their company. They cleaned retail spaces. Not much glamour in that.

One of the more successful tools I used in my creative process was to jot down keywords and phrases my clients used during our initial discussions. To set the right tone for their plan, it helped to get to know them better.

In Lisa's case, she was all about professionalism. She'd said, "We want our teams to be quick and efficient but not at the expense of a job done well. We use the greenest and safest products on the market too."

Joe was adamant about great customer service. "It's a top priority. Our people are taught to be personable and polite. I'm keen on employees dressing neatly too, and there's no smoking or cursing allowed." Between the two of them, one phrase stood out: *good character*. They both had it.

There was a rap on my door. It was Gordy. His eyeglasses sat cockeyed on his nose. It looked like the only thing he'd run through his hair all day was his hand.

"Casey, I'm curious, did the Ianellas get back to you?"

"Yes. Their attorney is going over the contract. 'Just a formality,' they said."

"Super! I like that couple. I know you'll do right by them."

Before I had a chance to respond, Lyle Wexler walked in. "Do right by whom?"

"Casey's new clients, the Ianellas." Gordy squared his shoulders like a proud parent.

Lyle sauntered over to the window behind my desk and took in the panoramic view. He surveyed my office like he was sizing it up. Leaning over my desk, he began to read my notes. "What's all this? Personable and polite. Dress neatly. No smoking or cursing. Are you planning to teach an etiquette class?"

I shuffled the papers into a pile and stuck them in a manila folder. "All part of my creative process. Not ready for primetime viewing yet."

"Casey's longtime clients, the Obermanns, referred the Ianellas," Gordy said. "They own a professional maintenance company."

Lyle sneered. "Maintenance? What's their annual revenue?"

I knew it wouldn't impress him, so I didn't plan to answer.

Gordy rubbed his hands together fast enough to spark a fire. "Close to three mil, but they're growing."

"Pfft," Lyle sputtered and walked out of the room.

The juxtaposition of this couple and Lyle only underscored his lack of character.

21

I wasn't home fifteen minutes when my landline rang.

It was Roberta. "Where have you been? You didn't answer your cell."

"It was turned off."

"You can do that?" she asked.

"Sure. You push the button—"

"You know what I mean," she said. "I left you a message."

"What was it?"

"Things are happening. I need to speak with you and Griffin, some place private."

We expected a call like this from Roberta every six months. When Griffin couldn't make it to the last sports show interview in Watertown due to an impromptu teachers' meeting, I knew it would come soon. The show's hosts were gracious, but I could tell they were bummed. Even I knew that a Double Header guest appearance meant double guests, not a single one.

Part of me was glad Griffin couldn't make it. I needed a few more cool-down days away from my brother. Yet I knew it wouldn't sit well with Roberta.

I suggested we meet at my place the next day around seven.

Roberta, her signature suit, nicotine patch, and attitude arrived on time. She got right down to business, starting with a slam. "It's grand that the two of you could make it."

We didn't react.

"I've been stalling on offers from *Red Sox Nation*, *From the Bleachers*, and *Playbook*, mainly because I don't know what to tell them. When one of you can commit, the other can't. Since you're billed as a team, that won't cut it. There's no sense in my going crazy drumming up business you can't handle."

On the defensive, I tried to respond. "We never—"

"Let me finish. Another thing, your last few columns stunk. There was a tone in them I didn't like. If I can hear it, your readers can too. I don't need to know what the problem is, but something's bugging you two and you need to fix it. Got it?"

Griffin and I avoided eye contact.

Roberta pushed. "I said got it?"

"Got it," I said to keep her from asking again.

Griffin and I sat there like school children who'd been summoned to the principal's office. I wanted to remind her that she worked for us, but I didn't dare.

"For the record, I am your agent, not your publicist. Casey, you should know the difference since you work for a marketing firm. You've done little promotion on your own and virtually no social media posts. You have to decide how much time you can give to your career."

"Which career?" I snapped. "The one that pays a lot or the one that pays a little?"

"The one I'm trying to promote. As long as you brought up money, let me remind you that I've been working darn hard for the fifteen percent of the little you do make. The fact that you're making a paltry sum is not my fault. You act like you're doing me a favor when you can show up for a TV appearance or a fundraising event. And what happened to those biographies you talked about writing?"

Griffin tried to schmooze her. "You see, we have these jobs—"

"And I don't? Right now I'm passing up opportunities for you that might not come around again. In case you've forgotten, I have other clients—clients who are hungry, clients who aren't satisfied with desultory results."

"Geez, don't let tact hold you back." Griffin's sarcasm turned to a smile. "Roberta, we know you're the best agent ever."

"Cut the baloney, McGee. Don't waste that charm on me. Save it for your public. I've been around too long. I know you think I'm dictatorial. Most of my clients do. And if you tell me one more time that you like my hair, I'm going to puke."

That shut Griffin up faster than jamming both feet in his mouth.

Roberta leaned forward. "Transition time from hobbyist to professional is just around the corner. I want to know how far I can push and how much I can sell. If you tell me to back off, I'll back off."

Griffin sat up straight and looked at me for a sign. I had none.

The only thing I said was, "Do you expect an answer tonight, Roberta?"

"Not tonight, but soon. I'm being sincere here. Only you two can decide whether to go for it all or lose what you've got."

Our beating wrapped up around eight.

Roberta slapped her hands on the arms of the chair and pushed herself up. We followed her to the door, tripping over each other like clumsy colts. Before we could see her out, Sam walked in with Tommy on his heels.

"Sam! You're home." I felt like I was being rescued. "I didn't know you were off tonight."

Sam hesitated when he saw Griffin and Roberta. "I thought I told you. We had a class today. Then we went to the gym and stopped for Mexican. Are we interrupting?"

"Nope, meeting's over," Roberta said, standing in the

threshold. "I've given my clients enough to think about." She turned to her nephew. "Speaking of thinking, Tommy, are you still seeing that girl, Gina?"

He took a few seconds to reply. "Why?"

"Why, indeed?" Roberta said. "Everyone knows that girl is nothing but a sucking hole of want." Without another word, she turned and walked out.

Roberta's one-two punch had knocked Griffin and me to the mat, and her right hook had left Tommy wobbling. The three of us plunked down, speechless.

Sam policed the scene for bruised egos. "Wow. If that woman is tough enough to silence you three, SWAT might want to recruit her."

"Yeah, Aunt Bobbie doesn't pull her punches. It's gonna sting for a while."

It was now or never, so I forged ahead and asked Tommy what I'd been dying to know. "Since Roberta brought up Gina, may I ask what attracted you to her in the first place?"

He shrugged. "She worked dispatch for a while in Revere. She had me at 'Reveeya PD. Can I help yous guys?'"

I tilted my head for a better read of his face. "Really?"

"Stupid, I know. She sorta reminded me of Marisa Tomei in *My Cousin Vinny*."

I paused, trying to imagine it. "Does she still?"

"Not so much. More like Audrey II in *Little Shop of Horrors*."

"Then you might want to rethink your—"

Sam interrupted, his way of telling me to mind my own business. "Anyone want a cold drink?"

"I'll take one," Tommy said.

Griffin raised one finger. "Me too. Hey Sam, I hear Tommy's your new spotter at the gym. Must be a huge weight lifted off your shoulders."

I looked at Griffin and groaned. "How long have you been waiting to use that lame line? Ignore my brother, Tommy. He can't help himself—or won't."

After Griffin and Tommy left and Sam headed for the shower, I reran the evening's discussion with Roberta in my head. First I was mad, then embarrassed, and finally ashamed. Roberta was right. We'd taken her for granted, let her fend for us like we were five-year-olds, and acted like spoiled brats.

In the early days, writing Double Header had been fun. Now it was a job. When Roberta first approached us, we wanted it all and we told her so. The player interviews, the promotional appearances, the possible money to be made, and the recognition all drew us in.

Now what? Were we prepared to make the sacrifices it would take? Where would we find the time? My commute and my job ate up fifty hours a week. Griffin's job wasn't as demanding because it was local, but I knew him—he'd never give up family time for fame.

Griffin and I each had a lot to think about before we talked.

The next day, as part of my decision process, I went back to Dad's collection. I'd already begun filing things away and jotting down book ideas, but now it took on a more businesslike tone. I opened a new spreadsheet and began filling in headings: Name, Sport, Team, Years Active, Notable Achievements. I added the information I had scribbled on a notepad then began hunting online for more facts. Some things were as simple as copying and pasting, but other things required digging deeper through news clippings and personal interviews.

I found more than a few curious facts about retired pros. Besides those who'd traded in their player status to coach, manage, or do color commentaries during televised games, others retired and never looked back. Some used their fame to help charities and nonprofits. Many made millions in advertisements. A few had gone into the ministry or become baseball chaplains. Some reports were sad, others inspiring.

I lifted a *Sports Illustrated* out of the cardboard box. It was from 1988. Larry Bird was on the cover, and the caption read, "The Legend Lives On." As I did with everything in Dad's collection, I handled it gently. When I turned to the table of contents, something fell out. It wasn't one of those irritating renewal postcards, but an envelope simply addressed to "Ned." The note was still inside.

When I unfolded the paper, I was struck by the opening words:

How did this happen? What have we done? How can I make this all go away? These are the questions I've been asking myself. I have no answers. I feel nothing but shame. Enough for the both of us.

My hands were shaking. This was a note to Dad from Lisa.

I turned in my badge and gun last night, citing personal issues. I don't know where I'm going. All I know is I need to start over. I don't know what you'll decide to tell Annie. Every time I think of her, I cry. I am so sorry, Ned, and ashamed. Maybe someday we'll find forgiveness—for ourselves and from others. I wish you and your family well. L

Why had Dad kept the letter? Here it was, serving as a witness to their affair and its aftermath. She gave up her home, her job, maybe even her career, because of this indiscretion while Dad got to move up in rank and move on with his family.

What would I have done in her place?

22

At 4:42 a.m., the ring of the bedside phone sounded more like a siren. My fog-brain asked, "Why would anyone call at this hour?" Fear provided a list of reasons and names of loved ones.

Sam picked up fast. "Hello . . . Tommy? Slow down." He swung his legs out from under the covers and sat up straight on the side of the bed.

I turned the bedside lamp on and came around to sit beside him.

"I'm so sorry. When did you find out? Where are they transporting him?"

Sam put his hand over the mouthpiece and whispered to me, "Nick. Tommy's brother. Wounded."

My heart quivered at the thought of Tommy's family. No one could prepare for this news.

Sam reassured Tommy. "No apology necessary. I'd be upset if you didn't call. Whatever you need, brother, let me know."

When Sam hung up I asked, "How bad is it?"

"He was injured, but they don't know how badly. They're shipping him out of Afghanistan but didn't say where."

"Life doesn't come with warnings, does it?" I leaned into him.

Sam put his arm around me. "No, and not knowing the details with their son on the way to some hospital overseas will make for a long wait for the Colettis."

Unable to go back to sleep, Sam and I got up. We sat together over coffee, alone in our thoughts. I didn't know the Colettis well. Still, I wished I could do something but I wasn't sure what. I could only imagine how helpless Tommy and his family felt.

Before I left for work, I hugged Sam tight. "Tommy's lucky to have a friend like you."

"Thanks. Do you think Griffin and Jillian have left for school yet? All I can see is that Memorial Day table Jillian set up. Remember when Tommy asked if he could put Nick's picture there? I feel like I should tell them."

"They don't leave for another half hour. I'm sure they'd want to know."

Sam called them, and I left for work. I phoned Mom when I got to the commuter lot. Even if my mother didn't know Tommy that well, if there was a slight chance that prayer really did work, I had to tell her.

"An early morning call. What a pleasant surprise!"

"Wish my news was good. You know Sam's friend, the young statie you met at Griffin and Jillian's cookout?"

"He was the one with Gina, the girl I spoke with?"

"That's him. He called Sam early this morning to tell us his brother Nick was wounded in Afghanistan. They don't know how serious it is yet."

"How awful for his whole family. Web and I will pray."

"I figured you'd want to know."

"You were right. I'll get it on the prayer chain too. Call me when you know more."

"I will."

I'd only been at my desk for ten minutes when Roberta called. She sounded stuffy. "Did you hear about my nephew?"

Had she been crying?

"Yes, Tommy called Sam. I'm so sorry. Any news?"

"None. Ramona is a wreck. Nicky was due to be discharged in less than two months." There was a catch in her voice then a pause. "I had hoped you'd get to meet him one day."

I'd never been privy to Roberta's vulnerable side, so comforting her felt, well, uncomfortable. "I'm sure we will once he's home."

"No way can I go back to New York now. Ramona needs me."

I doubted the rest of the Coletti family felt the same. True or not, I said the first thing that came to mind. "You're a good sister."

"I know."

Before I could say another word, Roberta hung up.

A barrage of random thoughts about the Coletti family pummeled my creative process the whole morning. I got little done. When I phoned Sam for an update, there was none.

Other than Dad, I hadn't lost a family member. Both sets of my grandparents were still living and active. If something happened to Griffin, how would I feel? I hadn't been the nicest sister lately or the most understanding. What if I never got a chance to make it right? Finding no value in second-guessing, I put that thought aside and went back to work. I tweaked my presentation for the Ianellas, who arrived right on time for their second appointment. Based on our initial interview, I'd come up with a simple slogan for their cleaning company: "Pure clean, pure green."

My plan to rebrand the company's image included changing their charcoal gray uniforms to colors of ocean azure and moss green. Joe loved the crisp logo our graphic design team created, and Lisa was pleased I'd included employee policies as part of the overall marketing plan.

She smiled and pushed her glasses atop her head. "Casey, it's like you were in our heads."

I started to respond when the conference door flew open, Lyle Wexler hanging on its doorknob. "I need to see you now, Casey. It's important."

Important? More important than our clients?

He wasn't going away, so I excused myself and met him in the hall. "What is it, Lyle? I'm in the middle of presenting." I held myself back from saying it, but I'm sure my face read, "Somebody better be bleeding."

"The janitors can wait. I need to find the files on the Cambridge pharmaceutical firm Gordy's been working with. He told me to check with Nora."

My fingers tapped my folded arms. "And?"

"She's not at her desk. You're the closest thing to her."

Could he be any more of a jerk? Did he think we were interchangeable? "I can't help you, Lyle. I'm sure Nora will be back shortly. Sorry."

That was a lie. I wasn't sorry.

"Tell you what, kid, I'll poke around Nora's files and you check her desk."

My mouth dropped open. Remarkable. So he *could* be more of a jerk. I tried to come up with a nonhostile response but stopped when Nora stepped off the elevator.

She stood in front of her desk and put her fists on her hips. "May I help you find something, Lyle?"

Anxious to get back to the Ianellas, I didn't wait to hear his answer.

As was Kincade's practice, I told Joe and Lisa to take the marketing plan home to review. "We won't start implementation until you've had time to digest it and only after you sign the contract and give us the go-ahead."

Joe shook my hand and thanked me. Lisa held my eyes with hers. "We're glad to be working with *you*, Casey."

I pretended I didn't know that her emphasis on "you" was in reference to Lyle.

23

The first day of summer was a week away. It wasn't the heat I craved as much as the light. It meant I could go for a run when I got home from work, which not only cleared my head of the day's junk but used up a chunk of alone time. Having time to myself at home was a good thing, but too much of a good thing was too much. I rarely admitted it to myself or to Sam, but our work hours were lousy.

After my run and a shower, I zapped a Lean Cuisine, choosing convenience over low sodium content. It was tasty. I smiled when I thought of Griffin and me teasing Mom about the frozen dinners she let us have a few times when we were kids. If she could see me now.

I was flipping through channels when my cell phone rang around nine thirty. It was Vanessa. We hadn't spoken since our lunch almost a month ago. "My, my. If it isn't Attorney Vance summoning me at this late hour."

"Late hour? Oy vey, you are getting old, aren't you? I remember being subpoenaed to go clubbing no earlier than ten when we were roomies."

I laughed. "Then we ruined it all by becoming reputable members of the establishment."

"Ain't it the truth, girl." After a pause, she got to the reason for her call. "Any new developments in the case of the half brother? Solved the mystery? Reached a settlement?"

"You know me, Vanessa. I don't settle unless I can get my way."

I loved her laugh. It came from a hearty place deep down inside her.

"I guessed as much, but I thought I'd check in. So how's it going with Griffin?"

"I'm not on his favorite person list. It's weird how differently we've reacted. Griffin can't wait to meet him. I, on the other hand, wish he'd disappear."

"As your pragmatic friend and legal counsel, may I point out the slim-to-none chance of him disappearing?"

I sighed. "I know. Just running out the clock."

"Game over is coming, honey. If I were you, I'd make my play while I still had the ball."

"Ooh, your sports metaphors are improving. I'm impressed."

"I'll ignore your condescension. Tell me, any more clues as to the identity of this young man?"

"Nope."

"Let's see what we have so far. His mother's name is Lisa Erickson. Sounds Scandinavian. What does your mother remember about her looks?"

I hated to admit it, but I'd never thought to ask Mom.

Vanessa saw through my stall. "You haven't asked her, have you?" Her tone told me she considered me a hostile witness. "Let's proceed. We know where her PO box is, so she probably works or lives nearby or both. She was a state cop twenty-five years ago. Maybe she still is."

"First of all, Erickson is her maiden name, so that's no help. And hundreds of people go in and out of that post office branch every day. Trust me, I've seen them."

"You might have seen *her* if you had a vague idea of what she looked like."

I bellowed, "Objection!"

"Overruled. According to the time table, the kid would be around twenty-four. Met any males around that age lately?"

"You asked me that last time."

"Okay, how about women named Lisa old enough to be the mother?"

I pretended to ponder her question. What I was really thinking was that if I mentioned Lisa Ianella she'd have her on the stand before I could say "mistrial."

I was sitting up in bed reading when Sam came home. He looked like he'd spent eight hours chasing a week full of bad guys. "Rough day?"

"Yeah, long, too."

"I hate to ask, but any more news about Tommy's brother?"

He sat on the foot of the bed and rubbed his face with both hands. "They found out he's being evacuated to Ramstein, Germany but nothing more about his condition. His parents are catching the first flight over they can get."

"Roberta said her sister was a mess. I would be too. How's Tommy holding up?"

"They're close, he and Nick. He's feeling guilty, I think. Mumbled something about not trying hard enough to talk Nick out of joining the Marines."

"Oh, because being a state cop is such a cushy job?"

Sam shrugged. "What can I say? He's searching for answers. He'll be okay. I only hope his brother is."

Sam was asleep within minutes while I lay awake thinking about the Coletti family and what they might have to endure. If Nick did make it home alive, what physical condition would he be in? What emotional scars would his injuries and this war leave behind?

In light of these ruminations, my disagreement with Griffin about our half brother seemed pale and petty.

And I could fix it with one call.

The next morning over coffee I pushed my arguments aside and picked up the phone. "Griffin, it's me."

"My high IQ is showing 'cause I figured that out when I read the caller ID. What's got you calling me so early?"

"I'm going to write Lisa Erickson and tell her we're willing to meet her son."

Griffin gagged. It took a few seconds for him to speak. "Agh! You made juice come through my nose." He cleared his throat. "Casey, are you sure you want to do this?"

"No, but you are."

I hung up and rummaged around for the same note cards I'd used when I responded to Lisa's first letter. After I wrote the note, I called and read it to Griffin.

Dear Lisa,

Thank you for your patience in all this. The additional time helped Griffin and me sort through our feelings. We agree that we're ready to meet with your son. I've enclosed the phone and email contact information. I expect we will hear from him soon.

Sincerely,
Casey Gallagher and Griffin McGee

On my walk from the T to my office, I dropped the card in the slot at the post office branch I called Lisa's. It wouldn't be long now, but I knew it would feel like forever.

24

The middle of June had passed, and Lyle Wexler was still lurking around. If he hadn't told me otherwise, I'd think he was settling in. After plying Nora for answers she didn't have, I decided to talk to Gordy.

"Got a minute, boss?"

"Boss? Ha! You must want something." Pleased with his guess, Gordy leaned back in his chair and folded his hands behind his head. "Come on in."

I entered and shut the door.

"Must be important if we need the door closed. What's bothering you, Casey?"

"I've narrowed it down to two words: *Lyle* and *Wexler*."

Gordy laughed. "Irritating, is he?"

"Yes, and add rude and condescending. He's interrupted me twice during presentation meetings. He told me he'd be gone by mid-June. It's past that. What's going on?"

Gordy felt around the papers on his desk then patted his shirt pocket before he found his glasses on top of his head. "Let me check the calendar. You're right. He was scheduled to be back in New York by June 15. Although, when I mentioned him to another VP at the home office last week, the woman acted like she didn't know him. Maybe they don't want him there either."

"Viable assumption."

"Casey, you do know that Lyle and I are both VPs and that I'm not his superior? I can't order him back to New York."

"I know. But isn't there a way you could gently suggest to the little twerp that he keep his nose out of my accounts?"

Gordy laughed. "I could try, but I might not use those exact words."

"Thanks. I appreciate it."

I opened Gordy's door and bumped into Lyle at the threshold. "On your way in or listening at the door?" I tried to act like I'd cracked a joke, but he didn't laugh.

Once Lyle was in with Gordy, I grimaced at Nora. With her palms up and her mouth curled down, she signaled she'd been helpless to warn me. I escaped to my corner haven, hoping Gordy would be able to geographically take away the thorn in my side.

Ensconced in my comfy chair, I reviewed those of my clients whose contracts were coming up for renewal. Each and every year I strove to add some fresh ideas to their marketing plans. Since they'd already expressed their appreciation, I fully expected them to renew.

In my eight years at Kincade I'd only lost one account, way back in my first year. That loss still goaded me. No one else at Kincade had a better retention record. My goal was to keep it that way.

For inspiration, I turned my chair around to take in the cityscape. That morning the weather man had predicted heavy fog and low visibility. Perhaps he'd been describing my brain. A surprising option broke through—maybe Mom could help. She'd been working for that small marketing company for twenty-something years, a family enterprise which dealt mainly with small-to-midsized regional businesses. Even though many of Kincade's clients were Fortune 500 companies with national markets, marketing is marketing. She could have some useful input.

My conscience mocked me. *How altruistic of you, Casey, to give your poor, old mother some credit.*

I dialed her number. "Mom, got a minute?"

"Sure. What was it Dad used to say? 'What can I do you for?'"

Even with the recent drama, our quoting Dad hadn't changed and I liked that.

Without breaking their confidentiality, I explained what I'd done for my clients to date. Mom said she'd had some similar-sized companies and shared what had worked for her. Our call was more like a couple of professionals brainstorming than mother and daughter chatting.

"Thanks, Mom. With some minor changes, I think we've got some ideas that will work for both our clients. Love you." I turned back to my desk to record a few notes of our conversation.

Startled by a grunt, I turned and found Lyle Wexler leaning against my door frame.

"I see you've moved on from discussing your next major marketing event with Gordy Ackerman—a middle-aged VP who can't get beyond Kincade's Boston office—to talking things over with Mommy. Is that a lateral or vertical move?"

I reached for my pink, gel stress-relief ball and squeezed. I tried to calculate how hard I'd have to throw it to wipe that smug look off Wexler's face.

"I'm serious, Sam. Wexler is a rat. I don't know how he got to be a VP in a company the size of Kincade. Gordy's more of a professional than he'll ever be, yet Lyle takes every chance he can to belittle the man. It's infuriating!"

"Gordy's a grown-up, Case. I don't think he'd want you fighting his battles, do you?"

"Probably not. Besides, I'm starting to suspect this might be one of those blood-is-thicker-than-résumé situations. Wexler's not experienced or old enough to be this cocky."

"If it's nepotism, it's a no-win situation for everyone on his radar."

Poor Sam. I'd started his day off by venting about work before we were even out of bed. "Sorry, I didn't mean to spend the little time we have together griping. Can we start over again?"

"Depends. What did you have in mind?"

"Well, we can either clean the basement or . . ."

He pulled me closer. "I'll take the *or*."

It was an easy decision—since we didn't have a basement.

25

Mike was pulled during the second game against the Mariners on the Sox road trip. The reports said he strained a tendon in his pitching arm, bad enough to be put on the disabled list. I called to see how he was doing.

"It's no biggie. The prescription is ice and heat and ibuprofen until it heals."

"Has the trainer predicted how long you'll be on the DL?"

"Nah, but I don't think it'll be too long. It's starting to feel better already."

"I'm sure your parents are pleased to have you around. Then there's Tess."

"Having extra time with Tess is huge." I could tell by his tone he was grinning. "But my parents are driving me nuts. Mom fusses and Dad hovers."

"That's what parents do."

"On the plus side, it's been over a month since Dad has had a drink. You wouldn't know this, but prior to his recent backslide, he'd been sober for almost twenty years. I was so young my memories of him drinking are faint. It was a shocker."

"What do you think triggered it?" I asked before I caught myself. "Or is that too personal?"

"It can happen to anyone. One day we're walking around so sure we've risen above the problem, and before we see it coming, we've slipped into pride or fear or complacency. Haven't you ever done that, Casey?"

"Do you have to ask?"

"Dad says his main problem was that for years he'd acted as his own higher power, as they say in AA. When fear took hold, he lost his sobriety. Thankfully, he recommitted his life to Christ. Now his motto is one day at a time with God. Probably should be everyone's."

His bringing up God surprised me. "God talk, huh?" I teased. "Now you're sounding like Darin."

"I'll take that as a compliment. You know, I never talked openly about my faith. Always said it was a private matter. Bull. It's pride."

"What changed your mind?"

"Wait a minute. Let me get my Bible."

I groaned inwardly then switched the phone to my other ear and braced myself.

"Tess showed me a verse in the Gospel of Luke where it talks about God being ashamed of us if we're ashamed of Him. I don't want Him to be ashamed of me. He's given me a lot in this world, but not as much as I'll have in the next."

"Yes, but doesn't God want you to enjoy what He's given you?"

"What I'm saying is it's more important that I follow Christ than do my own thing."

"Do your prayers actually get answered?" The question flew out of my mouth before I could catch it.

"Yes. Why? Do you have something you want me to pray about?"

With no fallback answer to that question, I tossed out the story of Nick Coletti.

Mike promised to pray, which I suspected would do more to make him feel useful than change Nick's condition.

Once we hung up, a thought goaded me like a stick: If you

don't believe praying helps, what makes you think "sending kind thoughts" and "wishing good luck" will be more effective?

I defended myself: Nothing wrong with encouraging words and common courtesies.

Mike's words rattled in my brainpan: "Bull. It's pride."

It had only been a few days since our attitude-adjustment meeting with Roberta, but a lot had happened since then in Roberta's life and in ours. Griffin and I knew we couldn't postpone the discussion about our future forever. Roberta's ultimatum would not go away.

We scheduled our round-table talk for the next Saturday Sam had off, ten days out. To avoid any last minute game changes, during the wait time Griffin and I promised to go over the various scenarios and their respective ramifications with our spouses.

With a baby on the way, I pretty much guessed what Griffin and Jillian would do. He would keep his teaching and coaching positions and, therefore, his benefits. Jillian would become a stay-at-home mom. She might consent to sub occasionally, but that's about it.

I wrote a list of questions for Sam and me to go over, like how much more do we need before we can buy our dream home? What amount did that mean putting away each week? Could we cut our expenses even more now to get into a new home sooner?

Maybe if Sam picked up a few extra shifts, I could take time to work on the biographies. Could I handle writing with a full-time job and the column and all it entailed? What about our personal time? What about starting a family?

All the scenarios I came up with involved us working longer hours to make more money, which meant less time together.

For months, I'd been ignoring the possibility that Double Header and the brother-sister driving force behind it might not survive. I thought seeing the facts on paper would help me find a simple answer. Wrong. I had more questions and fewer answers than before.

If the answer was so simple, why did it elude me?

I stuck my running shoes on and took off down the bike path behind our development. I didn't often get to run in the early morning hours. Since I had a nine-thirty meeting south of Boston this morning, I caught a break.

It was dry and a little chilly, perfect running weather. I thought how happy the birds seemed with all their chirping—until I recalled a recent article I'd read which explained that chirping wasn't early morning aviary chitchat but territorial screeching. "Get out of my tree! Leave my eggs alone! You think you can leave for the winter then start where you left off? Not in my backyard!"

I was amused at how alike humans and other species could be . . . which brought me back around to Lisa's son.

Lisa's son. Aloud I asked, "Casey, are you ever going to be able to say my half brother or Dad's son or even my brother?" I couldn't answer.

It had only been a few days since I'd mailed the second note to Lisa. I'd included my business card, knowing I would be the one they would call. No way was I going to let Griffin blindside me with a luncheon date with this kid before I had a chance to find out more about him.

I took a deep breath then let it out.

Too many changes, too fast. Dad's death, Mom's remarriage, Roberta's ultimatum, the future of Double Header. The biggest, Lisa's son.

By the time I was ready for work, I realized my run and shower hadn't relieved my stress. I tried to focus on my job, usually a source of distraction. It didn't work. What had happened? Oh, yeah, Lyle Wexler had happened. Why wasn't he gone? Why did he irritate me so much? Why couldn't things stay the same?

Maybe one day at a time with God oughta be *my* motto.

After my meeting, I took the T the rest of the way into the city. The ride wasn't memorable. I didn't even bother with my game of imagining what other passengers did for a living. I needed to figure out what *I* was supposed to do for a living first.

My cell phone beeped at the exact moment I was passing *the* post office. It creeped me out, like there was a sniper-caller out there. I was relieved to see it was Griffin. "Yes, little brother?"

"I haven't heard anything. Have you?"

"It's only been two days. Let's give 'em time to check their mail. I'll call you as soon as I hear something."

"You gave them my number, too, didn't you?"

I hedged. "Griffin, they know us, so I'm sure they can figure out how to get ahold of us."

"I'd be willing to bet that Ms. Control Freak only gave them her cell and email. Am I right?"

"What difference does it make? Since Lisa Erickson contacted me, it seemed logical. Don't worry."

I hated being so transparent.

The bright spot of my morning was when Nora told me Lyle Wexler was back in New York.

"For good?"

"Not sure, but he flew out last night without a nice-to meet-you or see-you-later."

"He was probably expecting a going away party, which I will gladly throw him this afternoon."

"You didn't like him much, did you, Casey?"

"Did you?"

Nora was smart enough not to answer.

With Wexler gone, I could leave my office door open without fear of him skulking nearby.

So why did I close it?

I knew why. Because of the call I anticipated receiving. I was worse than Griffin.

I opened my laptop and went to my client files. I scrolled through my cell phone's contact list, but used the landline to call those who were due to renew contracts. After we agreed upon a meeting date, I hinted at a few of my ideas so they'd know I had something fun in the works. With the element of surprise on my side, my presentations were an effective event.

I jumped when my cell rang around noon. My pulse rate sped up when I didn't recognize the number.

"Casey Gallagher." I don't know why I didn't just say hello like I usually did.

It was Joe Ianella with bad news, not for me or Kincade, but for him. His mother had taken ill, so he was flying to Chicago to be with her. He assured me that they were pleased with the contract and overall plan but would feel better waiting to execute it after he returned.

"You do what you need to do, Joe. I'll be here when you're ready."

A week had passed since our scolding from Roberta, so I figured I'd touch base to give her an update. "Hi, Roberta."

"What do you have for me?"

"Not much. First, any more news about your nephew? The last news I had was that he was being evacuated to Germany and that your sister and brother-in-law were flying over."

"Ramona and Vincent are at Logan right now. Got a nonstop on Lufthansa." Weariness weighed down her words. "Ramona's an RN, so she'll be able to tell us more about Nicky's condition once she sees him and talks to the doctors."

"Are you still in Boston?"

"Yes, I wanted to be there when Tommy and his sister Ali got more news."

"I understand." I segued uncomfortably. "I know this isn't important considering all that you have going on, but I want you to know that Griffin and I heard you the other night. We've got a sit-down planned with our spouses this Saturday. That's the earliest Sam could get off."

"I suppose it's a start."

Before I could end our conversation with a few words of comfort, Roberta hung up.

For the rest of the day, every time my cell phone rang it chipped a few seconds off my life. When would I learn that the expected only happened when you stopped expecting it?

26

"Hi, Casey. It's Mike. I'm trying to reach Griffin. I tried his cell, but he's not answering."

I marveled again at how others expected me to keep track of Griffin. "Griffin turns his phone off during school hours."

"Right. I guess I'll try later."

"Is it something I can help you with, Mike?"

"Don't think so. Griffin invited Darin and me to come by and meet his high school team Thursday afternoon."

"They'll be so excited!"

"You're welcome to join us."

"Can't. Unlike you, I'm not on the DL, so my boss expects me to be here."

"Bosses can be funny like that."

"Besides, this is Griffin's thing. He doesn't need me running his play."

After Mike and I hung up, I called Jillian to firm up our plans for Saturday. "Jillian, I forgot, are you and Griffin coming here on Saturday or are we going to your house?"

"Why don't you come here? I've got a new recipe I want to try."

"You haven't come up with a theme for the occasion, have you? If so, I might have to give you a wet willy."

"Eww, you would do that to the mother of your niece or nephew?"

"Only if you scrapbook about the dreams and goals of the McGees and Gallaghers."

"Why, Casey Gallagher, I think you're poking fun at me!"

"I am, but only because I'm jealous. Someday when I have kids, I'm afraid they'll want all their birthday parties at Auntie Jillian's."

"Casey, would that be such a horrible thing?"

The vision took form. "On second thought, have I told you lately how generous and talented you are?"

"No, and you haven't told me if you've heard back from Lisa or your brother either."

Griffin had rubbed off on her. I wanted to ask, "Which brother?" but that would require an admission on my part. "No. I told Griffin I'd call as soon as I did."

"If you hear back before Saturday, maybe we could ask him to stop by after our meeting? We'd all be together."

Jillian should have been named Pollyanna. "I'd rather save that for another time. The discussion about our future and Double Header will be enough for one day, don't you think?"

"I guess. It was only a thought." She sounded a little hurt.

"As usual, Jilly, you think of everyone. But I'm not as nice as you, remember?"

"That's what you want us to believe, but you don't fool me."

The truth was I wasn't nearly as nice as Jillian, but I decided not to argue. "One more thing. Tell your husband that even though Mike invited me, I won't crash his team pizza party on Thursday. I'll let him play the hero without interference."

When another three days passed with no response from my note to Lisa, I started to question my actions. Did I put a stamp on the envelope? Drop it in the right slot? Remember to add my return address?

Yup, I had done everything right.

If they were so hot to meet us, what was taking them so long? I was irritated and sick of jumping every time my phone rang or my email beeped.

If one more person asks me . . .

My phone rang again. "Hello."

"Honey?"

"Hi, Mom."

"Any word from Lisa or her son yet?"

Grrr.

Saturday arrived before Sam and I were ready. Our attempts to discuss things before our meeting with Griffin and Jillian had been waylaid by our schedules. Since we weren't due to land on their stoop until noon, we had time to talk over breakfast.

I fried up some link sausage, scrambled four eggs, and toasted a couple of bagels. When the food was plated, I got us each a cup of strong coffee. No mild breakfast blend this morning.

Sam took a bite of the sausage. "Real sausage? No fake turkey stuff?"

"Don't get used to it. We're back to healthy tomorrow. It's a treat to keep you going during our marathon talks. I know how you dislike these things."

"And you don't?"

I took a bite of sausage. "Mmm. Let's enjoy our breakfast. I promise not to bring out my spreadsheets until after our second cup of coffee."

At the word spreadsheet, he stopped chewing and his eyes rolled.

"Sam, you know this is how I think best. Work with me, please."

He agreed to try.

When the table was cleared, I handed him a copy of my

notes and spread out my pie chart like a delicious dessert. This time Sam looked straight at me, but his eyes had the fresh glaze of a donut.

"Trust me," I said. "It looks worse than it is."

"If you say so."

I opened with the good news. "By putting fifty percent of our income aside for the past four and a half years, we've saved close to $275,000 toward a house. I figure we need another 100K."

"What did you say? How much? Why do we need more?"

"Because our decision to buy our forever home in a preferred neighborhood before we start a family doesn't come cheap."

Sam stretched across the table to reach my hands. "Not exactly the way I remember it, Case. The whole plan for a dream home and waiting to have kids was more *your* decision than ours."

"We talked about it ad infinitum, Sam." My tone sharpened. "How could you forget?"

Sam took a slow sip of his coffee and set his mug down before he responded. "Since the whole purpose for this talk and the meeting with Griffin and Jillian is to get everything out on the table, let me suggest that I might not have been *in* on the plan as much as I was part of your plan."

"Now you tell me?"

"I tried to tell you that the whole 4,000-square-foot house with the high-end finishes was not at the top of my wish list. I'd be thrilled to start a family earlier in a less than grand abode."

"Where was I when you told me that?" I pointed to our original budget. "Besides, even if we put the issue of buying a home aside for now, how can we handle children with our demanding jobs, my long commute, and your crummy hours?"

"That's why we're talking." Sam leaned forward and folded his hands around his mug. "Listen up, Case. You tell me what you want and I'll tell you what I want. Total honesty, okay?"

I said "Okay" but I wasn't okay. "Our plan . . . or my plan, if you prefer to put it that way, was to save for a few more years to afford the house we want, preferably in Duxbury or Hingham. That means having our first baby when I'm about thirty-four or five. I could cut back on my hours in the city, write part-time, and do Double Header."

"Is that realistic? When would our family have time together? I don't want to wait until I'm in my late thirties to be a father. By the time our kids are in high school, I'll be old. Raising our kids in a germ-infested daycare with us passing each other on our way to work is no way to live."

"People do it every day, Sam, and they manage."

"You're right, they do. But I want to do more than manage. We have one life, and I want to share mine with those I love—you and our children." He reached for my hand again. "Isn't *how* we live more important than where?"

I pulled away and crossed my arms. "I don't want to raise a family in some rundown shack in a neighborhood where we need bars on the windows."

"It doesn't have to be either-or, Casey. A solid-built Colonial would do. Another thing, even without a family and a bigger house to care for, how do you plan to commute to Boston every day, work on your biographies, and continue with your Double Header column and activities—especially if Griffin backs out?"

I leaned back hard against the seat. All Sam was doing was speaking the truth, but his solutions came up short of the miracle I wanted—one that would add another eight hours to my personal twenty-four-hour day.

Sam held his hands out, palms up. "Listen, Case, we can't even make some of these decisions until after we know what Griffin and Jillian are going to do."

"You know exactly what they're going to do." My lower lip protruded about the time my frown showed up. "He'll keep his job for the benefits, and Jillian will opt to be a stay-at-home mom."

"You say that like it's a lesser profession."

"I didn't mean that. It's just that . . . well, it's . . ." I gathered my papers into a pile and rapped them on the table, this way and that way, until their edges were even.

Sam covered my hand with his. "I know, it means change, and you don't do change well."

I picked up our mugs and walked to the sink. I had to admit it was true—to myself. But not to Sam, at least not right away.

27

Deciding to start our meeting with Griffin on a positive note, I asked, "How did your team react to your celebrity guests on Thursday?"

"I felt like Coach of the Year. They were so excited to meet Hennessey and Flynn. When I first told them they'd be joining us for pizza after the game, I thought they were gonna carry me on their shoulders into the pizza house." Griffin paused like he was picturing the night. "Not every pro ball-player would take the time to do that. Ya know, more and more, those two impress me."

I nodded. "Me too."

From the kitchen Jillian called, "Griffin, did you tell Casey about meeting the Red Sox chaplain?"

"Oh, yeah," he said. "He was at the restaurant. Cool guy. He sat with us a few minutes. Asked Darin about his siblings."

"Which ones?"

"Don't know. Darin might have said something about changing his mind. The chaplain told him to keep praying."

"About what?"

"Don't know."

Agh! I should never send a boy to do a woman's job.

Since I'd seen Darin a couple of times recently, it seemed unlike him not to mention a problem with his family. Of course it wouldn't occur to my "don't know" brother to find out what it was.

I sighed. "Did it ever occur to you that you don't know the answers because you don't ask the questions?"

Griffin mimicked my sigh. "Casey, did it ever occur to you that I don't ask because it's none of my business?"

Before I could slap him with a response, Jillian announced, "Okay, everyone, take your seats. We can talk over dinner."

I was amused watching Jillian maneuver around the kitchen and dining room. Normally able to slide through small spaces, her belly now acted like a rolling roadblock, sending her on detours around the table and chairs.

"I don't know what's wrong with me today," she said. "I keep bumping into things."

"Nothing having a baby won't cure," I said, patting her stomach.

She tilted her head. "Oh? I've never heard that before. Do you think that will help with my equilibrium?"

Griffin smiled. "I'll bet on it, Jilly. Now come join us."

The news from Griffin and Jillian held no surprises. Jillian planned to take eight weeks maternity leave, then decide what to do after that. Griffin's job would remain the same.

The most difficult decision for Griffin was whether to continue with both Double Header and the biographies or choose between the two.

"I'd like to stick with the column, at least through the summer. I'll make myself available for TV and radio spots for as long as I can."

Even though I was disappointed, it made sense. After the baby was born, he knew both Roberta and I would want more out of him than he could give. As for the biographies, he agreed to do research between work and helping Jillian.

Me? I still wanted it all, including my job at Kincade and the salary and perks that came with it. Even more so since my main irritant, Lyle Wexler, had fled the state. Giving up Double

Header would be like giving up my first born. I loved writing the column and making the TV and radio appearances, but how could I continue both jobs and start on the biographies, not to mention pleasing Sam and starting a family?

As usual, decisions were simpler for Griffin and Jillian. They figured it all out in one conversation.

What was wrong with me?

In the end, I asked Sam to give me more time to think. It was easier for him, since none of the changes we had to make affected his career.

A thought sprang up like a weed: Had Lisa Erickson felt the same way?

I phoned Darin that evening, sure I could get more info out of him than my brother. "Griffin said he met your chaplain after the game at the pizza house. *Cool guy* was the phrase he used."

"Griffin's right. He played in the minors before he got the call."

"So he was called up to the majors too?"

Darin chuckled. "No, the call was from God, into the ministry."

"Oh." I decided to skip the subtlety and ask Darin what I wanted to know. "Is everything all right with your family?"

"As far as I know. Why do you ask?"

"Griffin said the chaplain asked about them."

"He always does."

I waited for more of an answer, but none was given. "Okay, then. Talk later?"

"You bet."

Griffin and I waited in the green room for the assistant producer of *From the Bleachers* to give us the high sign.

Griffin got up, fidgeted, and plopped back down. "This might not be the right time to bring it up, but it's been over a week since you wrote to Lisa. I'm not taking any chances, so I'm gonna follow up."

"Did it occur to you that they may have changed their minds?"

"Yes, it did. You read me the note you wrote, remember? It didn't exude familial affection."

"It wasn't supposed to. How do you plan to reach them, another note?"

"I'll think of something. Sam might be able to help us find her."

"You expect to use my husband to help you?"

"Help *us*, Casey, us."

The show's assistant producer opened the door and announced, "You're on!"

The taping went well. Griffin and I performed our bickering-siblings act successfully but hid the real friction, despite Roberta's suggestion. It wasn't about us; it was about sports. As professionals, we could separate the two. Most of the time.

We reached Griffin's car a little after six. It took him a while to maneuver his way out of the parking garage and through the congested streets. We didn't say much until we reached I-93.

"They invited us back," he said, "so I guess we did well, huh?"

"Guess so." I untwisted my seatbelt, turned my head right, and stared out the window.

"Still mad at me, I see."

"The word is *angry*. And, no, I'm not angry. I'm just thinking."

"Yup, that's what you always say when you're mad."

"I wanted to give you time to reconsider, that's all."

"Gee, that's all? How magnanimous of you."

The tension spring-released and my temper took off. "How come you think more of Lisa's son's feelings than you do mine?"

He took a deep breath and let it out slowly. I had to strain to hear him above the traffic noise. "Tell me, Casey, why is it acceptable for you to think more of your feelings than you do of his or mine?" His expression was calm, which made me madder.

Before I could formulate a rebuttal, Griffin yanked my arm, pulled me toward him, and yelled, "Get down!"

My thoughts were fuzzy. I wanted to wake up—but from what? Was it a dream, a nightmare? What was that beeping? It took all my strength to raise my eyelids. I saw a glimmer of white and a blur of stainless steel. Where was I?

"We're here, Casey."

Who was there? Through the dim light, I saw Sam sprawled in a chair across the room. He looked like he was dozing. When I tried to call him, I heard more beeping, this time louder. Sam rushed to my side. He touched my face. Someone else was there, but who? They talked, but I couldn't stay focused long enough to hear what they were saying.

All I remember thinking is *Sam's with me. I'm safe.*

I awoke again to the sound of Mom and Sam whispering, but about what? Did I hear Webster and Jillian too? I needed to figure things out before I spoke.

Willing the film from my mind, I remembered the crash. I felt pain first then panic. My eyes sprang open. I scanned the room and saw Sam, Mom, Webster, and Jillian. Their faces told me this was no party. I tried to speak but couldn't. I reached up and felt something taped to my mouth. Something was stuck in my throat. I pulled at it.

Sam ran to the side of my bed and took hold of my arms. "Easy, Case. Calm down. Everything's gonna be fine."

Mom patted my shoulder. "Web went to get the doctor, honey. Try to relax."

When the doctor arrived with a couple of nurses, she shooed everyone out of the room except Sam. She fiddled with the contraption I was connected to then spoke to soothe me. "It's called tracheal intubation, Casey. I'm going to remove the tube from your throat. It will feel funny. Do you think you can handle it?"

I nodded, trying not to tense up, my hand squeezing Sam's. She lied. It didn't feel funny. It made me gag.

Mom, Webster, and Jillian were allowed back in the room. I tried to speak. My throat was sore and my voice raspy. I looked from Sam to Mom to Jillian. "Please. Where's Griffin?"

28

Griffin sauntered into the room with a tray of Dunkin' Donuts coffees, a smile on his face, and a one-by-three-inch bandage on his forehead. "Good of you to finally join us, sis. Have a nice nap, did you?"

My panic receded. "You're okay? You weren't hurt?"

"Leave it to your brother to escape with only a scratch," Mom said.

"I wouldn't say only a scratch. I did get five stitches." He set the coffee down and touched his bandage. "I could end up with a quarter-inch hairline scar."

I cleared my throat to speak. It still felt raw. "I'd throw something at you if it didn't hurt so much."

The smiles that crossed between us told the truth.

"Listen, Casey, what do you remember?" Sam asked, always the cop.

"Not much." I glanced at Griffin. "We were, uh, discussing something, and Griff yelled. Then there was a loud bang. I don't know what happened."

"I do," Griffin said. "A teenage girl jumped onto I-93 going too fast off the ramp while texting. After she hit our rear panel and turned us sideways, her car spun back around and crashed into the front passenger door."

"Other than facing some serious charges," Sam said, "she's fine."

Jillian added, "You got the worst of it, Casey."

Sam pulled something out of his pocket. "Well, almost."

"What do you mean?" I asked.

"When the EMTs were getting you out of the wreck there was some collateral damage." He held up a plastic bag filled with my crushed smartphone. "One of them stepped on it."

I reached up and winced. My arm dropped to the bed.

Sam put his hand on my shoulder. "Easy, Case. It's only a phone. I'll get you a new one."

"It's not the phone. It's my contacts. If they can't be restored, I'll be lost."

"And we almost lost *you*." Sam caressed my cheek with the back of his hand. "Relax. You won't be calling anyone anytime soon."

I knew he was right, but I'd need to get ahold of Nora so she could notify my clients.

"On the bright side," Griffin said, "your granny satchel made it through unscathed."

"Oh, if it isn't Mr. Louis Vuitton himself critiquing my fashion sense. Where is Hildegard anyway?"

"Stop fretting, Casey. She's at home." Sam looked over at Griffin. "Am I gonna have to ask you to leave?"

I made a face at Griffin.

He stuck out his bottom lip. "Sorry, I'll behave. I promise."

Mom shook her head. "Seems like things are almost back to normal."

Lifting my hand to rub my eye, I felt a bandage. It was wrapped around my head. I hadn't thought about my injuries. Anxiety rose. "How bad do I look? Does anyone have a mirror?"

Sam said, "No facial injuries, thanks to your brother's quick thinking. You were banged up and bruised and suffered a concussion."

Mom bent over and kissed me on the cheek. "We've been praying, our whole church has." She released a stuttering breath.

"Thanks, Mom. I'll be fine."

She straightened my covers. "I know that now, but it's been a long week."

"A week? I've been here for a week?" I tried to raise myself up, but pain coursed through my side. A random question surfaced: What condition would I be in if Mom and Webster had *not* prayed?

Sam leaned over and touched my lips with his. "Yes, a week that felt like forever."

"Because of the swelling on your brain," Mom said, "they kept you in a medically-induced coma."

I tried not to stress about regaining a week of lost time. "How do they do that?"

Griffin raised a finger in the air. "I can field that one." He stepped closer. "The nurse comes in every hour on the hour and gives you a whack on the head."

Jillian yanked Griffin's shirtsleeve. "Nummy, don't make your sister laugh. It hurts."

She was right; it did. And it felt good.

Besides the pain caused by two broken ribs, a cracked collar bone, and more bruises than were visible to me, I was a little nauseated. The nurse said it could be the pain meds or the head trauma, which was the doctor's main concern. Three days after I came to, they felt it was safe to move me out of ICU.

By the time I got to my semi-private room, another patient had claimed the bed with a view. After my family left and the nurse got me settled, I thought about turning on the television to catch the ten o'clock news. I didn't want to hear it as much as I wanted to avoid thinking. I had banished angst, but I sensed self-pity lurking around the corner. I knew depression wouldn't be far behind.

I peeked over at my roommate, an older woman with

silver-white hair in a short, spiky Newbury Street cut. She was reading the *New England Review*, her tortoise-shell glasses low on the bridge of her nose. Her manicure looked fresh, her long nails painted a rich shade of ruby red. The only lines on her face were those between her brows.

"Excuse me," I said, "would you mind if I watched the news?"

She peered over the top of her glasses. "Are you sure you want to do that, dear? It's never very good."

"It isn't, is it? I suppose a stay in the hospital is bad enough news."

"Yes, I agree." She put her magazine down. "My name is Olivia Price. And you are?"

"Casey Gallagher."

"It's delightful to have the company, Casey. I've been here four days, and it's been abominable." She took off her glasses and leaned over her bed railing. "And I haven't even started on the menu yet!"

Even though hospital cafeteria humor was standard issue, I chuckled. "Will you be here much longer?" I debated how much interest I should invest in a roommate who may be gone in the morning.

"Not sure. They're running more tests tomorrow. I think I pay my doctor to be a pessimist."

I smiled. "It's good that you can joke about it."

"Who's joking?" Mischief danced in her eyes.

Before I could find out any more about Olivia Price, my pain meds kicked in and I fell off the radar.

With the news out that I was alive and awake, cards and flowers streamed in over the next week. Darin and Mike sent an iTunes gift card and a note that read, "Casey, we're praying overtime for you. Stay 'tuned' for God." I wasn't sure how I was supposed to do that, but I thought it was sweet.

Roberta sent me a vintage copy of the *Sporting News*. Maybe I wasn't being fair, but her "Hurry up and get well" card sounded more like an order than a heartfelt message. Good ol' Roberta.

When an arrangement arrived from Kincade, I noticed that my roommate had no flowers. "Olivia, I've run out of room. Would you mind if the orderly put this bouquet on your window sill?"

"Not at all, dear. Gracious! It's been a long time since I've received flowers." She laughed. "And these weren't even intended for me."

"Well, they are now. I suppose it's different when you're in for tests."

"No, dear, I mean it's been decades. My corporate job kept me so busy that my personal life took a hit. My husband got tired of waiting for me to come home."

"Oh, I'm sorry. Did you have any children?"

"A daughter, but we've been estranged for some time now."

I didn't want to say "I'm sorry" again, so I said, "Oh." I couldn't imagine being estranged from my family. I was sure they wouldn't allow it.

"I don't deserve sympathy. I made my choices, not all wise." She sighed. "Now here I sit in the exciting life I built, alone, having tests ordered by a pessimist." She scrunched her hair and perked up. "The good news is that I'm making headway with my daughter. She's flying in for a visit next week."

"That's wonderful. I hope things work out. Mind if I ask where you work?"

"Gannett in Boston."

"Gannett Mergers & Acquisitions?"

"That's the one. How about you, dear?"

"I'm at Kincade Marketing Solutions. They've got a decent sick-day policy, but I must be pushing my limit by now. Does Gannett give you a hard time about taking time off?"

"No. It helps that I'm the CEO."

Olivia was the type of strong woman I admired, one I could learn a lot from. Of course, I believed being happily married and being a CEO were not mutually exclusive as long as you had the right spouse, which I did. We exchanged phone numbers and agreed to have lunch once we were both back to work.

"I plan to step down at the end of the year. No clue what I'll do after that." Her words got hung up on the way out of her mouth. "Take my advice, Casey, don't do this whole end-of-life thing alone."

"You've met my family. I don't think I'll have that option."

She laughed. "They do hang about, don't they, dear? But it's the love that counts."

"You're right. It is."

After hearing Olivia's story, I vowed to appreciate it more.

On my second day home, Mom offered to come by so Sam could work his usual four-to-midnight shift. He'd taken a lot of time off, and I knew it would make both of us feel better to get some things back to normal.

Sam fussed over me, straightening blankets and arranging items I might need on the bedside table. "Be sure to listen to your mother, Casey." When Mom arrived he said, "If she doesn't behave, call me. I'll hire a burly nurse to take charge." He kissed me good-bye but seemed unsure of his decision to leave.

"I'll be fine. Now get going or you'll be late. Love you."

"Love you more. Call me if you need me."

Once he left Mom said, "You sure had him worried. He was a wreck."

"And you weren't, Mom?"

"Maybe a little. But I had the Lord to turn to—and I did. He gave me peace, which made all the difference." She put her hand on my cheek and smiled. "Can I get you anything?"

I wanted to say "Maybe some of that peace God gave you" but didn't. "What I want right now is sleep. I didn't get much those last few days in the hospital."

"Good idea." She moved the phone closer to the bed and

turned the ringer off. "When you wake up, don't shout. Call my cell." Then she tipped the plantation shutters, kissed my cheek, and closed the door behind her.

When I awoke a few hours later, Mom was at the door before I could call.

"Hungry? How about some tomato soup and a grilled cheese sandwich?"

"Sounds good." I smiled at the menu. It was the same thing she served me when I got sick as a child.

Griffin, scheduled to relieve Mom that evening, showed up with a frozen mocha drink for me.

"My favorite. How'd you know?"

"My wife pays attention."

"Yeah, that sounds like Jillian. But I'll give you points for listening to her."

"Thanks." He sat on the chair near the bed, leaned forward, and clasped his hands tight. "Just so you know, it wasn't our arguing that caused the accident. I had time to move when I saw the girl coming, but the lanes were full. I had no place to go. I'm so sorry."

"Griff, I don't doubt your decision for a second. If I hadn't been so stubborn . . ."

"Let's drop that whole subject for now and focus on you getting better."

"Okay."

"One good thing came out of this whole mess," he said.

"What's that?" Was he getting sentimental again?

"For once, my half of the column was in before yours."

I thought he'd finally one-upped me until I remembered I'd sent him two installments the previous week. "Hah! Now I can say that not only have I never missed a deadline, I've bested you every week, even the week I was in a coma."

He groaned. "Say it ain't so."

"It's so."

29

With only a few weeks left of school, Jillian used up her personal time to sit with me when Mom or Griffin couldn't relieve Sam. Although the one-on-one time with each of them was good, Jillian and I got the chance to share more than we ever had before about our dreams and goals, marriages and families.

"I brought you some books to read," she said. "This author is fabulous. Her writing reminds me of yours."

"Mine? All you've read are my Double Header columns."

"Not true. I save all your notes and cards. Your comments are always so clever yet heartfelt. Even your sales copy makes me want to hire your clients. With your talent and wit, you could write anything."

"I don't know about *anything*." I was touched that she saved my notes. I thought I was the only one who did that. "I'd like to start on the sports biographies soon."

"Go for it! Do whatever you can, whenever you can, to grow your dream."

Up until the accident I loved Jillian for putting up with my brother, but this friendship was different. "Besides having a healthy baby on your due date, Jilly, what are your dreams?"

"Someday, I hope to open my own shop and hold quilting bees, craft classes, and do party planning. I dream of walls filled with tiny prints and bright colors and little pieces of pretty. Probably sounds silly to you."

"No sillier than me moving words around until I like the way they sound." I suggested she make up some business cards and brochures to have on display when she and Griffin hosted their own events. "Your parties are the best form of advertising. It's a gift the way you decorate and pull things together into one cohesive theme without it ever looking cheesy."

"Thanks. I enjoy doing it."

She proved it when she set a tray in front of me that rivaled a Martha Stewart magazine layout—a crock of homemade vegetable soup, half a chicken salad wrap, and a mini-skewer of fresh fruit. She'd even folded the cloth napkin into a nurse's cap. "See, this is what I'm talking about!"

She smiled as she set her matching meal on a tray table nearby.

Later over a cup of tea, Jillian opened up. "Between you and me, Griffin was a mess after the accident, inconsolable. He blamed himself. He acts like a wise guy, but that's just it. It's an act. He loves his big sister, you know?"

"Now now, a lot of time and attention has gone into branding our sibling behavior. We wouldn't want to ruin it now with all that mush, would we?"

When Tommy dropped by the next day, he had some good news about his brother. "Turns out Nick was hurt in a freak accident on base, not in a firefight. They expect him to make a full recovery, almost in line with his release date from the Marines. Mom's trying to get him into Spaulding Rehab where she works."

Sam slapped him on the back. "Great to hear that! Your parents must be relieved."

"We all are. Dad came home last week so he could get back to work."

"What does your dad do again?" I asked.

"Postmaster. A position that's hard to get but easy to lose if you're not careful. Now that he's home—hallelujah!—Aunt Bobbie can return to New York!"

I laughed. "And your mother?"

"There's no way Mom's leaving Germany without Nick. The doctors said he might need a few more weeks."

After Tommy left, thinking about his brother's injury and my accident reminded me of the expression *bad things always come in threes*. Did it ring true because people insisted on counting bad things until they reached three?

I decided to start counting trios of good things, starting with Griffin and Jillian's baby, my recovery, and Nick's return to his family. Before I could stop counting or lose track, I reached for my journal and began writing. I filled a whole page before I could say "hand cramp."

Or think about Lisa Erickson and her son.

Outside of the de rigueur bouquet of flowers from Kincade and get-well cards from Gordy and Nora, I hadn't heard much from work. I wanted to check in before my clients thought I'd gone on sabbatical, so I called the one person who would know everything, Nora.

"Casey Gallagher. What are you doing calling here? You're supposed to be resting."

"I am resting. The least I can do is pick up a phone. How's everything going there?"

"Here?"

"Yeah, you know, at Kincade?"

"Business as usual."

"Good. I know a few of my clients heard about the accident because they sent flowers, but I'm not sure about the others. I left my laptop in my office, and my cell got crushed in the accident, so I'm handicapped in more ways than one."

"Casey, don't you worry. I've got your laptop locked in my cabinet. Everything is fine and dandy."

Nora knew everything. But I knew Nora. Something wasn't right. Why did she have my laptop locked up? When she said "fine and dandy," that meant things weren't.

"Can you transfer me to Gordy?"

"Gordy? Uh, he's out at the moment, but I'll tell him you called."

"Okay. If any of my clients call for me, feel free to give them my home number."

"Upon my honor, I will do no such thing." She sounded like she was reciting a pledge. "I have my orders."

"Orders from whom?"

"Your husband. He called a few days ago. The man knows you, Casey."

Sam had called Nora? He never called my workplace. I wasn't sure how I felt about his running interference. No, that's not true. I felt cared for.

It took another week of bed rest before I was able to get around the house well enough for my family to agree to leave me alone. Between Sam in the morning and the others in the afternoon and evening, I craved my space and privacy.

Before they consented, they cleaned my house, stocked my cupboards, and crammed thirty-six cubic feet of food into a twenty-eight cubic foot refrigerator. The only thing that surprised me was that Jillian hadn't started a scrapbooking project entitled "Casey's Close Call." That I knew of.

My first afternoon sans unlicensed homecare, I played jazz, read fluff, and daydreamed and dozed in my overstuffed chair. Restless after hours of uninterrupted relaxation, I decided a manicure was within my range of mobility.

While searching for a nail file in my bag, I found Olivia Price's phone number and decided to call.

"Hello."

It didn't sound like Olivia. "Hello. I'm calling for Olivia Price. Do I have the right number?"

"Yes, this is Olivia's number. I'm her daughter."

"Oh, hi! Your mother mentioned you'd be visiting. We were roommates in the hospital recently." I was so pleased for Olivia.

The young woman had more to say, but I missed most of it. The only words I heard were "I'm sorry. My mother died the day after she was released from the hospital."

I'd known Olivia for less than a week, yet the news left me weak. I mumbled my condolences and hung up. Sadness settled over me like a lead apron as I thought of the reconciliation that never happened and the life Olivia didn't complete.

30

Since the doctors hadn't cleared me to drive yet, after bugging him for days Sam took me into the city so I could pick up my laptop and some files. Truth is I didn't want to get behind the wheel; I was still sore and didn't trust my reflexes.

He dropped me off in front of the main entrance of Kincade's building. "I'll meet up with you after I park. Promise you won't lift anything heavy."

"I promise."

"Uh-uh, let me see both hands. Uncross those fingers." Satisfied I'd behave, he left to find a parking lot.

After being away for three weeks, the doors to Kincade's building seemed taller and heavier than I remembered. Once inside, every step on the marble flooring echoed hello. I felt like the lobby—with its twenty-foot coffered ceilings, mahogany furnishings, and plastered walls—opened its arms and welcomed me home.

After signing in at the reception desk, I embraced the feeling as I entered the elevator and pushed the button for the third floor.

When the doors slid open, I took one step out then backed

in again. "Oops, wrong floor," I muttered. "How did I do that?" I pressed the number three again. The doors shut and opened, but the elevator didn't move. I checked the floor again—three—and peeked out, almost afraid to exit.

Nora rushed over to me. "Casey, I didn't know you were coming in. Why didn't you call me?"

All I could see was stark white, sleek lines and hard edges. My brain was unable to compute. "What on earth is going on?"

"Come over to my desk and I'll tell you."

Her walnut burl desk had been replaced by a high-gloss white laminate one. Wavy glass partitions separated her space from that of others of various sizes.

"They're called pods," she said in response to the large question mark on my face. "Work stations for the account managers." Nora stumbled over her words. "I'm sorry, Casey, I should have told you. It happened so fast, and you were still in the hospital. I didn't want to upset you."

"But . . . but . . . why? The decor was updated a few years ago."

"I hoped Gordy might have called you before he left."

"Before he left? Left for where?" By the timbre of her voice and the gloom in her eyes, I doubted it was for a branch in sunny Los Angeles. "What's happening?"

"Already happened." She lowered her voice. "Kincade was bought out by WGM and Gordy was let go."

"What? Gordy? It can't be."

"Afraid it is."

My mind was racing too fast for whole words to come out. "Whe . . . wha . . . how?"

"Let me show you around." Nora put one hand on my arm and pointed with the other. "This is what they call the pod-slash-file area." She accented the word *slash*.

In the center of the floor there was an arrangement of low contemporary sectionals flanked by white laminate cubes. Huge brushed-nickel floor lamps arced over the couches.

"Is this an employee lounge or something?" I asked. "How's that going to work right in the middle of the work stations?"

"This is the reception-slash-ideation core where account managers hold client meetings."

"You're not serious. What about client privacy?"

"It's supposed to convey a feeling of freedom and trust to our clients. She pointed to a small counter area. "This is the coffee-slash-snack bar. The sixth floor holds the cafeteria-slash-employee playroom."

"With all those slashes, it's a miracle someone's not bleeding."

"*Slash*," Nora said, "is one of Lyle's pet words."

"Lyle Wexler? You mean he's back?"

"You might say that." Her whole body seemed to deflate a little. "Have any idea what WGM stands for?"

I knew I wouldn't like her answer.

"Wexler Global Marketing. Lyle is the CEO's nephew, and he's heading up their new Boston acquisition."

It took me a long, agonizing moment until I could speak. "I knew it. He was way too confident for someone his age."

I was so mad I was shaking. Gordy was gone, Kincade was no more, and Lyle was my boss. It was too much to take in. I remembered my purpose for coming and turned to walk down the hall toward my office.

Nora reached out to stop me. "Uh, sorry, Casey, but Lyle took over your office. Your client files are over here." She pointed to a pod then cleared her throat. "At least the ones he didn't give to Poppy Brandeis."

"What?" I was sure I'd heard wrong. "Did you say he gave some of my clients to Poppy?"

Before Nora could answer, the elevator doors parted and Sam got out. He stopped a few steps into the reception area. "Whoa, when did this change? Or did you already tell me, Case?"

I shook my head and raised my hands to block his questions. "Stay here, Sam, please. I'll be back." I marched down the hall toward my old office.

Nora called after me. "Wait!"

But I didn't.

Under the force of my knock, the door creaked open. I

leaned in before I stepped over the threshold. The walls were stark white and the furniture was a mix of royal-blue fabric and black lacquer. One of the two windowless walls was covered with an oversized piece of geometric art in monochromatic shades of blue. The other was home to a huge flat screen. Two black gaming chairs were centered in front of the TV on a neon-yellow shag carpet. Facing the panoramic view, a clear acrylic table sat where my desk used to be. There wasn't a thing on it.

The only pretentious and juvenile thing missing from this room was Lyle Wexler.

I spouted off to Sam all the way home. "If you think the reception area is over the top, you should have seen my office! If I had to put a name on it, I'd call it contrived-slash-tacky."

"And no one had a clue?"

"Nora said everyone was given the news one day and told to go home until further notice. All calls were routed to their New York office. The biggest clue should have been Lyle Wexler hanging around for months without doing any real work."

"Did the employees get paid?"

"I guess, at least those who didn't get fired. In hindsight, it all makes sense. Tailored suits showing up months ago, rubbing their chins and scratching their pointy heads. Hard hats examining structure and measuring walls. And that interior desecrator with his cape and his wand, shadowed by his sycophantic disciples."

"With all that going on," Sam said, "how could you not know?"

"We thought it was the usual paint and carpet updates, this time done by people who wanted to make their jobs look more important than they were. Apparently, it's not the first time WGM has done this. As soon as the sale was executed, their team pounced. It's built into their acquisitions handbook."

"What did Gordy tell Nora?"

"She hasn't been able to reach him, and there's been no response to her voicemails. Aah! I'm lost without my phone, but I got his number from Nora."

Sam handed me his phone. "Try him."

I called, but there was no answer. I left a message.

I leaned back against the headrest to sort things out. Since Nora had shown me my pod and files, I assumed my job was safe. Or was it? What else would change? How would I work with Lyle?

31

Of all the people I didn't want to hear from, Lyle Wexler was chief. But that's who called me the next morning. "Casey, Nora told me you came by yesterday. Does that mean we can expect your pretty face back at work soon?"

That answered my question about my job. "I'm seeing the doctor today. He'll give me his decision then."

"How about our new look? Über Arctic, right? Nora made me promise not to call you. I think she wanted to surprise you."

What an idiot.

"By the way, I hope you don't mind, but I took over your old office. I need a serene space to meditate, away from the action."

Meditate, on what? Your video games? Double idiot.

"No problem, Lyle. My pod is closer to the coffee-slash-snack bar, so it's all good."

I hung up and called my mother.

"What am I going to do about the clients he gave to Poppy? What do I tell them?"

"The truth," she said. "This is not your doing, so you don't have to feel guilty. No one saw this coming."

"Except Lyle. Some of my clients are due to renew their contracts, and two new clients are close to signing. I don't know what they'll do now."

"You've done your best for them. Once you explain the situation, the decision to stay or go will be up to them."

"You know, I always thought large companies were successful because they were built on good business practices."

Mom laughed. "And you've worked in marketing for how long? Businesses are run by people. Some are ethical. Some are not. My boss would have done things differently, but he has more integrity than most."

"I'll be back on the job in a few days, so I guess I better get used to it."

"Never get used to it, Casey."

Mom was right. Get used to it, no. Work around it, yes. Because I needed this job.

In my last days of recuperation, I lay on the couch and watched the Red Sox beat the Yankees. For a few hours, it took my mind off my return to work. The win put the Sox in a good position for the playoffs.

The Irish Twins played the final four innings. Mike was working on the win. When Darin jumped and caught a foul ball and picked the runner off at second, the color commentator called him a "spring-action kangaroo."

I called Darin that evening. "Hey, Flynn, would you prefer that I use the acronym SAK in my column or spell out spring action kangaroo?"

"First time I've ever been compared to a marsupial. If I were you, I'd go by SAK."

"It was a tough catch and a wicked throw."

"Thanks," he said. "My muscles will be moaning in the morning."

"Flynn, tell me you're not complaining to *me* about sore muscles."

"Not me. No way. How're you feeling anyway? We're still praying."

"Better, thanks. Speaking of praying, remember Tommy Coletti's brother, Nick? The one who was injured in Afghanistan? Looks like he'll make a full recovery."

"See? God does hear our prayers. Speaking of that, have you tuned in yet?"

Tuned in? Seconds passed before I realized Darin expected an answer.

He said, "If you want to hear His voice, Casey, you need to tune in."

He is right, Casey.

If you say so.

My first day back to work started with a rough ride on the T. Those ribs I thought had healed were telling another story. The walk to the office revealed that Lisa Erickson's pet post office branch had not burned to the ground. I assumed this meant she'd gotten my open invitation but had changed her mind about meeting us.

"Works for me," I grunted.

As soon as the elevator doors opened, Nora jumped up to greet me. "You're back! You have no idea how I've missed you."

"And entering this otherworld would be too scary without you."

"Now, how may I help?"

We walked over to my pod and beheld the wall of cardboard boxes, containing the complete contents of my office. "Where's Lyle?" I whispered.

"In your—I mean, his office. Why?"

"No reason. I want to get organized before I face him. Got time to help with these files?"

"I'm all yours."

We began unstacking boxes so I could examine their contents. We made one pile for my active files, one for files I could store, and the last for files I should surrender to Poppy. About a third of the way through on the edge of a box in the back, I found a cell phone and a pair of eyeglasses. Smiling, I shook my head and held them up.

"It can't be." Nora reached for the items.

"Yes, it can. And now we know why Gordy hasn't returned our calls."

She grabbed a padded envelope and dropped the phone and glasses inside. "Poor Gordy. He's probably feeling bad that no one's tried to reach him."

We spent the next hour sorting until I was as settled as I would ever be in my gleaming white pod. My city view was gone, replaced by laminate walls and slick motivational posters. I realized how much I'd taken that corner office for granted.

I put off reporting to Lyle for as long as I could. When Nora called ahead, I was told to come down.

"Lyle, about my clients—"

Before I could finish my question, Junior Smugness himself spoke. "I chucked a few of them Poppy's way to keep her around for a while. It's a bonus having someone to look at who hasn't reached the age of pluckin' and tuckin', if you know what I mean."

I ignored his remark and took a tack I thought he couldn't argue against. "It's taken me years to cultivate a relationship with these people. By tossing them over to a newbie, don't you think we could lose them?"

"No skin if we do. They're piddly compared to our clients across the globe."

Even if I had come up with a response, he didn't give me time to speak.

"The über cool way WGM works is there is no 'your clients' and 'my clients.' They're WGM's. We work as a team. That reminds me, traveling won't be a problem for you, will it?"

I didn't think he cared if I answered.

"One last thing, Gordy mentioned your little sports column. I'm more into extreme sports myself, but it might be a tool we can use. Keep me in the loop. I'm sure we have clients who'd love to catch Opening Day at Fenway."

Lyle stood, indicating our meeting had ended. When I

stepped out into the hall, I was sure I heard the sound of a rattle as he slithered through the shag carpet back to his gaming station.

32

When Sam got home that night, I was pacing like a wild cat on a hunger strike.

"You should see the sixth floor. They even named it"—I made quotations marks in the air—"The Level of Creativity. Pompous nitwits. They've Google-ized the space with foosball and ping pong tables and even have a video gaming section with a huge flat screen. I had to dodge interns rolling around in Heelys to get through the room."

"Heelys? Aren't those the sneakers with wheels? At work? I can just see the commander letting us do that."

"They say it helps keep their 'creative juices flowing.' If that's true, they better plan on mopping up after themselves, because I'm not gonna do it!"

Sam smiled then stretched, working the kinks out of his tired body. In the middle of a yawn he said, "Have you been able to reach Gordy yet?"

I sighed. "No, we're trying to find his home number."

"Anyone else you know get fired?"

"Yes, some good people who'd been with the company for years. Nora said they were escorted out like criminals."

"And you?"

"Maybe I was young enough to slip their noose, but I'm still surprised. It's not like I pretended to like Lyle. Jeepers, Gordy was nicer to him than I was."

After his third yawn, I let Sam go to sleep.

When I thought of Gordy, I got mad all over again. This was a man who cared about his employees as much as he did his clients. I didn't know if he'd been transferred or blackballed or what. All that broom sweeper Lyle would say was, "Casey, change is inevitable. Get used to it."

This whole employee-centered concept was a fad. Couldn't WGM see that? How long did any fad last? I wanted to scream at Lyle, "Look into the future! Imagine your super kids in twenty years, still wearing rolling footwear to get back and forth to their pods after 'solutioning' and 'ideating.'"

What a colossal farce.

I was realistic enough to know that if it could happen to Gordy and other good people, it could happen to me. Especially with an unprincipled company that valued their cool quotient over high standards.

I spent my first week back at work calling all the clients I had before the hostile takeover. The Obermanns' main marketing event had already passed, and they were ecstatic with the results. The next phase of their plan was in motion and running smoothly; they had no complaints.

When I called Joe and Lisa Ianella, I thanked them for the flowers they'd sent while I was in the hospital and engaged them in small talk. My intent was to smooth out their transfer to Poppy.

"Although we appreciate Poppy filling in for you," Lisa said, "we're glad you're back."

I hit a sacrifice fly to let the rookie get to second base. "Lisa, I'm sure your account is in capable hands with Poppy."

They didn't budge. "We both prefer to work with you, Casey."

I apologized and suggested they call Lyle because it was out of my hands.

One client refused to sign a new contract because of the increase in fees. The others were on the fence. I advised them as I would myself. "Wait and see before you decide if WGM is a good fit."

I felt like I was playing keep-away with the truth. There were moments during my conversations when I hoped WGM's policies didn't include wiretapping. When my phone rang for the umpteenth time I stared at it, fearful of what new problem it would bring. I took a breath before I picked up. "Good morning."

"How does the patient feel now that she's back at work?"

Phew. It was Vanessa. "You don't want to know, because you wouldn't believe it."

"Are you in need of a lunch date with your counselor? Will it be legal or mental health today?"

"Either will do. Where and when?"

With lunch as a reward, I finished my to-do list in no time. I double-checked my bag for my new phone and let Nora know I'd be back around two. Lyle exited the elevator as I entered.

"Where're you off to?" If it was possible, I believed he had more gel in his hair.

"Lunch."

"So, I take it you like the new sushi bar?"

"Actually, I'm going out."

"Out? With that über cool menu upstairs?"

"I need something warm for lunch." I pressed the down button and the doors closed. At that moment he could have fired me and I would have considered it an "über cool" mercy killing.

When I saw Vanessa walking toward me, I practically ran into her arms. "You're a lifesaver. You can't imagine what work has been like."

"Oy vey, girl. What's going on? Are you still on meds or something? This is Kincade we're talking about, your dream job."

"Dream-turned-nightmare. And it's not Kincade anymore. It's WGM."

"Whaa?"

"Let's find a table outside. I feel like a mouse who's escaped from a maze—a laminated one."

I waited until we ordered before I regaled Vanessa with my tale of low blows.

"This is a good thing, Casey. It makes it easier to separate the wheat from the chaff."

"What does wheat and chaff have to do with anything? How does working for a jerk make my life easier?"

"It doesn't. But if he was kind and understanding like your Gordy Ackerman, you'd never leave. This way, your decision about your future is easier."

I knew what she was selling, but I wasn't ready to buy it. After the waiter delivered our food I said, "Let's change the subject. Are you and Bryson coming to the surprise thirtieth birthday party Sam's throwing for me?"

"I don't know what you're talking about."

"Yes, you do. It's at Griffin and Jillian's house on August 30. I want to make sure you got an invitation. This is Sam I'm talking about."

She tilted her head and tapped the side of her cheek. "Now that you mention it, I do recall marking something on my calendar for that day."

"Good. That's all I needed to know."

"My turn to change the subject," she said. "Any news on your brother from another mother?"

"Cute." I made a face at her. "As a matter of fact, before the accident I sent his mother a note telling her we were willing to meet him. Haven't heard a word back since, and it's been over a month." I put my hand over my heart. "So much for his 'longing' and 'deep desire' to meet us. Must have changed his mind." I backhanded the air. "Okay by me."

"Sweetie, let me leave you with this quote I heard from a woman preacher the other day: 'Bitterness is like taking poison and hoping your enemy will die.' I suggest you think on that real hard." She kissed my cheek and was off, leaving me no time for a rebuttal.

Good thing, because I had none.

Wait. When did Vanessa start listening to women preachers?

I returned to the office by one forty-five and slipped back into my pod. It was pathetic that I now equated not running into Lyle a high point of my day. Was it just Lyle or was it a normal part of any transition? No, it was Lyle. I pushed those esoteric musings aside so I could get down to practical matters.

Until Lyle showed up.

He cracked his knuckles while standing at the opening to my pod. Was his plan to punch me? I stifled my amusement.

"So you told your janitors, the Iaccocas, to call me." The edge in his voice almost scratched the laminate. "Would've been better to have some warning."

"I recall telling you that we might have problems with some clients. Since the Ianellas weren't pleased with the change, I sent them to the only person who could turn things around—you."

"If you want them so bad, you've got them. Personally, I think Poppy is glad to be rid of them."

Nice.

To make up for the awkward inconvenience, I was determined to do even more for Joe and Lisa. I wanted to come up with a marketing event that would make a huge splash. The word *splash* brought me to *water* which brought me to *clean* which brought me to a dead end. I refused to stop brainstorming until I came up with an idea I could sleep on.

On my way home that night, my mind got stuck on Vanessa's comment "separating the wheat from the chaff." I took out my tablet and Googled the expression. One source said it meant "to separate what is useful or valuable from what is worthless" while another source said "to choose what is of high quality over what is of lower quality." It was somewhere in the Bible too.

How could I distinguish the wheat from the chaff in my life? I loved writing Double Header with Griffin. So he couldn't devote as much time as I wished he could. Did that make our co-venture worthless? Sam's hours and my long commute didn't allow us much time together, but that didn't make our marriage less valuable. My position at Kincade, er, WGM, paid me well and provided excellent benefits. So it was giving me fits lately. Did that qualify it as chaff?

As far as I could figure, there was some good in it all.

Even in your half brother, Casey?

Who said that?

33

After a good night's sleep and a couple of strong cups of coffee, I started the day with a better attitude. On the train into work I devoured the sports page, pleased to read Mike had another good outing against the Indians and that the Bruins had signed a long-term contract with the best center they'd had in years.

Following that good-mood maker, multiple marketing ideas for the Ianella account came at me in waves. By the time I reached my Back Bay stop, I had regained enough of my old confidence to ignore Lyle's cynicism and condescension.

I stepped off the T and headed to my office. The weather made the day one you wished you could bookmark. Slowing my pace, I let the sun warm me inside and out. The contrast of a few puffy white clouds made the blue sky look bluer. Was that a breeze off the harbor?

"Casey!"

I jumped and turned in the direction of the voice. It was Mike with Tess, standing in front of the post office.

"Hey! What are you two doing out so early? Oh, right. Tess, you work nearby. With Mike's mother."

"Yes, I'm on my way in now."

Mike stuffed the stack of mail he was holding into her backpack.

I turned to him. "I'm surprised you're up, Hennessey. Figured you'd be sleeping in after last night's game. Congratulations!"

"Thanks." He looked over at Tess like a goofy golden retriever. "We had an early breakfast. The team's got a long road trip coming up."

Had Tess and Mike's relationship progressed to the overnight stage?

"Some date, huh, Casey?" Tess giggled. "Meeting for breakfast at six thirty in the morning."

"I married a cop, remember? Our dates aren't much better."

They rushed off but not before Mike's cheeks turned red. So shy, young love. Something told me I was wrong about the overnight.

Breakfast at dawn. Sam and I used to do things like that. I checked my watch—he'd be up by now. When I reached the steps to my building, I called him before I went in.

"Hey, when was the last time we had a real date night?"

"Uh, it's a little early for a quiz, Case."

"It's not a quiz."

"Is 'I can't remember' the wrong thing to say?" He was smart enough to sound hesitant.

"No, it's the truth. I can't remember either. We're pitiful. When's your next day off?"

"Friday, but I had plans to . . ." He paused. "I think the operative word here is *had*. Is it a date, pretty woman?"

"It is. Pick me up at seven." I hung up and giggled, something I hadn't done in a long while.

Nora greeted me with a bigger-than-usual smile. "Excellent morning, isn't it?"

"It is so far." I knew there was more to this greeting. "Why is that?"

"For starters, Lyle called to say he'd be in New York for the rest of the week."

"Yes!" I double-pumped my fist. "That'll do it for me! I don't need another thing."

"No?" Nora looked over my shoulder. "Not even a visit from Gordy?"

Gordy came out from behind the coffee-slash-snack bar with his arms open wide. "Miss me, do you?"

"Do we ever! It's awful without you." I gestured to his glasses pushed atop his head. "See you've been to the Lost and Found already."

He hunted in his hair. "My wife kept telling me this is where I'd find my glasses and phone."

Nora said, "We would have called to tell you but . . ."

He held up his dead cell phone. "I'm sure there are a dozen voicemails from you two." He turned to me. "I understand your phone was DOA in the ER. Better it than you."

"I agree. So what are you doing now?"

"Thankfully, the one thing Kincade did right was negotiate a good severance package for those of us who got laid off. But that won't last forever."

"Anything lined up?" Nora asked.

"I've got a second interview next week with a smaller firm. Got a good feeling about it too. I'll keep you posted."

"Please do. Let's stay in touch."

"Okay. Then I'm out of here before I get you ladies in trouble."

I felt better after talking with Gordy. In some ways I envied him. He sounded positive and looked good—even a little less frumpled. I was glad to hear the company I had respected for years had fought for decent severance packages.

Of course, when my time came I'd be dealing with WGM, not Kincade.

The day ended almost as well as it began. I had a long chat with the Ianellas. They were pleased I was back managing their account. The only change they made to their contract was to shorten it from twelve to six months. They assured me it was not a reflection on me but that they wanted to be certain WGM had the same standards and principles as Kincade.

I couldn't blame them.

My husband was not skilled at orchestrating romantic events, yet I knew he would try his best. The thing is, he'd need a month and input from every female who knew me to do it. Since we only had forty-eight hours, I decided to throw him an easy pitch.

"Sam, since this whole date night thing was my idea, would you mind if I planned it?"

"Uh, okay, if you want."

Was that color I saw coming back into his face? "Thanks, hon," I said, turning so he wouldn't see my smile. I ignored what the Madison Avenue slicks said about romance and put myself in Sam's shoes. First, what would he *not* want to do? Go to the opera or symphony. Dine at a five-star restaurant with epicurean cuisine and tiny portions. Dress up in a suit and tie.

Outside of the dressing up part, I didn't want to do any of them either.

Then it came to me. The more I thought about it, the more excited I got. Before I left for work on Friday, I laid out our date clothes on the bed: my red dress and sparkly heels and his go-to wedding suit, shirt, and tie. That would misdirect any guesses he might have.

When I pulled into our driveway around six, I was pleased to see Sam dressed in his suit and standing at the door to greet me. I could tell he'd showered and shaved, his complexion rosy and smooth but for a red-splotched tissue patch.

I tapped his makeshift bandage. "What's this?"

He shrugged. "Close shave, dull blade, sharp girl."

His endearing efforts at primping tempted me to suggest we stay in. Instead, I raced to the bathroom to shower.

My red party dress earned me a whistle. He helped with my shawl and held the car door open for me.

"Wait," I said. "It's my surprise, remember, so I should drive."

I headed north on Route 3 and bore left onto 128. When I got off at Exit 6, he guessed a few restaurants. When I pulled into F1 Boston, an indoor Formular One racetrack, he looked over at my dress and down at his suit. "Is there something you're not telling me?"

"Yup. We can suit up inside. We're signed up for eighteen laps."

"Are you serious?"

"About you? Always and forever." I leaned over and gave him a kiss to last him the eighteen laps then pulled a duffle bag with our changes of clothes out from behind the passenger's seat.

After a brief beginner's class, we changed into jumpsuits and sneakers and headed to the track to wait our turn. The noise level only added to the excitement. I couldn't decide whether or not to go easy on Sam. In the end, I knew he wouldn't want me to. At least that's what my competitive self told my good-wife self.

The only thing my good-wife self didn't bank on was the good-cop husband smoking my competitive self by two laps.

When Sam climbed out of his kart, he had a smile like an eight-year-old boy with a frog in his pocket. "Sweet! All those car chases turned into an advantage! I'm gonna let you plan all our date nights."

"Not so fast, Andretti. You still have to take me out to dinner."

"Yeah, I figured the fancy clothes went with a fancy restaurant."

"You figured that out, huh?" I held up the duffle bag again. "Does that mean you don't want to change into your jeans?"

He looked at me to be sure he'd heard what I said. Laughing, he wrapped me in his arms. "Have I told you lately what a cool wife you are?"

"I know I am. Now careful of my ribs!"

He loosened his hold. "Oops, sorry. You okay?"

I kissed his cheek. "I'm way more than okay and you know it."

I tried to set the tone over dinner by not talking about my job at WGM. We covered everything from the New England Patriots draft pick to crème brûlée to sex. Yet somehow the subject of work kept intruding.

"Please, tell me what you think I should do." I reached for his hand.

"If I do that, I'm afraid you'll resent me. I think the decision has to be yours."

"A few weeks ago, I would have agreed. But when you said the other night that my plan was not necessarily our plan I realized you were right."

"And because I want you to be happy, I haven't given you much input."

"What I'm saying is, I want our plans for the future to be just that—ours. Let's sort things out."

"Are you sure you want to hear what I have to say?"

I did a final gut check. "Yes, I'm sure."

"Okay, this is the way I've envisioned our lives since the day we said 'I do.'"

34

I listened as Sam described a life I wanted and wondered why I'd never seen it before. He was right. We didn't need the mansion in Duxbury or Hingham. A two-story in Plymouth or Kingston would do.

Maybe it was easier to see in the light of almost dying and turning thirty. Meeting Olivia Price was like looking into my future. Losing her before I got to know her showed me how fragile life was. If I were to create an if-I-were-to-die-tomorrow list, would it include spending any more time with Lyle Wexler?

I didn't need to live like a rat, racing through city streets, jumping over roadblocks of stress. I could work from home at a job I loved. No more waiting another five years to start a family. Our kids could grow up with Griffin and Jillian's.

Suddenly, the so-called plans and dreams I'd carried for years seemed more like burdens and nightmares. With the possibilities before me and my husband's encouragement, I felt like I had the power to hit my future out of the park.

Either that or I'd had too much caffeine.

I had the weekend to contemplate all Sam and I had discussed. When he left for work on Sunday, I decided a run would do me some good—my first since the accident. It was hot and humid, but I managed a few miles at a reasonable pace with no great discomfort. It was the burst of hope my body needed. It also cleared my head.

Later, I checked in with Mom.

"Hey, how was your date night? Sam surprised?"

"I got him good. Even made him wear his suit and tie so he wouldn't suspect a thing. It was a blast. You and Webster should try it."

"The F1 racetrack?" She laughed. "I can't see that ever happening. Did you go out to eat after?"

"Yes. We talked at length about our future and everything."

"Care to share?"

"Hard as it may be for you to believe, I'm coming around to Sam's vision for our future. It may mean a decrease in income but an increase in contentment."

"You can probably guess which I think is more important."

"Yes, but these decisions are major and life-changing, Mom, and you know me."

"I do. But you and Sam are in sync now. I'll pray the Lord gives you the peace."

I don't know what made me ask. "How will I know when He does? I don't even know if He's real."

"I asked the same question a few years ago. Then one of my friends showed me a Bible verse, Isaiah 7:11. 'Ask the Lord your God for a sign, whether in the deepest depths or in the highest heights.' I asked for confirmation, and He gave it. He'll do the same for you."

I didn't respond.

Listen to your mother, Casey.

What? I am! At least give me credit for not looking for a brick to build my wall higher.

If I had been leaving Gordy and Kincade, I would have given

them at least a month's notice, but two weeks was all Lyle would get. I saw what he did when people gave notice. I had no reason to believe he'd treat me any better.

When I called Gordy to tell him my news, he cheered. "I'm proud of you, Casey. Things have a way of working out. Did I tell you I got the job?"

"Congratulations! What's the company?"

"You may know them. JB & Son Marketing. Their main office is in Boston, but they have a satellite office on the Cape."

"You're kidding? That's the company my mother's been with for over twenty years!"

When I told Nora my news and Gordy's, she offered congratulations but her eyes said otherwise. "Casey, can you understand why I'm conflicted? I'm delighted for you both but afraid at my age I won't be able to find another position."

"One more thing, Nora. Gordy said to give him a call." I winked. "He's interviewing for an executive assistant." A slow-motion smile moved across her face.

The sports reporter for the eleven o'clock news said, "Pitching star Mike Hennessey was having trouble with his pitching arm in the third inning of tonight's game. He's off the roster for the next few weeks." They showed a clip of Mike leaving the field holding his upper arm.

Well aware that my concern for the Irish Twins had grown more personal over the months, I called Darin the next day to get a report. "Hope you don't mind, but I had to check in on Mike."

"Not at all, Casey. Looks like he'll be out for a few games. They're doing some more tests to find out what caused the injury."

"Wouldn't 100-miles-an-hour pitches be enough to do it?"

"Might be, but something's got the doctors bothered."

"How's he doing?"

"Fine. He knows whose hands he's in. He trusts the Lord to work it all out for his good."

Sheesh. Again with the Lord.

"So he's sure he'll get better?"

"Nope, didn't say that. I said Mike is sure the Lord will work it all out for his good."

Tomatoes, tomahtoes. What's the difference?

Since surprising Sam had been such a high, I decided to go one further by making some changes in our home office. As soon as he left for work on Sunday, I removed everything from the walls and wrapped Dad's pictures, plaques, medals, and awards and placed them in a storage bin. I only kept a few photos to display—one of him in his uniform, the other walking me down the aisle.

Taking a cue from my mother's gallery in her home with Webster, I hung a collage of photos and made sure to include both sides of our family. Positioning our wedding and honeymoon pictures in the center brought focus and balance to the room.

While framing Sam's citations to hang above his desk, I thought of the fight we'd had when I first told him about Dad's affair and Lisa's son. Shame still needled me when I recalled him saying no husband feels great about living in the shadow of another man. I remembered my own thoughts of protestation: Can't he understand that it's all I have left of my father?

In a flash, it hit me. Besides Griffin and his unborn child, I had a half brother who was part of Dad too.

I went to my room and polished Dad's boots one last time. After packing them in a large box with the Kiwi polish and rags, I enclosed a picture of Dad in his uniform. And a note to Lisa:

> *These boots belonged to my father when he was on the force. I'd like your son to have them, whether he decides to meet us or not. The picture was taken a year before Dad died. I am praying.*

I don't know why I added that last part. I wasn't

praying…or was I? Could silent wishes to an invisible God be classified as prayer?

Later, when Mom stopped by to see my completed project, I handed her the box on her way out and asked her to mail it so I wouldn't have to carry it on the T. The truth was I was afraid I'd change my mind. She looked at the address but didn't say a word. She didn't even ask what was in the box.

She knew.

"I hope Griffin won't mind," I said.

She hugged me. "I'm sure your brother will approve."

The last thing I did before I climbed into bed was post a sign on the office door which read: "For the Most Important Man in My Life." To be sure he didn't miss it, I left the hall light on in case I was asleep when he got home.

I heard him come in, put his revolver in the lockbox, and turn on the TV. About ten minutes passed before he headed down the hall. He paused. I assumed he saw the sign. It took a few more minutes before he entered the bedroom. Leaning to kiss me, he whispered, "You asleep?"

"What do you think?"

"I love the wall . . . and you for doing it."

When I came home from work a few days later, I found a gift-wrapped package and a card attached. It was an electronic picture frame. Sam had scanned and uploaded all the photos of Dad and even included his citations and awards. The note simply read, "A good man and a great father, one any daughter would be proud to have. You both were blessed, and now so are we."

My cop wrote that?

35

Roberta, when will you be in Boston next? Griffin and I want to schedule a sit-down with you."

"I'm flying in Tuesday to check on my sister's place before she and Nicky come home."

"So they'll be back soon then?" I hadn't thought of Roberta as the domestic type so it struck me funny, although that might not be how it struck the Coletti family.

"No release date yet, but I bet they could use my help."

Uh, bet not.

We scheduled a six o'clock Wednesday dinner at her favorite steakhouse.

Griffin and I were waiting when Roberta arrived.

"Wow," she said. "Must be important if Griffin's on time."

Griffin fired back, "It's just that I couldn't wait to see what you've done with your hair."

I couldn't believe he dared say that, but I saw her smile as she stepped forward to follow the hostess.

Once our drinks arrived, Roberta took a sip of her Manhattan before she asked, "So what's it going to be, kids?"

Strengthened by my recent decision, I spoke first. "Here's the long and short of it. Griffin and I want to continue Double Header and get started on our biographies."

Griffin straightened in his seat. "For the rest of the summer I will make myself available to do any radio or television guest spots you book."

Roberta said, "After that?"

"When school starts and Jillian has the baby, my priority will be my family and my teaching and coaching jobs. I can write from home, but my PR appearances will be limited."

"Okay." Roberta took another sip of her cocktail.

I spoke before she could pounce on Griffin. "The major change is that I'm giving up my full-time job, which will give me the time I need to write." I was surer each time I said it.

She put her glass down. "Oh?"

"I've been bound and gagged by that job for too long. I'm ready to commit."

Roberta slapped the table. "Good girl! About time you figured it out! Now let's get started."

We drew up a timeline for the year beginning right after my last day at WGM. As my tribute to irony, I chose Labor Day as my formal departure date. It would give me time to finish the projects I'd already begun. It also fell a month before some of my clients were set to renew their contracts. We nailed down our first biography too, Carl Yastrzemski.

Roberta almost bubbled like soda water with a spritz of lime. "I can easily switch my focus to traditional publishing houses instead of newspaper syndicates. Before I signed you, they're who I dealt with mostly. Casey, your marketing background will give you an edge once we get you two published."

When the meeting ended, I bounced out of the restaurant like a kid on a sugar high. Okay, the pie á la mode might have helped.

Maybe turning thirty wouldn't be so bad after all.

Sam was on the phone when I returned from running errands the next day. "Here she is. Let me check." He held the phone out about six inches from his mouth. "Listen, Case, do you mind if Tommy comes by to watch the game this afternoon?"

I hollered, "That pain in the neck. Why would I want him over here?"

Sam hurried to bury the receiver in his shirt and gave me a puzzled look.

I laughed and picked up the extension in the kitchen. "Did you hear that?"

"Sure did. So it's okay then?"

He arrived about an hour later. "I had to get out of the house. Aunt Bobbie is on a cleaning rampage, as if my brother will care about my dresser drawers being 'neat and tidy.' She's got Ali dusting Nick's trophies and Dad moving furniture around to make room for his wheelchair."

I put some chips and salsa out on the coffee table. "When are they due back?"

Sam passed him a cold drink.

"Early next week, if all goes well. He'll need some rehab once he's back in the States."

"If it makes any difference, Roberta thinks she's needed. At least that's what she told us the other night."

"I know. My mother's her only sibling, and since she never had any kids of her own she's like a mama grizzly around us. Don't get me wrong, it's nice that she cares, but sometimes she weighs in where it's not needed. Like now. Mom says if she wasn't in our stuff, she'd be in someone else's."

"Sam told me you and Nick are close."

A commercial came on and Sam pressed the mute button.

"Yeah, as kids we did everything together. Then he joined the Marines and I went off to college then the police academy. A lot's happened since then. Sometimes I'm afraid it won't be the same as it used to be."

"Why do you think that?" I asked.

"War has a way of changing people. Plus, since he's been gone some family issues have come up."

Sam responded before I could. "We respect your privacy. Don't feel you need to tell us anything."

My husband knew me too well.

When the game came back on, I noticed Darin was catching for the new southpaw. After the Sox won, I had to admit it had a good deal to do with the duo's performance. I thought about poor Mike nursing his injury. "How do you think Mike feels watching Darin work so well with another pitcher?"

"Mike's a pro," Sam said. "He'll deal with it."

Tommy added, "The little I've been around Mike tells me he's more apt to be elated for them."

I nodded. "Good observation. You're probably right."

"I am? That doesn't happen often." Tommy got up off the couch. "I'll think I'll leave before I break my streak."

I stood. "Is it possible to have a streak of one?"

"Come on, play nice," Sam said. "Say good-bye to Tommy, Casey."

I waved both hands and echoed Sam, "Good-bye to Tommy, Casey."

He shook his head and smiled. "See you guys later."

After he left, I asked Sam, "What do you think he meant by family issues?"

"That it's personal."

"I know it's personal, but what do you think he meant?"

He tossed a throw pillow at me. "Nosey-pants, don't you have a column or a biography to write?"

I threw it back and followed with another. "Guess so, since I'm not getting anything useful from you."

I called Mike a few days later. "You up for some company?"

"Sure. When d'ya have in mind?"

"It's short notice, but Sam's in the city for training today. Any chance we could stop by later, maybe around six or so?"

"That works. I can't promise I'll be alone though. My parents and Tess are tag-teaming, watching my every move."

"Want us to pick up a couple of pizzas?"

"Sounds great. Since Flynn won't be here, can you skip all those veggies and add extra pepperoni on one?"

It was easy enough to find Mike and Darin's place in Southie. Even with the pizza stop, we arrived by six. Tess greeted us at the door. "This is perfect timing. Mike's been craving pizza."

With his right arm in a sling, Mike extended his left hand to Sam. "Good to see you again, Sam."

"Same here. How's the arm?"

"Better. The sling's just a precautionary measure." Mike extended his free arm, inviting us into the living room. "Hope it didn't put you out, coming all the way over here. You both must've put in a long day already."

The townhouse was not what most would expect from two newly flush pro ballplayers. But this was Mike and Darin. It was more IKEA than high-end design. A large charcoal-gray microfiber sectional divided the open space and faced the flat screen. In front of the sofa, an oversized barn board coffee table sat on a bright patterned area rug. An extra wide bookcase filled with books and family photos took up one whole wall.

Mike continued toward the dining area. "So, you wanna eat while it's still hot?"

Tess laughed. "I told you! His mouth has been watering for pepperoni since you called."

The rustic dining room table was long enough to seat twelve. "Wow," Sam said. "You entertain a lot?"

"Not unless you count family." Mike smiled at Tess. "And we do."

After the four of us were seated, Mike and Tess bowed their heads and closed their eyes. Sam and I did likewise.

Mike spoke. "Lord, thank you for friends like Casey and Sam who took time out of their day to visit. And thank you for the pizza they brought. Please bless the food and our time together in Jesus's name. Amen."

I nabbed a slice with extra cheese.

Sam and I had decided on the way over not to ask Mike a lot of questions about his injury or his future. It was Mike who brought up the subject.

"Ya know, I don't know what this injury will mean long-term. I'm not being negative, just realistic. I've gotta prepare for the worst."

"And expect the best," Tess said, giving him a nudge with her elbow.

Mike nudged her back. "Yeah, that too."

Something told me they'd had this discussion before.

"Either way," Mike added, "my future's in God's hands. There's no better place."

How could he feel like that? He'd worked his whole life toward a career in pro ball. It would take a lot to forgive a god that would take it all away. A whole lot. Yet Mike didn't wring his hands, hang his head, or even sigh when he spoke about his injury. I think he believed what he said.

We'd just finished our first slice when the door bell rang. When Mike came back from answering it, his parents were on his heels. "Look who smelled the pepperoni. My parents, Kevin and Lisa. Casey, Sam, I told you about them, didn't I? They're like humanitarian drones, hovering over me, dropping food and supplies, picking up laundry."

"I became well acquainted with that drone model after my accident," I said. "Nice to meet you both."

Kevin said, "It's the famous sportswriter! And is this your young man?"

Sam stood. "I'll take that as a compliment, sir."

Tess jumped up. "Take a seat. I'll get more plates."

"Sit, dear. We just came by to drop a few things off," Lisa said. "We're not staying."

Kevin looked confused. "We're not staying? I thought you said we could watch the game with the—"

Lisa interrupted him. "No, no, dear, we have to get back."

"At least stay for a piece of pizza, Dad. It's your favorite."

Kevin looked to Lisa for a change of heart but got none. Lisa held her purse in front of her with both hands. "Mike, give your father a slice on a paper plate, so we can be on our way."

"What's the rush, Mom?"

"We have some things to attend to, that's all." She took the plate from Mike and said, "Good meeting you two. You kids have fun."

When the door closed behind them, Mike said, "Sheesh. That was odd. It usually takes an act of Congress to get them to leave."

"I've seen that behavior before," I said, "from my drones. I don't think they wanted to impose on us 'kids.'"

Sam and I stayed about an hour longer. Mike was right; it had been a long day. We were quiet on the way home, each keeping our thoughts to ourselves.

My current conundrums: First, if I thought it would take a lot to forgive a god that would take Mike's career away, did that mean I believed in God?

Second, was it my imagination or did Lisa Hennessey seem uncomfortable around me?

36

While opening the mail over my morning coffee, I found a second note from Lisa Erickson. It was short and typed. No genteel cursive, no watermarked stationary, no polite subterfuge like her first letter. And mailed to my home address.

> Dear Casey,
>
> Even though I promised to keep your identity hidden from my son, time and circumstances prevented me from doing so. He is in your life now—I believe for better, not worse. But he fully understands your hesitancy in this situation.
>
> I am the one pleading his case. Please reconsider.
>
> Sincerely,
> Lisa Erickson

So much for the promise of an adulteress. Hadn't I offered to meet with her son before my accident? What the heck was this all about? Hadn't she gotten my notes? How about Dad's boots? Where were they?

"He is in your life now," I said out loud. Was she saying that our half brother knew our identity? If so, why the subterfuge at this late stage? Initially, I might have been satisfied with a level playing field, but this was a game-changer. I had to discover who he was before I agreed to anything. I didn't trust this whole drama or any of the characters in it.

I pounded around the house, tempted to wake Sam to show him the note, but I let him sleep because I needed to think. I knew I'd have to tell Griffin, but I wanted a plan in place first. And I didn't want my brother's brand of common sense to get in my way.

"Vanessa, can you meet me for lunch today—no wait, what are you doing after work?"

"Sounds serious, girl."

"I can't talk here." I stood and looked over the top of my pod to see if any nosey ears were leaning in my direction. "Can you do dinner or not?"

"All right, all right, dinner it is, but you're scaring me."

"Sorry. Let's meet at our usual place."

I had a full schedule of meetings that day, which would help the eight hours pass at a bearable speed until my meeting with Vanessa. Despite my plans to give my notice in a few weeks, my resolve to do right by my clients remained strong. I had no choice; good work ethics were in my bloodline.

Which is more than I could say for Lyle Wexler.

As far as I could determine, he spent most of his time three floors up on the Level of Creativity, playing ping pong and video games. Insisting it boosted morale and productivity, he often encouraged others to leave their work to join him. It seemed like every day had a theme or scheme attached to it: Mad Monday, Game Day Wednesday, Fantasy Friday. I couldn't keep up. The whole company philosophy had gone from being customer-centric to Lyle-centric.

In the middle of my internal rant, the elevator doors chimed. I peeked out from my pod and saw Lyle step out swinging a fistful of Nordstrom bags.

Oops. I was wrong. Must be Personal Shopping Day.

He dropped the bags in the middle of Nora's desk. "Be a doll, Nora, and cut the tags off my purchases. I have a few things to do before my meeting."

Nora pushed herself up, walked around the front of her desk, picked up the bags, and handed them back to Lyle. "Unless you plan to change clothes here, I think this is something you can do at home. Besides, it's personal, not business—at least not my business."

Whoa. Good for you, Nora.

"Cranky, aren't we? And so sensitive. Having hot flashes too?" He laughed as he walked down the hall.

I was dumbfounded. "Nora, does he do that often? That's grounds for harassment."

"He's testing me, seeing how far he can go. Believe me, it won't go on much longer." She pulled a small digital recorder out from under her tissue holder.

"Way to go!" I looked around before I spoke. "Have you called Gordy yet?"

She raised one eyebrow and smiled. "I have an interview next week."

When five thirty came, I headed for the elevator and prayed no one would slow me down. It worked. I decided to walk the six blocks. As I neared the bistro, I quickened my steps when I saw Vanessa.

"I reserved a table in the back," I said. "More private."

She took hold of my arm. "Case, are you in some sort of trouble?"

"I don't think so. I'm not sure."

Once we were seated, I slid the note across the table to her. She read it in seconds.

"This isn't right. Didn't you send a note weeks ago offering to meet him?"

"I did. After that, I sent my dad's dress boots and photo. Now I'm wondering if she got either of them." The thought of Dad's boots buried in a mountain of dead letters made me ill.

"Why would she keep his identity from you at this point? It doesn't make any sense."

"I want to know who he is. If this is some kind of sick game, I don't want to play."

Vanessa leaned in on her elbows. "How can I help?"

"I'm not sure. I wanted to talk with someone who'd understand. I'm pretty sure Sam and Griffin will say I'm acting like a silly woman."

She laughed. "They wouldn't dare."

"Maybe not, but they'd think it."

"Okay, we have to go about our investigation objectively. Let me see the note again. And the envelope."

I handed them over.

Holding the paper up to the light, she looked for a watermark but found none. "Cheap copy paper." Then she checked the envelope and printed address labels. "Why would she go to the trouble to print an address label?" She read the note again. "The line 'He is in your life now—I believe for better, not worse' suggests he knows more than your name."

"That's how I read it too. I have no idea who he might be."

"Girl, let's go through the process of elimination, *again*. Maybe we missed something the last time we tried."

She reached for her briefcase and pulled out a legal pad and pen. "Let's list everything we know about this suspect. It's probably more than you think."

I talked; she wrote. We didn't come up with much. "Caucasian, around twenty-four. Mom's name is Lisa, and he must live in the area since he may have met me."

"Did you ever ask your mom what Lisa looked like?"

I sighed. "No."

"Wait." She pulled out her laptop and connected to Wi-Fi. She talked as she typed. "Massachusetts State police females." She looked over the screen then typed again. "Female Mass state cops." She waded through a few pages. "Or Massachusetts police academy graduation 1980s?"

"Graduation?" A chill made me put my jacket over my shoulders. "You know, Mom gave me all of Dad's stuff from the force. I've seen photos of graduating classes. I'll check when I get home."

"Okay. Let's move on to the unusual suspects. Who do you know who fits the description? Someone you've met around the time she sent her first letter?"

"I told you, I've only met three, maybe four, young guys in the past few months: Flynn and Hennessey, Sam's probie friend Tommy Coletti, and Lyle Wexler. Wexler may act like a juvenile, but I think he's close to my age, so he's out. Oh, please, let him be out."

"Any new clients? How about coworkers? Did you meet anyone at a party or an after-hours work event?"

"The last party I went to was Griffin's Memorial Day cookout. I met one guy there, Ethan Harte. Mom and Webster met him at their dinner club over a year ago. Again, he's too old."

Vanessa wrote something on her legal pad. "So who does that leave us with?"

"The only ones who fit into that age group are Darin, Mike, and Tommy. And I don't believe it's any of them."

"Maybe talking about them will shake something loose. What exactly do you know about each of them?" She poised her pen to record our findings.

I went on to tell her as much as I could about Darin, his parents, his siblings, and his faith. When I got to Mike, I told her he was an only child who had spent much of his time at the Flynns' house as a kid. She was like a bloodhound on an escaped convict when I told her his mother's name was Lisa.

"What? When were you planning to tell me this?"

"Vanessa, I met his parents for the first time the other night at Mike's condo. I'd seen Mr. Hennessey once before at a tavern in Southie. He was going through a rough patch."

"What do you mean?"

"He'd fallen off the wagon after years of sobriety."

"Perhaps triggered by his son's desire to find his biological father?"

"I don't think so. I mean, I didn't get that feeling."

She sighed and shook her head then drew a big star by Mike's name.

I gave her an overview of the Coletti family. "He's got a brother in the Marines who's in Germany recuperating from an injury and a sister in college. His aunt is Roberta Herzog, our literary agent."

Vanessa's head popped up, ready to interrupt.

I held up a hand. "I asked already. Tommy's mother's name is Ramona."

"Oh."

After another hour of examining clues, Vanessa's word for a bunch of random tidbits of information, we were no closer to identifying Lisa's son.

"None of these three guys bear any physical resemblance to Dad, Griffin, or me. There's something else. Wouldn't I feel something? You know, some sort of connection when I met him?"

"I'm thinking you'll feel foolish when we solve this case and ask ourselves why it took so long."

Right.

37

Even though I was exhausted from my dead-end sleuthing with Vanessa, I had to search for the picture of Dad's police academy graduation or I'd never hear the end of it from her. His graduation photo was one of the few that was never framed or hung on the wall, which would make it more difficult to locate.

Since I'd already gone through many of Dad's boxes, I sought out the ones I hadn't touched. I found more sports magazines and newspaper articles in one box but no photographs. The second box held paperwork, most of which I could safely junk. It was nearing eleven, but there was only one box left so I stuck with it.

Jackpot! I think Dad had a picture of every graduating class since he'd joined the force. Thankfully, there wasn't a class every year, so there was only one photo in the time period that would work.

I scanned the sea of resolute faces half hidden under hats emblazoned with metallic shields. Even a magnifying glass didn't help that much. Except for the front row, I could hardly distinguish between males and females.

I found Dad in the seventh row, second from the right. He looked like a kid, but his square jaw, straight nose, and deep-set eyes gave him away.

Wait. Look at the names on the bottom of the photo, dummy.

My finger ran across the names and stopped on *L. Erickson.* She was second row, fifth from the left. Her hair was tucked into her hat, but it looked light, which seemed to go with a Swedish name. Her visor cast a shadow, so it was hard to see her eyes or nose. Her face was kind of narrow, her skin fair, nothing I hadn't surmised before this. She looked to be about 5 feet, 8 or 9 inches and trim. What I could see of her face was pretty.

Laying the photo on the dresser, I closed up the box and stuffed it back in the closet. I was tired, and it was too late to call Vanessa.

As if on cue, my landline rang. I stared at it like it was a Komodo dragon. "Yes?"

"Did you find it?"

It was Vanessa. "Don't you know any better than to call a cop's wife late at night? You scared me half to death."

"Oh, sorry. Did you find it?"

"Yes, but it was hard to see her face." I told her all I knew and promised to call Mom for more details.

When I told Mom about the latest letter from Lisa, she agreed it sounded odd.

"Not that I don't trust you, Mom, but you mailed the package I gave you, right?"

"Yes, I mailed it the next morning. And the return address was clear, I remember. It's strange that she wouldn't mention the package. Did you include a note?"

"Nothing chatty, basically saying that he might like to have them. I included a picture of Dad in his uniform too."

"In the note, did you ask if he still wanted to meet you and Griffin?"

"Not in so many words. I figured he'd either changed his mind or was making me wait like I had him."

When I asked Mom about Lisa Erickson's looks, her

response was not unlike what I imagined. "A little taller than me, slender, blonde. She was definitely attractive but tough-looking. I think the female officers felt they had to prove something to the men back then."

"Do you think you'd recognize her if you saw her?"

"I'm sure I would. Why?"

"I don't know. I'm still trying to get a grip on this whole thing. I feel like I've lost control."

"What does Griffin think?"

I curled my hair around my finger. "Oh yeah, about that. I haven't had a chance to tell him or Sam yet. I wanted to do some investigating first."

She sighed. "Casey Nicole, for your own sake and theirs, let them in."

I put aside my thoughts of Lisa Erickson and her son to work on a Double Header extra. These were the columns we used when the week in sports was less than exciting or when the papers put out a supplement. I checked my list of possible topics. The story of Darin and his family seemed perfect, so I called him. "A-yo. Casey."

"A-yo back, Flynn. What would your parents think about Griffin and me writing a column about you and your family?"

"Depends. As long as the focus isn't on the difference between their biological and adopted children. They're sensitive about the whole adoption issue. They tell us we're unique, but they don't want us to feel it has anything to do with how we became Flynns."

"From what I've gathered, they've been successful. Besides, the only ones I know for sure are adopted are the two sisters I met at Griffin's cookout—Tess, because she's Asian and Elena, Hispanic."

"I'll run it by my parents and get back to you."

"How about this? I write out a list of questions and they only answer the ones they want? They get final approval before I submit it for publication."

"Might work," he said. "Let me ask you a question, Casey."

"Sure."

"A while back I told you my parents each had a child before they married. How do you know for sure Tess or Elena isn't Dad's biological daughter?"

I thought it was obvious, but then I realized both biological parents didn't have to be Asian or Hispanic to have an Asian or Hispanic child. "I guess I wouldn't know unless I'd been told or had met your parents."

Darin laughed. "Not easy, is it? One big pot of Irish stew. That's the way we like it."

After we hung up, I thought about what Darin said: "My parents each had a child before they married." I'd learned from Tess and Elena that their brother Shawn had been adopted, so the only one who could possibly be Lisa's biological son was Darin.

Right?

Either way, as far as I could tell, I wouldn't mind having any of the Flynns as a sibling.

38

I slipped out of bed and dressed without disturbing Sam. He'd come home even later than usual, so I figured he needed to sleep. Near the coffee machine, I found an envelope with a Post-it stuck to it which read "Could you please mail my parents' card on your way out? I forgot, and their anniversary is the day after tomorrow. Love, Me."

I was impressed. Sam had remembered to buy the card. His mom had done all the card buying in their family, so I had some training to do when we got married. Looked like I'd made some progress.

I put the card where I'd see it on my way out. I'd drop it in the mailbox box at the end of our road.

While sipping my juice and coffee breakfast, I finished the list of questions for Darin's parents so I could get it to Griffin. Not that I expected him to change anything. To avoid an argument, he'd tell me it was fine. Personally, I thought my brother gave in too easily.

I rinsed my cup and Sam's dishes from the night before. (I admitted I still had some training to do.) When I peeked in on him he was sleeping hard, so I blew him a kiss and backed out of the bedroom.

On my way out, I tucked my in-laws' anniversary card into Hildegard's front pocket then locked the door behind me. It wasn't until I was on the T that I saw the card peeking out. I groaned at my memory lapse.

Well, at least I knew a post office where I could mail it.

I got off at my usual stop and made my way to Lisa's post office. Standing on the sidewalk outside the entrance, the double doors looked intimidating. I walked through them, feeling brave and nervous at the same time, which didn't make any sense.

As long as I was there, I decided to ask if sending the card Priority mail would speed the delivery. I took my place in line behind the blue velvet rope. There were two people ahead of me, a man with a pile of packages and an elderly lady ahead of him squawking at the postal clerk to repeat himself.

"Next!" called a man from another window. His voice echoed off the marble floor and tile ceiling.

Package Man in front of me made a brief attempt to push his stack of boxes to the next window but decided it wasn't worth the effort. He told me to go ahead. I walked up to the window where a middle-aged man was waiting, his dark, bushy eyebrows shading his deep brown eyes from the glow of the fluorescent lights.

"Good morning." I slid the card toward him. "Could you tell me if this will get to Cape Cod by tomorrow?" I read his nametag: "Vincent Coletti."

Vincent Coletti? At this post office branch? Was this supposed to mean something?

He picked up the envelope. "You might get lucky with first class. Priority won't get it there any faster."

"Thanks." I turned to see if there was anyone behind me. "Excuse me." I pointed to his nametag. "I have a friend named Tommy Coletti."

"And I have a son named Tommy Coletti. How 'bout that! How d'ya know my boy?"

"My husband is on the state police force with him, Sam Gallagher." I watched for a reaction.

"Yes, Gallagher. Tommy's mentioned him." He picked up a few packages and tossed them into a bin behind him.

"I pass this post office every day on my way to work. Tommy told us you worked for the post office, but I had no idea this was your branch."

He looked up from sorting a few pieces of mail. "Quite the coinkydink, huh?"

"Quite. He's been updating us on your son Nick's progress. Says he'll be home soon."

His smile stretched the full width of his face. "Yes, thankfully, any day now." He opened a drawer and straightened the stamps inside.

"In rehab for a while, I hear from your sister-in-law, Roberta. She's my agent."

"Oh, is that right?" When someone bellowed from the back room, he took a step backward and placed the closed sign in his window. "You'll have to excuse me. Work's calling my name."

"Sure. Glad we met, Mr. Coletti."

"Me, too, Casey." He disappeared into the back.

Was he abrupt or just busy? I left the building. Was it my imagination or my intuition telling me something? I knew Tommy's father was a postmaster, and I knew the Coletti family lived in the city. Tommy would have no reason to tell us which branch, would he?

I shook it off and chalked it up to the "it's a small world" theory. I quickened my pace then stopped short about a block away.

When did I tell him my name was Casey?

The look of vague alarm on my face must have concerned Nora, who got up when I came in. "Everything okay, sweetie? You look confused."

"Maybe because I am confused."

"Anything I can help you with?"

"No, I'll work it out once I find a logical explanation." I turned down my volume to a whisper. "How'd your interview go?"

Lyle Wexler came out from behind the coffee-slash-snack bar wearing a smirk and carrying his usual double espresso. "What are you coconspirators whispering about?"

"It's a surprise, Lyle," Nora said. "You're not allowed to know about it—yet."

Lyle flapped his hand around like he was shooing flies. "I get it, I get it. No more questions from me. I'll figure it out, you know. That's what we bosses do."

He spoke like he'd been a member of some exclusive boss club for years when in truth this was his first executive position. When talking to one of her fellow administrative assistants in New York, Nora had discovered that Lyle's uncle had been resistant to this promotion but that Lyle's mother had pressured him into it.

Knowing the truth behind Lyle's promotion almost made me feel sorry for him until he said, "Chop, chop, Casey! Complacency is suicide in this business. There's always someone to come along and take your place."

"So true, Lyle." Pointing to the motivational banners hanging over the seating area, I gave him the best straight face I could muster. "You might want to put that on one of your flags."

His eyes followed the line of my finger then turned back to me. "Too late, Casey. Already on my to-do list. Hard to get one by me, isn't it?"

His pinhead status was secure.

Once he was in his office I said to Nora, "What was he smirking about? What surprise?"

"His birthday's coming up soon. He thinks we're planning something special for him." She winked at me. "And we are."

I took that to mean that her interview at JB & Son had gone well. Pretty soon both Gordy and Nora would be working for the same company as my mother. Life threw some interesting curves.

That thought prompted me to call Vanessa. "Get your legal pad out and add this news under the half brother heading. Point one, Darin's mother was either pregnant or had him before she married her husband, and they don't like talking about their biological children versus those adopted. Point two, Tommy's father works in the same post office branch where Lisa Erickson has her post office box. I spoke with Mr. Coletti, and I swear he was hiding something."

"Look, I have written down here that Tommy's mother's name is Ramona. What's Darin's mother's name?"

"Uh, Mrs. Flynn."

"I'll ignore that. And whose mother's name is Lisa?"

"I know, Mike's. All of them seem right, then all of them seem wrong, all at the same time."

"Oy vey."

Indeed.

39

Poppy Brandeis was pacing near my pod when I arrived at work the next morning. "May I speak with you as soon as possible, Casey?" She fidgeted with the gold chain around her neck.

I stopped and set my things down. "Now's good. What's on your mind?"

"You know Mr. Yokum, the elderly man who owns the tire stores?"

"Yes, he's one of the clients Lyle gave you while I was in the hospital." I expected to see guilt on her face, but she didn't look uncomfortable at all.

"Yes, him. He's on his way over, and I don't think he's going to be pleased with my ideas. Would you mind taking a look?"

Was this some sort of trick? I wanted to say "Yes, I would mind," but then I remembered what it was like being twenty-two and new. "Let's see what you've got."

I scanned through her marketing strategies. "Poppy, these are terrific."

"Really?"

"Yes, really. With a tweak here and there, they'll be a good fit for Mr. Yokum."

We spent the next thirty minutes huddled over her laptop making minor changes. When Yokum came in I whispered to Poppy, "Don't let the old goat scare you. He's all bluff."

"Good to see you again, Mr. Yokum. Poppy just showed me her new ideas to promote your company. You've got one of WGM's brightest working for you."

As they walked toward the conference area, Poppy turned and mouthed "Thank you."

My final month at WGM might be tolerable.

Then in strolled Lyle Wexler with his skinny jeans and fat head.

"Casey! WGM does not agree to six-month-long contracts. So tell your friends the Panellos we have no deal."

"It's Ianella. They're nervous because of all the changes, that's all. I assured them six months wouldn't be a problem this one time."

"Who are you to assure them?" Lyle snorted. "You're not in Kansas anymore, Dorothy." Then to Nora he barked, "Hey, Auntie Em! Get the Panellos on the phone." He looked down his turned-up nose at me. "Now, do you want to tell them or do you want me to?"

I raised one finger in the air. "Wait right here, Oz the Great and Powerful."

His chest puffed up like I'd given him a compliment.

I went around the corner to my desk, plopped down in my chair, and put my head in my hands.

Now what do I do, God?

Put it in My hands.

A peace came over me. I printed out my precomposed letter of resignation and signed my name. When I rounded the corner Lyle was right where I'd left him, arms folded across his chest, rocking back and forth on those $900 Ferragamo heels.

"So what will it be, sweetie?" he said, trying to make his voice sound ominous.

I handed him my letter. "Consider this my two weeks' notice. Guess you'll have to tell them yourself."

He blinked. "Oh, come on, Casey, can't you take a joke? I could possibly make an exception if it's such a huge deal."

"Really? You would do that for them?"

"No sweat." Turning to Nora he said, "You! Get the janitors on the phone. Stat!"

She looked at Lyle then at me. "Wait, Casey."

"See, even Auntie Em here wants to talk some sense into you."

Nora slipped a piece of letterhead out of a pod cubby and scribbled a short message. She walked around her desk and handed it to Lyle. "Not as formal as Casey's but just as binding. My two weeks' notice."

Lyle's face turned purple as he scrunched the letters in his hands. "If that's the way you feel, you can both leave now! I'll call security to escort you out."

Since we'd seen him do it to others, that's what we expected.

I packed my personal belongings and laptop into Hildegard and headed for the elevator. Nora boxed her personal items and joined me.

Lyle snarled, "And don't expect a severance package. I don't care what your contract says."

Nora held up her digital recorder and stared him down. "No problem. I'm sure an age-slash-sex discrimination lawsuit will net us more."

A simple push of a button closed the doors on a pivotal chapter in my life—and the dumbstruck expression on Lyle's face.

I looked over at Nora. "I sure hope this means you got the job with Gordy."

"I did. And a raise."

"Are you really going to sue Lyle?"

She grinned. "Probably not. But he doesn't know that, does he?"

"Let's celebrate!" I said. "Where do you want to go for lunch?"

"Anywhere that doesn't serve sushi."

After our emancipation lunch, I called Sam on my way to the T. "Hope you're ready to execute your vision for our future, 'cause I pulled the trigger at WGM today."

"Geez, Casey, I hope you didn't shoot Wexler. I've got a full caseload already."

"Nah, it was more of a walkout than a shootout. He was only going to get worse."

"I'm glad. Now we don't have to wait to list our condo."

"Whoa, Sam, slow down. I haven't even gotten home yet."

"Let's schedule an appointment for tomorrow."

I bit the side of my thumbnail. "I don't know. It's kind of sudden."

"Listen, Case, putting it on the market by mid-August instead of late September will attract buyers who commute to Boston or attend one of the many colleges in the city."

"Can't we talk about it in the morning since I won't have to leave for work?"

He laughed. "Sure, we can talk—with a real estate agent."

Sam got his way.

I rushed through my breakfast since the real estate agent was due to arrive at ten. Standing over Sam, I waited for him to take his last bite of cereal so I could get his dishes into the dishwasher.

"Can I at least have a second cup of coffee?" he said, holding his mug out of my reach.

"I want to make one last run with the vacuum and dust cloth before she gets here."

"I don't know why you're worried, Case. This place is spotless."

He was right, but I chased him around the house with the vacuum anyway.

It didn't take long to show the agent around 1,100 square feet. Based on the economic climate, I was concerned about its current worth. We'd been there for less than four years, but the agent assured us our prime location would save us. When she asked about our mortgage balance it was Sam who was shocked, not her, when I said zero. She left us with a contract to review.

The minute she was out the door, Sam faced me with arms crossed. "We had a fifteen-year mortgage. When and how did we pay it off? Don't you think this is something I should have been in on?"

"When the interest rates dropped on our savings, it made sense to double up on the mortgage payments, so I did."

"Even with that, we still have $275,000 in the bank?"

"Close to it."

Sam scratched his head. "To think I've been driving around in that junk of a truck. I don't know whether to be happy or angry with you."

"Please choose happy. I wanted it to be a surprise."

"Okay, but don't ever do that again," he said, wagging his finger at me in a mock-scolding.

I laughed. "I doubt that will be an option now that I've left my substantial salary behind."

"You're not getting off that easy. You're on the hook for a bestseller, remember? How about writing a detective mystery for me instead of a sports biography?"

"Ooh, speaking of mysteries, you'll never guess who I met yesterday."

"You're right. I won't, so tell me."

"Tommy's father."

"Tommy Coletti's father? Where?"

"He's the postmaster at Lisa's post office."

"Huh? Lisa's post office?"

Sam could be such a guy. "Yes, the branch where Lisa Erickson has a post office box."

He rubbed his chin. "Are you suggesting that his father has something to do with Lisa Erickson?"

"He knew my name."

"For Pete's sake, Tommy probably mentioned you. You're jumping at shadows. What's this all about?"

I told him about the second letter I'd gotten from Lisa.

He held his hand out, palm up, and wiggled his fingers. "Give it here. Let me take a look."

I got the letters from Hildegard and surrendered them. I included the note that Lisa had written to Dad all those years ago.

Sam read her note to Dad first and put it aside. Then he unfolded her first letter to me and read it slowly and did the same with the second. After examining the paper, he checked the addresses on the two envelopes. He brought the envelopes up to his nose and sniffed. "Second one smells like smoke."

He looked at the address label on the second envelope. Tilting his head back and forth, I could almost hear his thoughts falling into place like change in a coin separator. "It's addressed to Casey Gallagher and sent to your home address."

"And?"

"The handwriting on the note you found in your father's things matches the first letter, which was addressed to Casey McGee and sent to the *Lowell Sun*. The style of the second letter is different. One was thoughtful, the other abrupt. One was parchment, the other copy paper. No one would go through the trouble to print an address label when you already had a sample of their handwriting. Different M.O. This second letter wasn't written by the same person. Maybe the son or another interested party."

"Wow. You're good, Detective Gallagher. "Now all we need to do is find this guy before he finds us."

Sam grumped. "What difference does it make who finds who first?"

"It's about unfair advantage."

"Why does everything have to be a competition with you?"

I bristled. "You wouldn't understand."

"What's not to understand? You didn't want to meet this kid, then you agreed to meet him, then decided not to meet him because he didn't respond to your generous offer to meet him in the time period you allotted. Where is his unfair advantage in all this?"

I mumbled, "I'm not talking about this anymore." Sam's comments made me feel childish and petty and I didn't like it.

What I disliked most was that he was right.

40

Can you afford to take a day off work to get pampered?" Mom asked. "I've got a gift certificate to the new spa in Plymouth."

Oops. I hadn't told my mother about my job. "That's the second best idea I've heard lately. The first was giving WGM my notice earlier than I'd planned."

"What did you say?"

"My last day was the day before yesterday, mainly because staying might have jeopardized my spotless police record."

"I'm sure there's a story behind that. How about tomorrow? You can fill me in."

We met at the spa the next morning around ten. We chose the couple's room so we could experience the relaxation together. I hoped their motto "We'll massage your stress away as far as the East is from the West" was more than marketing.

Now relax, Casey.

"I will," I mumbled.

"You will what?"

"Relax. Like you said."

"Oh," she said. "I must be losing it."

We spoke little during the massage but started up once we moved to the pedicure chairs.

Mom stuck one foot in the sudsy water and asked the question I was expecting. "So tell me what prompted you to leave WGM sooner than you planned?"

"Nora and I simultaneously gave our two-week notice, but Lyle thought it was best we leave immediately." I handed the girl my polish and kicked off my sandals. "My clients knew change was on the way. Believe me, it was for the best."

Mom reached over and patted my arm. "I'm impressed."

"Why? Because I have no job?"

"No, because you did what you thought was right. Tell me, now that both Gordy and Nora are moving over to JB & Son with me, have you thought about joining them?"

"I'd be lying if I said it hadn't crossed my mind. But I feel like I've got to take this chance to write or I might lose it."

"Now I'm doubly impressed."

"Thanks. You'll be pleased to know Sam and I met with a real estate agent yesterday to list the condo."

"How'd it go?"

"Better than we thought." At the tap of the technician's hand, I pulled one foot out and submerged the other. "It's still nerve-racking."

"It shouldn't be. Your place is in mint condition in an ideal location. It'll go fast."

"What if we sell the condo and can't find a house?"

"Then you'll be homeless, sleeping on cardboard flats, and dumpster diving for food."

"Not funny, Mom."

"You're the funny one, Casey. You've always disliked change. You were only a toddler when Dad and I moved the first time. You cried for two weeks because your stuffed animals were not in their right place. You had a major meltdown every first day of school."

"Was I that bad?"

"Let's just say, while it's natural not to like change, your aversion to it often escalated to hysteria."

"My husband and brother might say those major meltdowns haven't stopped."

Mom looked me in the eye. "So what are you doing about it?"

"I'm trying, Mom, but it's hard."

We scuffed across the floor to the manicure station in our disposable flip-flops.

"You've started the transition already. Quit your job, stuck with your decision to write, and now selling your condo. Want to know what will make it easier?"

"What?"

"The peace of God. That's what helped me cope with life after Dad died. I assure you, losing a husband is a major life change."

"It's not like I can order peace online, Mom."

"No, it's simpler. When I asked the Lord to give me a sign that He existed, He answered in a way that was personal to me and my situation. He'll do the same for you. Once you believe He's real, you can ask Him for peace."

Listen to your mother, Casey.

"I *am* listening," I said.

Mom gave me a quizzical look. "Well, good."

We passed the rest of our time together planning how to decorate the new house I didn't know if I was ready to buy yet.

I was awake when Sam got home from work. When I asked him to sign the listing agreement so I could fax it to the agent right away, he blinked twice. "Are you sure? It's one thirty in the morning."

"I'm sure." He took the pen from me and signed it. I blew on his signature until it was dry then faxed it.

Although I had a hard time falling asleep, it wasn't fear that kept me awake. It was excitement. Big difference. I thought about what type of house I'd like to live in. Colonial or Cape? Cedar shingles or clapboard? Red or blue front door? If our place sold as quickly as the agent thought it would, in a few weeks we could be looking for a house to raise our family. Our family. I knew I was projecting. I didn't care. I was in a good place and ready for this new stage.

Are you ready to accept your brother too?

Back to this whole brother thing, huh? By the way, it's half brother.

Even though I'd narrowed my choices to the three rookies, I had no idea if my draft picks were right. Wasn't I supposed to feel a familial vibe or biological connection? And if it did turn out to be one of them, how would I feel about him deceiving me?

You can overcome it, Casey.

Are You sure?

41

Griffin actually added some good questions for our interview with Darin's parents: Have you always encouraged your children to build on their strengths and pursue their own interests? At what age do you think they're ready to make that decision?

I cleaned up the copy and sent it to Darin to pass on to them.

When I first came up with the idea to interview the Flynns it was prior to putting Darin on the half brother short list. Interviewing his parents would eliminate him or not.

A few days passed before I got a call from his mother. "Hi, Casey, this is Jaclyn Flynn, Darin's mother."

Jaclyn. The elimination process had begun.

"Hi, Mrs. Flynn. Good of you to call."

After some polite chitchat about her son and the Red Sox I said, "So, Mrs. Flynn, I gather you're getting back to me about the interview?"

"Please, call me Jaclyn. And you're right. My husband and I are agreeable under one condition."

Uh-oh, here it comes. "What might that be?"

"You and your brother must come to dinner. Being interviewed won't be nearly as intimidating that way."

"Are you sure you want to go to all that work?"

"Casey, adding two more plates to our table is not work."

"Okay, give me a date and I'll check with Griffin."

Every time I interacted with a member of this family I liked them more. My intuition also told me something else. *There is no way you're related to Darin Flynn. His family's too nice, and that would be too easy.*

Basking in the freedom of working from home, I settled into my comfy chair with my laptop, research notes all around me. I was feeling good about the progress I'd made and glad for the uninterrupted time. Then my phone rang. It was Roberta. I hesitated before answering. "Hi, Roberta."

"The plane has landed!"

"Your plane?"

"No, Nicky's. The whole family is breathing easier now that he's on American soil. He's on his way to the rehab hospital, but my sister says he's doing well."

"Wonderful! Speaking of your family, did your brother-in-law mention that I met him at the post office last week?"

"Vincent? No. So what'd he have to say?"

"Not much. We talked a little about Tommy and Sam working together and about Nick coming home. To be honest, he wasn't that talkative."

"That's Vincent. It doesn't matter, because Nicky is home! And since my sister is back, I'll be able to spend more time in New York. My Marvin is an understanding man, but he's missed me."

I'd almost forgotten Roberta was married. "I'd like to meet your Marvin someday. Does he ever come to Boston with you?"

"Not often, but he'll be here sometime soon to visit Nicky. You'd love Marvin. He's nothing like me."

How was I supposed to respond to that? A comment on how opposites attract didn't seem appropriate.

I was still searching for the right words when Roberta said, "Have you and Griffin been sticking to the new timeline? When can I expect the full proposal for your bio on Yastrzemski?"

This wasn't a personal call. No surprise.

"Roberta, the new timeline begins the day after Labor Day, remember?"

"Yes, but you're not at WGM anymore, so the timeline has changed."

"How did you know that?"

"You know me. I like to stay abreast of things in case I run into an interested editor. I pride myself in being prepared."

And pushy.

In the six weeks since the accident, the most I'd managed to run was two miles. That afternoon I attempted my first five-miler. The third mile mark was tough, but once my endorphins kicked in the pain faded and my head cleared. As I rounded the corner toward home, I checked my watch. My time was lousy, but I didn't mind.

Why was Sam's truck in the driveway? He'd left for work less than two hours ago. I cooled down a bit before I went into the house, mainly because I didn't want him to see me winded. He'd worry.

"Sam?"

"In here," he said, his voice coming from the bedroom.

"What're you doing home?"

"There was a last-minute opening in the anti-terrorism class in DC, and the commander offered me the spot."

"How long will you be gone?"

"Leaving in a few minutes. Be back in four days."

"Anti-terrorism, huh? Does that mean your job description is changing?"

"It might." He pulled his carry-on off the bed. "Don't look at me like that, Casey. You almost got killed by a texting teenager."

I scratched my police-work-is-dangerous speech, knowing it would be ineffective now.

Lean on me.

"Lean on you?"

Sam looked up. "Are you talking to me?"

"Uh, I guess." My answer wasn't convincing.

"Is there something going on that you're not telling me?"

"No, not really."

"What do you mean, not really?"

"It's nothing. It's just I keep hearing this voice. Well, not exactly hearing. More like sensing." I hadn't meant to tell him, but the words fell out.

"When did this start?"

"I don't know. Maybe a few months ago."

"Before or after the accident?"

"After, I guess. It's nothing, Sam. I've had a lot going on."

"That can do it." He threw some socks in his bag. "Any headaches or vision problems?"

"No," I said, waving the topic away with back of my hand. "Finish up your packing. You don't have much time."

Sam managed to fit everything he would need for his trip into his duffel bag and laptop case. He stopped before he opened the door to give me a new version of his listen-up speech. I could drive a four-wheeler through the furrow in his brow. "Listen. While I'm gone, I want you to check in with the doctor."

"It's not like I'm seeing visions."

"No, you're hearing voices."

"Actually, there's only one."

"What's it telling you?"

"That it's time for you to leave or you'll miss your flight." I kissed him hard enough to distract him and nudged him toward the door.

It didn't work.

"All joking aside, Case."

"It's not like I actually hear a voice, and it's not all the time. It's only when I'm trying to figure something out. Stupid things, like meeting my half brother."

Sam smiled. "That's the first time I've heard you do that."

"Do what?"

"Talk about meeting your half brother." I put my hands on my hips and gave him the look. Because my husband knew what was good for him, he left without another word.

I suspected it wasn't the end of this discussion.

42

It was close to six when Griffin and I rang the doorbell at the Flynns' gray and white triple-decker. From the stoop, we heard footsteps pounding and voices shrieking, "I got it! I got it!" The front door swung open under the strength of three kids pulling on it. "Hi, I'm Casey and this is my brother Griffin."

"I'm Shawn." The teen shook our hands then gestured to the younger children. "This is Fiona, that's Wyatt."

Fiona stepped forward. "I'm nine. Wyatt thinks he's four years older than me, but he's not thirteen yet."

Wyatt, a wiry preteen, nudged her with his elbow before he yelled, "Mom! Company's here!"

Jaclyn Flynn walked through the living room to greet us, drying her hands on her apron. "I see you've met three more of our eight blessings."

"Quite a welcome too," Griffin said, winking at Fiona.

"Sorry, we're running a little late," Jaclyn said. "Patrick is picking Craig up, and Andrew should be along soon. His shift just ended."

Patrick? Craig? Andrew? Which one was her husband? I

tried to recall the association game I used to play to help me remember names. Patrick is the husband. *Phew.*

"No problem," Griffin said. "Casey always likes to be early."

I elbowed him when she wasn't looking. "Smells delicious."

"Thanks." Jaclyn motioned to the sofa. "Have a seat, please." She put her hand on Wyatt's shoulder. "Your turn to set the table, sweetie." Addressing Shawn and Fiona, she said, "Will you two please entertain our guests while I finish up?"

"Sure," Shawn said as Fiona squished in next to him in a Papa-Bear-sized recliner.

Their house had character. The dark walnut-stained trim, wainscoting, and floors contrasted nicely with the antique white walls. Any remodeling that had been done over the years hadn't diminished the charm of this old working class home.

Griffin spoke easily with both kids about video games, American Girl dolls, and skateboarding. Unless I wanted to sound like a boring adult, I had to step up my game.

While Griffin oohed and aahed over the new skateboard Shawn had gotten for his birthday, I reached over to a stack of middle reader books on an end table, bookmarks sticking out like a colorful bouquet. "Are these yours, Fiona?"

She joined me on the oversized sectional, which was a perfect shade of army green to camouflage the living of a large family. "Yes. I'm going into third grade, but my teacher told Mommy to get me fifth grade books."

"That shows how much you like to read." She looked satisfied with my response.

I surveyed the rest of the room. "To Our Son" and "For My Brother" birthday cards crowded each other on the mantel. Family photos hung inches apart, climbing the wall of the staircase.

One day Sam and I might have a home like this. A family too.

Patrick arrived with a young, freckle-faced teen sporting a tee shirt that read "A Joyful Noise Daycare." A few minutes later, a stocky young man with red hair like Darin's came in wearing a uniform with "Andrew Flynn" embroidered above the shirt pocket.

During introductions to Craig and Andrew, my phone beeped. It was Vanessa. I shut it off, thankful it had happened before dinner. Something told me there'd be no phone calls and texting at the Flynn table.

"Since everyone who's coming home is home,"—Jaclyn placed a deep wooden bowl on the table—"let's not keep our guests waiting any longer."

The bunch of us streamed into the dining room and surrounded the long mahogany table. Griffin and I waited until Patrick pulled two chairs out and said, "Better take a seat. They fill up fast around here."

Under the noise of scraping chairs and chatter, I leaned over and mumbled to Griffin, "Grace. Don't forget grace."

Griffin's head popped up. "Who's Grace? How did I miss her?"

I kicked him under the table.

"Ouch! What was that for?"

I folded my hands in front of me and prayed he'd shut up.

Patrick laughed. "I think your sister is trying to tell you that we say grace before meals."

Griffin griped, "I probably would've figured that out without a kick in the ankle."

Jaclyn smiled and reached for the hands of the children on either side of her. "Looks like you both will fit right in. Now let's all bow our heads."

Patrick said a brief prayer, thanking God for the food, family, and new friends. Together the whole family said, "Amen."

I don't know what I expected this family to serve for dinner—maybe corned beef and cabbage and boiled "p'dayduhs"—but I was pleased to see the meal set before us: tossed salad, lasagna, and Italian bread. The lace tablecloth, monogrammed linen napkins, and china looked old enough to have been passed down through the generations. Were they always this formal?

I got my answer when Fiona held up her napkin and asked, "Mommy, can I wipe my mouth on this like at Christmas?"

Jaclyn smiled at Fiona then winked at me. "Yes, dear, it's a special occasion."

While Jaclyn plated food for the younger kids, I looked at her more closely, trying to determine if she looked anything like the grainy police academy graduation photo. Her hair was strawberry blonde now, but had it always been that color? Her eyes were blue, which didn't help me since I didn't know the color of Lisa Erickson's. She looked a little heavier than the new graduate, but that would be normal for someone over fifty.

How long could I stare at her without getting noticed?

I got back to the dinner conversation. The topics ranged from rebuilt carburetors to Veggie Tales to tattoos. Mostly, Griffin and I listened. Once the main meal was over, the kids who weren't on cleanup duty retreated to the living room. Jaclyn, Patrick, Griffin, and I stayed seated at the table.

Jaclyn handed me a stapled packet. "Thanks for sending the questions ahead of time. You'll see we had no problem answering them."

Patrick added, "We hope you understand why we're cautious. Years ago, a reporter did a story about our family for a local paper. In his article, he separated our kids by saying 'their own children' and 'their adoptive children.' Somehow those who were adopted got the idea that they weren't our own."

"Yes," I said. "Darin filled me in a little."

"The truth is," Jaclyn said, "even our biological children have little in common. For instance, Andrew likes to get dirty and work with his hands, Wyatt loves music, and Fiona is a voracious reader."

When Darin had first mentioned his parents each had a child before they married—his father a girl and his mother a boy—I never asked who the boy was because it hadn't mattered then. It did now. I worded my next question skillfully, or so I thought. "So, who does Darin get his athleticism from?"

Patrick shook his head. "Not from me or Jaclyn."

Told me nothing there, Patrick. I knew I'd need to tack. I let Griffin jabber on while I pretended to look over our list of questions.

Jaclyn lifted a shamrock-painted teapot. "Would anyone like more tea?"

"Sure," I said, picking up my napkin to make room for her to pour. I took a sip then dabbed at the corners of my mouth, the embroidery touching my lips. I refolded it, monogram out.

I looked down at the stitching. It was an *F* in formal script. I thought how odd it was that this no-frills family would have monogrammed linen.

I looked at it again. Wait. I was wrong. It wasn't an *F*. It was an *E*.

I choked on my next sip. The letter *E* got larger, at least in my mind. Could it possibly be an *E* for Erickson?

Before I could investigate, Andrew called from the living room. "Mom! Dad! Darin just threw a runner out on second again!"

Although he tried, there was no way Patrick could stretch his neck around the corner to see the TV.

Jaclyn said, "Sorry for the interruption. That's the downside of having a son's job televised."

Griffin perked up. "We can catch a few innings, if you want. We're in no hurry."

Of course Griffin was amenable to watching the game; his ear had been tuned in since the national anthem. I had no choice but to agree.

The family jostled around, making room for the rest of us. The couch and floor filled up. I stared at the screen, but I was blind to the game.

If Jaclyn Flynn was in fact Lisa Erickson, then she knew all along who we were and what she was doing. Could it be true? Was Darin our elusive half sibling?

Sheesh, get a hold of yourself, I thought.

At the seventh inning stretch, the four of us returned to the table. With no idea how to proceed, I fumbled through my notes.

Patrick said, "As you can see by Darin's performance tonight, nope, that boy didn't get his talent from us. He came with it."

I looked at Patrick, trying to understand. "He came with it? How do you mean?"

"You know, when we adopted him."

"Darin was adopted?" I had trouble closing my mouth.

Griffin choked on a sip of his water. "Wow. Darin told us it wasn't easy figuring out where all the children came from. Now we know what he meant."

When Jaclyn picked up some dishes and headed toward the kitchen, I followed with my cup and saucer rattling in my hand.

"Jaclyn, mind if I ask you a silly question?"

"Not if you don't mind a silly answer."

"The *E* on your monogrammed napkins. What does it stand for?"

"*E* for Emmanuel is what I tell my kids. It means God is with us." She smiled. "Really, I have no idea. I bought them at a garage sale."

One out. Two left on base.

43

As soon as Griffin and I were in the car, I turned my cell back on to text Sam. Vanessa rang in before I had a chance.

"Is your boy Flynn still in the running?"

"Tell Vanessa I can hear her," Griffin said, pulling away from the curb. "Flynn's in the running for what?"

"You haven't told Griffin about our undercover work?"

Griffin raised his voice. "What are you two up to?"

"Put your phone on speaker," Vanessa said. "We need full disclosure."

Griffin poked me. "Yeah, what she said, Casey. Let me hear."

I pushed the speaker key. "When Vanessa and I reviewed our half brother possibilities, Darin made the cut."

"Darin? But he's adopted."

"Yes, Captain Duh, we know that *now*, but we didn't before tonight."

Vanessa's voice boomed. "What? Darin was adopted?"

Griffin came to a Stop sign. "Who else do Holmes and Watson have on the short list?"

I answered before Vanessa could. "Only Mike and Tommy."

He jolted through the intersection. "Mike Hennessey and Tommy Coletti? Are you serious?"

"Did your sister show you the other letter?"

I winced. "Thanks, Vanessa."

"What letter?" He had a hard time keeping his eyes on the road.

"Read it to him, Casey."

"Wait." Griffin pulled off to the side and put it in Park. "We've already had one accident. I'm not risking another."

I took the letter out and read it aloud.

Griffin looked as puzzled as I was. "It doesn't make any sense. She makes it sound like we know him and he knows us."

"Exactly." I folded it up and stuck it back in my bag. "That helped us narrow it down to those three."

Vanessa said, "Looks like we're back to Mike, which was my guess all along."

I held the phone closer to my lips. "If your guess is based solely on his mother's name being Lisa, I think you've got a weak case, Counselor."

"Huh? Mike's mother's name is Lisa?" Griffin bit the edge of his lip then smiled like he'd discovered buried treasure. "Wow. It would be kinda cool to have a Red Sox player for a brother, don't you think?"

"Yeah, cool." I wanted to pinch him.

"Circumstantial evidence is often more trustworthy than eyewitness testimony," Vanessa said. "Have I taught you nothing in all these years?"

"Oh, you've taught me plenty. Much of it I hope to forget. I'm hanging up now, Vanessa."

The next morning I awoke with a mission, to call Mike Hennessey and outright ask him if he was our half brother. If I smoked, this would be the moment I'd light a cigarette to offset my jitters. Since I didn't, I popped a piece of dark chocolate into my mouth. It still took me until noon to pick up the phone.

Mike answered on the second ring. "Thanks for calling, Casey. It means a lot."

"Sure," I said, not sure at all.

"I guess that's the reporter in you. You want to get the whole story."

Yeah, I wanted the story. Did this mean he was ready to talk? "So what is the whole story, Mike?"

"The doctor says I need surgery. They'll know more after that."

"Surgery?" I was lost. "On what?"

"You didn't know? Injured my pitching arm in the ninth inning last night. Looks like I'm out for the season."

"Are the doctors sure?"

"As sure as they can be," Mike said, "without being omniscient."

"How're you doing with all this?"

"Better than my parents and Tess. Maybe because I sensed the Lord was preparing me."

Not ready to hear how he could have "sensed" that, I closed my ears and mouth. After a brief exercise in self-control I asked, "Is there anything I can do?"

"Nothing I can think of. Except pray."

"I will, Mike. I promise." I meant it when I said it. Even if I wasn't sure it would help.

"Casey?"

"Yes."

"What did you call for anyway?"

I thought quickly on my feet but tripped. "Uh, we're doing a column on your new batting coach. Thought I'd get some inside info."

Asking an American League pitcher who seldom got a turn at bat for inside info on a batting coach was almost like asking Griffin about fashion trends.

"I've created a monster," I said to Vanessa when I answered her call. "And it's you!"

"I am not amused. Now let's finish our conversation and get back to Lisa Hennessey. Have you ever met her?"

"Once. A week ago when Sam and I stopped by to visit Mike. His parents only stayed a few minutes."

"Ugh. Why do I always have to pry this information out of you?"

I ignored her question. "They didn't hang around long enough to talk much. Her husband wanted to stay, but she was in a hurry to get home."

"Ah-ha!"

"Ah-ha, what?" I said. "I think his mother pretended they had something to do because she felt like they were intruding."

Vanessa went into full cross-examination mode. "Tell me, did Lisa Hennessey know you and Sam would be there?"

"No, but—"

"Just answer the question."

I made a face at the phone. "No."

"Could it be that your presence caught her off guard?"

"Could be," I said. "But anything is possible."

"And could it be that her husband's lapse from sobriety was due to his fear he would lose his only son to his biological family?"

"I doubt that was—"

She didn't let me finish.

"Yes or no, please."

I growled. "Yes."

"Now this is what we call circumstantial evidence. And it's building our case for us."

"Vanessa?"

"What?"

"If I'm ever in a courtroom waiting to be questioned by you, remind me to plead guilty and throw myself on the mercy of the court."

44

Now that I was working from home, I felt the need to create a timeline for my various projects. I even factored in four days a month for radio and TV spots. The hit-and-run work I'd completed to date on the biography had given me a good foundation. I had a preliminary outline and organized research files. The complete proposal would take another three weeks or so.

With Griffin off for the summer and me making my own hours, finding time to go over our work together would be a snap.

Or so I thought.

"Not today, Auntie Casey. Jillian has an ob-gyn appointment."

"Sorry, Case, I'm coaching Little League tonight."

"No can do. I've picked up a tutoring gig on Fridays."

I did the only thing I could do—called Mom to complain. "I'm busting my butt over here trying to get this project off the ground, and Griffin doesn't seem to care about it at all. Was he always like this?"

Mom chuckled. "If by 'like this' you mean sidetracked by

a bunch of things that were different from what you wanted him to do, then my answer is yes."

I was irritated. "Has Griffin called you to complain?" The second I asked the question, I saw the irony and groaned. "Don't answer that."

"Casey, I don't want to get in the middle of my children's business, but let me ask you a few questions, okay?"

I said "okay" and sounded like I meant it, but I suspected this would lead to a not-so-happy place.

"Whose idea was Double Header?"

"Mine."

"Whose idea was it to do the radio and TV appearances?"

"Mine in the beginning, then Roberta's. But Griffin agreed to them."

"Whose idea was it to write sports biographies?"

"What are you trying to say, Mom? Has Griffin told you he doesn't want to collaborate?"

"No, he hasn't. I'm making an observation, that's all. Perhaps the old adage *actions speak louder than words* may apply."

"Why doesn't he just tell me?"

"He might not realize it. When he was a little boy, he looked up to you. Following in the steps of his big sister became a habit. Now that he's older, he needs to take time to figure out where his skills fit best."

"What should I do?"

"Talk to him. Give him an out. Then see if he takes it. You and I both know you can write those biographies yourself."

Griffin and I had a morning TV interview in Boston. I took my own car so I could spend the rest of my day in the city doing research at a couple of sports museums and shopping for an outfit for my surprise birthday party.

We both arrived early and went directly to makeup. Once we were settled in the green room, we had a few minutes to talk before the taping began.

"Tough news about Mike," Griffin said. "How'd he sound when you talked to him?"

"Like he always does. Worried more about others."

"Doesn't seem fair, does it?"

"It isn't," I said. "By the way, when today's panel members ask about him—and you know they will—let's put a positive spin on it. No sense adding more worries to the pot."

Turns out the show's panel had already talked to the Red Sox front office about Mike's condition, so they covered that topic first and fast then moved on to the Patriots. Sometimes being friends with the Irish Twins worked against us. Today we escaped without a challenge to our objectivity.

On the way to our cars Griffin said, "Have you had a chance to bring up Mike's candidacy?"

"Candidacy?"

"Didn't you and Vanessa say he was in the running for half brother of the year?"

"That's the reason I called him yesterday. As usual, my timing was off so I didn't bring it up."

My recent conversation with Mom about Griffin popped into my head. "Hey, have time for lunch? That steakhouse where we usually meet Roberta isn't far from here."

"Works for me."

I spent the few miles to the restaurant comparing Mike's attitude with my whining to Mom. Here was this young kid facing serious surgery that could change his entire future while I was complaining about Griffin being too busy to help me. The moments I didn't like myself were crowding each other.

I hadn't kept my promise to Mike either. About praying. Maybe if I did, it would make me feel better.

It is not about you, Casey.

All right. I'll pray.

Since I couldn't bow my head or fold my hands while driving, I figured praying out loud might make up for it.

"Dear God, please help Mike. Help his parents and his friends deal with it, and help his father stay sober and help the surgeons do what needs to be done."

I stopped before the amen. Did that prayer even count if I wasn't sure I believed?

"God, I want to believe you're real. I do. Mom said to ask for a sign, so that's what I'm doing now. Thank you. Uh, amen."

I drove the rest of the way in silence. Waiting. Wanting. Wavering.

45

Griffin and I were seated at a table by a window. We ordered beverages then critiqued each other on our TV appearance.

"Didn't you see your hair in the monitor?" I pulled a clump of my hair straight out. "Are you still going to that same barber?"

"You betcha. He's the cheapest around."

"And old. It's a race to see who dies first, him or his business."

"Trying to get inside my head again, I see."

"Not me," I said. "It's way too lonely in there."

"By the way, did you have to be so obvious about your disapproval of Ulander taking Mike's place in the roster?"

My back went up. "What're you talking about? I didn't say a word about that."

"You didn't have to." He huffed. "They can interpret smirks and grunts."

The server dropped off his Pepsi and my raspberry iced tea.

"Okay, are we through here?" I said, picking up my tea. "Because I want to talk to you about something else."

"What'd I do now?"

"I've been thinking, that's all. About my life goals and yours."

"You're not going to pull out a list of talking points, are you?" He leaned back in his chair and stuck his fingers in his ears. "Blah, blah, blah."

I put my iced tea down. "This is serious, Griffin. I need you to tell me honestly how you feel about working on the column, the radio and TV shows, the biographies, everything."

"What d'ya mean? Thought we talked about this already."

"What I mean is I don't want to be dragging you places you don't want to go. If you've got other things you want to do with your life, you need to man up and tell me."

"What brought all this—" Griffin was in the middle of a sentence when a familiar laugh drew our attention to the restaurant lobby.

"Is it my imagination," I said, "or does that sound like…"

Griffin grimaced. "Roberta?"

We looked toward the entrance. Sure enough, Roberta was on the arm of a tall silver-haired man who was wearing a well-tailored suit and an engaging smile. The man squeezed her waist and whispered in her ear.

Roberta giggled. "Oh, Marvin, stop your teasing."

Marvin? This was her husband? He wasn't what I expected. Actually, I don't know what I expected, but it wasn't a mature James Brolin look-alike. His gaze never left her face, like she was the only person in the room.

Roberta spotted us when the host led them to a table nearby. "Talk about a small world!" She turned to Marvin. "These are my clients, Casey Gallagher and Griffin McGee." She rested her hand on his chest. "This handsome man is my Marvin."

"A pleasure to meet you both," he said. "Roberta Lee has spoken highly of you."

"And you as well," I said. "Won't you join us?"

It was Griffin's turn to kick me under the table.

"Certainly," said Roberta. "You don't mind, do you, sweetie?"

"Of course not, lovey." Marvin kissed her cheek and pulled a chair out for her.

"Marvin's such a dear. He surprised me by flying in this morning so he could be with me when I see Nicky for the first time."

"Right. Nick's back," Griffin said. "How's he doing?"

"We'll find out when we see him this afternoon. He's at the new rehab facility in Charlestown where my sister works."

After we ordered, the small talk resumed, mostly Roberta nudging Marvin to tell us about himself.

"Marvin, tell them about your real estate consulting firm in New York."

"Marvin listens to smooth jazz. What are some of the artists' names, sweetie? Maybe they'd recognize them."

"My Marvin loves hiking the Appalachian Trail. Dear, tell them how many miles you hiked last time."

When Marvin refused to be the main topic of conversation, Griffin and I told Roberta about the morning talk show we'd taped and the work we'd completed on our book.

Roberta leaned her shoulder into Marvin. "Didn't I tell you Casey and Griffin were go-getters?"

Who is this woman and what has she done with Roberta?

Griffin excused himself right after our lunch plates were cleared. "Sorry, I told my wife I'd be home in time to help her with some things."

"What things?" I knew full well he was trying to leave me alone with these unlikely canoodlers.

Ignoring me, Griffin shook Marvin's hand and said to Roberta, "I hope your visit with your nephew goes well. Give him my best."

"Thanks," she said. "Maybe you both could come by to meet him one day. I'm sure Tommy would like that too."

"Sounds good." Griffin turned to me and said in a low voice, "I'll call you later so we can finish our talk."

Roberta used this break in the conversation to go to the ladies room, leaving me alone with her Marvin. He stood until she was out of sight then sat and slid his chair in close to the table. "Since Roberta Lee and I never had children of our own,

Ramona and Vincent's three mean the world to us. We were worried sick about Nick."

"Considering where he was and what he went through, it's understandable."

Sensing an awkward silence coming, I decided to dig for details on Roberta while I had her husband alone. I positioned my elbows on the table with my chin in my hands and started with her name. "So Roberta *Lee*, huh? Is Lee her middle or maiden name?"

"Middle. Her father was a Civil War buff, a rebel sympathizer actually."

"Ah, I did not know that. So her family was from the South?"

"Her father was born and bred in Virginia, but his wife was a Connecticut Yankee."

"And Roberta's sister, Ramona? Named after a lesser known Union general?"

"Not exactly." He chuckled. "My mother-in-law had the privilege of naming their second daughter. As an art history major—you know how they can be—Mrs. Erickson decided on Ramona Lisa."

Mrs. Erickson? My chin fell out of my hands about the time my elbows slipped off the table.

Ramona. Lisa. Erickson.

46

Worried my facial expression would trumpet my shock, I scrambled to regain my composure. "Ramona Lisa. What an unusual name."

Marvin narrowed his brows. "Oh, my, I may have broken one of Roberta Lee's cardinal rules: Never reveal family secrets. Be a dear, Casey, and forget we had this little conversation."

I choked on my good fortune. "What conversation?"

He smiled and winked then expounded on the rigors of his last Appalachian adventure. I endured the wait for Roberta's return from the restroom by planning a smooth exit, one that wouldn't arouse suspicion. I didn't know how much, if anything, she knew.

A minute after Roberta got back, I pretended to read the time on my phone. "Uh-oh, I'm late for a date with a friend." I stood up before she could ask with whom. "It was a pleasure, Marvin. Talk to you soon, Roberta."

A nightmarish Jack-in-the-Box melody played in my head as I walked to my car. Ramona Lisa Erickson Coletti, Ramona Lisa Erickson Coletti, Ramona Lisa Erickson Coletti. Pop goes the weasel. And the weasel was Tommy.

Did Tommy know? Sure he did. Why didn't he say something after we sent the note agreeing to meet him? How about Roberta? I would bet on it. This whole thing was too coincidental to be a coincidence. That would explain Mr. Coletti's behavior in the post office too.

I started the engine and turned the AC on high. A blast of hot, sticky air hit me in the face. I gasped for a clean breath. Lingering in the restaurant parking lot was not an option since Roberta and Marvin would see me. I entered traffic and drove, trying to find a place to park so I could think. Not an easy feat in Boston on a weekday. I kept driving.

Why was it hard to believe Tommy was Dad's son? Truth is I'd have been equally surprised if it had turned out to be Darin or Mike. Something in me figured I'd know him when we met. In spite of my cynical self, I had hoped to feel a connection. It wasn't supposed to be this way.

A FedEx truck pulled out in front of me on Boylston Street. I pulled into the parking space it left behind. This was news I didn't want to text. I called Sam. As I suspected, since he was in the middle of his conference I had to leave a message. "Sam, call me, please. It's important."

My calls to Griffin, Mom, and Vanessa went to voicemail too. If I'd been a conspiracy theorist, I would've built a strong case for myself. In reality, Griffin was on the road and Mom and Vanessa were still at work.

I tapped the steering wheel to the rhythm of my impatience. Had Tommy used Sam to wheedle himself into our lives? My insides twisted. The pictures in my mind taunted me. Tommy at Opening Day at Fenway, in the batting cages thwacking our troubles into the outfield, at the 9K run, at Griffin and Jillian's Memorial Day cookout and the Bruins game with Mike. When I recalled how I welcomed him into our home only a few days ago, I slammed my palms against the steering wheel.

I wanted to call him right then and there, but I didn't have his number. That made me madder. I spoke through clenched teeth. "Call me back, Sam. Please!"

Immediately my phone rang. It was Sam. "What's up, Case? Are you all right?"

"No, I'm not." Before he could ask, I hurried to say, "It's not physical."

"Is it the voices?"

"Voices?" It took a split-second for it to register. "No, Sam. And it's singular. I'm not hearing voices, just one voice."

"Did you go to the doctor?"

"Sam, this is not about that!" I wished I'd never told him. "It's about Tommy Coletti."

Sam's voice slowed. "Something happen to Tommy?"

"No, but something might. Turns out your so-called friend is my so-called half brother, Ramona Lisa Erickson Coletti's son."

"Huh? Lisa Erickson? Ramona Coletti?"

"They're one and the same." When I explained how I found out, Sam was as confused by Tommy's behavior as I was. He offered to call him.

"No, Sam. Let me have that pleasure myself."

"Go easy, now. There may be more to the story than you know."

"Like what? Sam, give me his number, okay? I just want to talk to him."

And catch him off his guard.

"Casey, let me ask you this, are you more upset that it's Tommy or that he knew first?"

"Please, Sam, his phone number."

"Answer me first."

I growled into the phone. "It's hard to say what I feel. One minute it's anger, then confusion, betrayal, even disappointment."

"Disappointment?"

I sighed. "The truth is I was almost looking forward to meeting this half brother of mine. I guess part of me thought when I met him it would feel right. But this doesn't."

I scribbled the number Sam gave me on the back of an envelope and made him promise not to give Tommy a heads-up. "I know how you cops can be."

"You're my wife. I wouldn't do that. Keep me posted."

"I will."

Before punching in his number, I held the phone against my heart and prayed he'd answer. He did.

"Hey, Casey. To what do I owe the pleasure?"

"I need to meet with you. Alone. Where are you?" I knew my manner was brusque, but I didn't care.

"Is something the matter? Is Sam all right?"

"Sam's fine. How soon can you meet?"

"Um, uh, I'm off in a half hour, but from here I'm heading over to Spaulding to visit Nick."

"Is that on First Street?" I asked.

"Yeah. We could meet in the lobby, if you want."

"Good. I'll see you then." I hung up before he could ask any more questions.

Genius move. Agreeing to meet at a location crawling with his relatives, some of whom would recognize me.

Griffin rang in seconds later. "Sorry, Case, watching Roberta and Marvin fawn over each other was more than I could take."

"You're gonna have to take a lot more than that. I know who he is."

"Who *who* is?"

"Our half brother." I told him about my conversation with Marvin.

"No way! You think he knows?"

"What do you think? I'll find out for certain when I see him this afternoon at Spaulding Rehab in Charlestown."

"Why there?"

"Long story. Don't suppose you want to meet us there?"

"Turn around and drive back into Boston?"

"It's either that or let me handle it on my own."

Griffin sighed. "Give me the street address."

47

I entered the expansive lobby of the sleek new rehabilitation facility built on the site of the old Charlestown Navy Yard. There were pockets of people milling about, some at the information desk, others on their way in or out. No one I knew.

A two-story, ocean-colored glass installation drew my eye. Sitting in front of it was an elderly lady hugging a purse on her lap. By the expression on her face, I doubted the glass art feature was much comfort to her.

A young man in a wheelchair, wearing a New England Patriots hat and aviator sunglasses, sat off to the side in the light of the full-length windows. Sound bites of the Red Sox broadcast echoed from his phone. The getaway day game in Detroit was underway.

I took a seat away from the traffic yet close enough to the young man so I could hear the commentator. With my eyes fixed on the entrance, my plan was to catch Tommy as soon as he came in and drag him away from here.

Since no one had any reason to expect me to be in this lobby, it was possible hiding in plain sight might work. I took a cue from the Tom-Cruise-in-*Top-Gun* patient in the wheelchair and put my sunglasses back on.

The young patient held his smartphone up and pleaded, "Come on, Kiku, don't let me down!"

Kiku? How had I missed this new addition to the Sox lineup? I cleared my throat and said, "Excuse me."

He looked in my direction and said, "What can I do you for?"

"I'm curious. Who's Kiku?"

He gave me a sheepish grin and pointed at his phone. "I believe anything that costs this much warrants a name. I chose Kiku. Too weird?"

Ha! I wished Griffin was here to witness this.

"Not to me." I smiled and lifted my bag. "Kiku, meet Hildegard."

He grinned. "Pleased to meet you, Hildegard."

Before Kiku and Hildegard could get acquainted, my phone rang. It was Roberta. I choked on a breath before I answered. "Hello."

"Casey. Forgot to tell you I spoke with one of my New York editor friends. They like the sound of your biography series. How soon can you get that proposal to me?"

"Um, can I get back to you on that?"

"Sure, but soon."

I wanted to know how much time I had before they showed up. "How was traffic going through town?"

"Don't know. We left only minutes ago. Send me that proposal."

Good. Tommy should be here before they arrived. I turned to the young man. "Any score yet?"

"Tied at two, bottom of the second inning."

"Who's on the mound for the Sox?" I scanned the sidewalk that led to the main entrance.

"Ulander. Flynn's catching. Shame about Hennessey."

"Yes, it is." Where the heck was Tommy?

"I want the Sox to win. I just don't want Ulander to push Hennessey out of a spot. Is that crazy?"

I smiled. "Not to me. You said what I've been thinking."

"So you like baseball, huh?"

"What's not to like?" I scanned the hallway and craned my neck to see outside.

He looked where I had looked. "Waiting or hiding from someone?"

Now this is the reason I didn't usually engage strangers. "Waiting."

"Me too. My brother."

Yeah, me too, I thought sarcastically. Since I wanted to keep this conversation superficial, I said nothing.

In a voice mimicking a convict from a prison flick, the young patient said, "He's bustin' me outta this joint for some fresh air."

He cocked his head in the direction of a pair of crutches leaning against the wall then turned down the corner of the cotton blanket on his lap to reveal his camo pants. "All dressed and ready for the harbor walk around the building. If I had my pole, I could fish off the rail."

"Good day for it."

"For sure. Hey, were you telling the truth?"

"The truth?" I squirmed in my chair. "About what?"

"Loving baseball."

I exhaled, releasing some tension. "No lie, I do."

"What's your take on Hennessey's condition?"

"The surgery is pretty straightforward. I have faith he'll be ready by next season."

"Mind if I piggyback on that faith? That kid's got a slider as slow and smooth as a southern drawl."

"Colorful way to put it." I placemarked that line to use in my next column.

"Signing the Irish Twins was the best move the Sox have made in years, for sure."

"Ditto." I fist-bumped him. Why? I never fist-bumped anyone.

We returned to the game. The Sox were at bat in the top of the fourth. The broadcaster announced, "Two outs, bases loaded with a three-two count on the batter." I moved a little closer.

My new fan friend cheered. "Put some wood on it! Bring 'em home!"

I leaned forward, listening for the bat to connect with the ball just as my cell phone chirped. I jumped and missed the play.

"He hit it outta the park!" The young man raised his hand for a high-five.

I slapped his hand then read my text. *Sorry. Running late. Tommy.*

Then it hit me. If Griffin was on his way here, my plan to leave with Tommy wouldn't work. *Sheesh.* All in all, one of my worst thought-out schemes.

Whoa! They're here already! Hand-in-hand, Roberta and Marvin walked toward the entrance.

48

Abandoning my plan to hide in plain sight, I sprang up and scanned the lobby for restroom signage then fast-walked my way to the women's room. I made it to the door a split second before Roberta entered the lobby. As an extra precaution, I hid in a stall. Then it occurred to me that I could miss Tommy if I stayed in there too long.

I needed to see if Roberta and Marvin were still in the lobby. When I cracked the door, Roberta, phone to her ear, passed by. I heard her say, "Marvin and I are here now. What room did you say Nicky was in? When are you and Vincent coming over?"

I waited another half minute before I re-entered the lobby. Scanning the perimeter, Roberta and Marvin were nowhere in sight.

I returned to my seat in the corner.

"Everything okay?" my fan friend asked.

"Could be better."

Was I complaining to this man in a wheelchair? I looked at him and said, "Sorry. I'm sure it's nothing compared to what you're going through."

"I'm okay. Injured myself in a freak accident at Camp Leatherneck in Afghanistan."

There was something familiar about his manner.

"Tommy calls me one lucky Marine."

Did I hear him right? "Did you say Tommy?"

"Yeah, my brother. The one I'm waiting for."

Somehow I knew this was no coincidence. "Is your name Nick?"

He lowered his head and peered through the narrow gap between his glasses and hat. "Yeah. How'd you know?"

"I didn't, but I know Tommy. He's the one I'm waiting for too."

Nick stretched his neck to see over my shoulder to the entrance. "Looks like we won't have to wait much longer."

Tommy waved on his way over. "Hey, have you two met?"

"Sort of," I said, resigning myself to the fact that I'd have to wait to confront him.

"All right! Now before I make good on my promise to get the patient some air, what did you want to see me about, Casey?"

Could this drama get any worse?

Nick adjusted his ball cap. "Your name is Casey?"

Tommy looked puzzled. "Thought you said you'd met."

Nick said, "Not formally."

Only our accessories had been introduced, but I hoped he'd keep that to himself.

"I can fix that. Casey Gallagher, meet my brother, Nick. Casey's husband Sam is the lieutenant on the state police force I wrote you about."

Before I could comment, Griffin sang out behind me. "Hail, hail, the gang's all here!"

Tommy slapped Griffin on the back. "What're you doing here, bro?"

Griffin chuckled. "Why, *bro*, joining my sister for the family reunion, of course." Turning to Nick, he said, "Ahh, now I know why we're here. You must be Nick. You look like the picture."

"Picture?" Tommy said.

Griffin said, "Dude, the one you showed us on Memorial Day."

To cut off Griffin's blabbermouthing, I sliced my hand across my throat when only he was looking. "May I speak with you for a moment, Griffin?"

He followed me a safe distance away before he said, "I take it this means you haven't talked to him yet."

"You showed up before I had a chance. Besides, his brother was here waiting."

"So whaddya gonna do now?" he asked.

"I'm not sure. Give me a second to think."

I glanced back at the brothers. Nick did a three-point turn in his wheelchair. He removed his hat and cut his hand back and forth across his flattop. His square jaw reminded me of Tommy's. He took his aviators off then folded them up and slipped them into his shirt pocket. He wheeled a few feet toward us, looked at Griffin, then back at me.

I took hold of Griffin's arm.

"You all right?" he said. "You've gone all pale on me."

I whispered, "There's something strange about Nick."

"Geez, Casey, the guy just returned from a war zone."

"I don't mean that. Look at him. Look at him closely."

Nick raised his chin a bit when Griffin looked in his direction.

"Now that you mention it, he sort of looks like me. Ruggedly handsome . . ." He stopped mid-sentence. Light grew in his eyes. "This might sound crazy, but his eyes remind me of Dad's."

"Midnight blue marbles splashing through an icy sea is how Mom used to put it." I took a few steps toward him, like I was walking on stilts, all crooked and off balance.

Nick rolled up his lap blanket and tossed it onto a chair. Was he going to stand?

Then I saw them. My throat constricted. It took some work to get my words out. "Hey, Marine, where'd you get those boots?"

He wheeled closer to us and extended one leg. The faded red heart and initials I'd drawn as a child came into full view.

His eyes were level and his voice steady. "My sister sent them to me. They were my father's. Hope you don't mind if I wear them."

49

I felt for a chair and sat down. Griffin plunked down near me. We stared at Nick and he stared back. After a silent pause that seemed to last forever, all three of us started to speak at once.

"Sorry. You go." I said.

Nick wheeled in closer. "No, you first, please."

"Are we arguing already?" Griffin said. "Guess we are siblings."

Dad's smile broke out on Nick's face. I wondered if the joy reflected in Griffin's eyes was his or mine. I suspected a little of both.

"You have Dad's eyes and his smile," I said.

Tommy stiffened, standing trooper-style. His tone was sharp when he addressed Griffin and me. "Why didn't you tell me you knew about Nick? Have you two been playing me all along? Was Sam in on this too?"

I'd almost forgotten he was there.

"Us?" I said. "Up until this moment, we had no idea the guy we were looking for was Nick."

"She's telling the truth," Griffin said. "I'm here because Casey told me our half brother was you."

Tommy poked his chest with his thumb. "Me?"

Nick reached out and touched his brother's arm. "Tommy, Mom didn't find the note and the box until late last night. She only brought it to me this morning. That's the first I heard about Casey and Griffin."

I looked down at the boots then back at him. "Now I get why we didn't hear back from you or your mother. You weren't home to get the mail."

Nick said, "My dad would've found your package sooner if my sister Ali hadn't stuck it in a closet during one of Aunt Bobbie's cleaning missions."

"Speaking of your aunt," I said, "how did Roberta and Marvin miss seeing you in the lobby?"

He put his hat and glasses back on. "You're not the only one who can hide."

As if the moment wasn't awkward enough, Vincent Coletti walked in with his wife—Ramona Lisa Erickson—making awkward an understatement. When they noticed us, they stopped and stared, first at us then at each other. He whispered to her and she took his arm before approaching.

She extended her hand to me then to Griffin. "Ramona Coletti, er, Lisa Erickson. I don't know whether Nick contacted you or if you found him, but either way, thank you both for coming."

Mr. Coletti looked a little embarrassed when he shook my hand. "I'm thankful, too, 'cause I'm not so good at keeping secrets."

It was hard to look at Lisa and imagine her with Dad. Just as he'd changed over the years, I suspected she wasn't the same woman either. I mumbled something unintelligible, while Griffin handled the clumsy moment with grace. "Thanks. Both of you. I've always wanted a brother."

They smiled at him like everyone does.

Mr. Coletti put his arm around Tommy. "Sorry to blindside you, son. We were going to tell you, but we thought Nick should be the first to learn who his other siblings were."

"Tommy," I said, "how much *did* you know?"

"Nick and I have always known he had a different biological father, but we had no idea who he was."

Something was still off. "Help me understand how you became a member at the same gym as Sam. First the police force then the gym. It seems like too much of a coincidence."

He rubbed the back of his neck. "I can't. That gym membership was a gift from—"

"Are you having a party without us?" Roberta and Marvin had re-entered the lobby. "Even Casey and Griffin are here! And your mother made me, your own aunt, wait two whole days to see you." Roberta leaned over to hug Nick. "How's the patient now that he's on terra firma? Marvin, doesn't Nicky look terrific?"

"Sure does!" Marvin shook Nick's hand.

Tommy's eyes locked on Roberta. "Aunt Bobbie. The gym membership was a gift from Aunt Bobbie."

Roberta spoke up. "So now it's a crime to give someone a gift?"

Tommy said, "I know how you work, Aunt Bobbie. There was more behind that gift. Spill."

Roberta threw her hands up. "Okay, so I got you the membership when I found out Casey's husband was a member. I needed a man on the inside. Besides, if I'd waited for the rest of you to figure it out, poor Nicky would still be waiting."

Tommy glowered at her. "Basically, you used me."

Roberta said. "Now, Tommy, used is a pretty strong word. Look at it this way, you paved the way for Nicky when you made friends with Sam and Casey and Griffin. It's a win-win for everyone."

One other thing bothered me. I asked Ramona Lisa about the second letter, the one that was typed and smelled like smoke.

"What second letter? I only wrote the one." She looked from me to her sister. "Roberta, was that your doing too?"

"So, you found me out," Roberta said. "But I wouldn't have had to write it if you'd kept me in the loop."

Ramona Lisa crossed her arms. "In the loop? We were in Germany!"

"I know," Roberta said. "That's why I stepped in to make Nicky's homecoming special."

"Aunt Bobbie," Nick interjected, "your infinite capacity to self-justify still amazes me."

Griffin said, "Roberta, did you know who Casey and I were before you became our agent?"

"Ramona Lisa is my little sister. Nicky's my nephew. I make it my business to know everything I need to know."

I was locked and loaded with Roberta in my sights. "Has our professional relationship been a cover all along?"

Roberta shook her head. "Absolutely not. I confess that may have been my initial idea, but you had talent, so it wasn't necessary."

"Think about it," Tommy said. "Aunt Bobbie would never have signed you if she wasn't convinced you'd make her some money one day."

"For sure," Nick said.

"No shame in admitting it," Roberta said. "I hope you'll forgive the subterfuge, but I needed to know what kind of people you two were before you met Nicky. I'm being sincere, Casey, when I say I wouldn't have stayed on as your agent unless I thought you had a future in the business."

It didn't take long for us to outstay our welcome in the serene lobby. Before someone asked us to leave, we retreated to the spacious cafeteria.

It helped when Ramona and Vincent insisted that Roberta and Marvin join them at a different table on the opposite end of the room.

The conversation between Tommy, Nick, Griffin, and me started out slow but picked up speed before too long. We meandered through multiple topics until we landed on our favorite, sports.

Nick said, "I'm a huge Sox fan, for sure. I even started a hot stove league in Afghanistan."

Tommy narrowed his eyes. "Hot stove league?"

Nick said, "That's what they call a bunch of baseball fans who get together in the off season to talk about the previous year."

Griffin said, "Like a bunch of Monday-morning quarterbacks."

"Yeah, sort of." Nick rubbed his chin. "You know what's kinda spooky? I often got my talking points from Double Header columns."

Griffin groaned. "Don't tell me you have talking points like Casey. Tell me it's not true."

I ignored Griffin and scowled at Nick. "By any chance, did dear Aunt Bobbie send you those columns?"

Nick shook his head. "Nope, I found them all by myself."

"Wow," Griffin said. "I didn't know the *Kandahar Clarion* ran our column."

Nick laughed. "Afraid not. Got 'em online."

I leaned forward. "Do you have an interest in writing, Nick?"

Nick shrugged. "I seem to gravitate toward it. Had a few pieces published in a sports report put out by *Military Times.* Nothing compared to you guys, though."

Tommy said, "Maybe that's why I felt at home with you two. It was like hanging out with Nick."

Griffin said, "Yeah, but what's our excuse for hanging out with you? Outside of Sam, our connection with you is Roberta."

"Being your agent and all, she's practically your family too." Tommy winked at his brother. "We'd be willing to share her on holidays, wouldn't we Nick?"

He grinned. "And weekends."

"Oh, no you don't," I said. "We'll claim Nick as one of our own, and we'll even let him drag you along, Tommy, but we draw the line at Roberta."

Nick's voice cracked. "You have no idea what it means to hear you say that."

I covered his hand with mine. "You're wrong, Nick. I do."

Griffin said, "Get used to it, Nick."

"Get used to what?" he asked.

"Being wrong." Griffin poked me. "Sister here never gives in."

In spite of Roberta's manipulation, my anger toward her

and everyone—including Dad—dissipated in the laughter between the four of us.

It was like Dad had figured out a way to give us another part of him. Or had God done that?

There was something else, something bigger. From the moment I'd approached Nick in the lobby, even before I knew he was my brother, I'd felt the connection I hoped to feel all along.

Here you go, Casey. Your sign.

50

Sam had been smart to accept Jillian's offer to host my thirtieth birthday party. Of course, I pretended to be surprised so as not to disappoint him. My only request for Jillian had been to keep the guest list short. When I arrived, only family and close friends were there to yell "Surprise!"

Jillian didn't have a smidgen of mean in her, so I knew there would be no over-the-hill cakes or Grim Reaper decorations. As party planner extraordinaire, she'd have a theme, but if I'd had to guess I would have guessed sports.

I would have been wrong again.

The theme was "Top 30." Guests had submitted their own top thirty lists, which Jillian transferred onto oversized scrapbooking pages and hung across the yard and house. I hugged and laughed my way around the yard as I read them: Sam's Top 30 Reasons I Married Casey, Griffin's Top 30 Ways to Make Casey Mad, and Vanessa's Top 30 Reasons Casey Needs My Advice. One of my favorites was hanging above the crib in the nursery: Top 30 Ways My Aunt Will Make Me Giggle.

A half hour into the party, Sam approached me with a

look of concern on his face. “Case, uh, Tommy’s here and I, um, it looks like someone’s in the car with him.”

“Didn’t he break up with Gina?”

“I thought he did.”

I think Sam was more relieved than I was when Tommy opened the door to help Nick out. We walked over to greet them.

“I hope you guys don’t mind,” Tommy said. “I sneaked Nick out of rehab for the celebration.”

“Mind?” I said. “Now all my favorite people will get to meet you!”

Nick hobbled on a foot and a crutch until Tommy got his wheelchair out of the trunk. “Are you sure? Tommy wouldn’t take no for an answer.”

“I’m sure. And since I’m the birthday girl, my wishes rule.”

Griffin joined us. “Haven’t you figured it out yet, Nick? Casey’s wishes always rule. It’s got nothing to do with her birthday.”

Sam shook Nick’s hand. “Sam Gallagher, Casey’s husband. Glad you could make it.”

“Good to finally meet you, Sam. My brother’s been bragging about you for months.”

We introduced Nick to the guests. I warned Vanessa about using her cross-examination tactics on him and begged my grandmother not to divulge anything too personal about me. Both of them ignored me. From what I could see, not one person gave Nick a reason to feel like an outsider.

Especially Mom, who hugged him and said, “Ned, your father . . . was a good man. If he had known about you, we would have welcomed you into our family much sooner.”

Nick and Tommy spent a good deal of time talking baseball with the Irish Twins. At one point Darin said, “You know the game, Nick. Maybe Casey and Griffin can draft you for their Double Header team.”

Tommy said, “Think about it, Nick. It’s not a bad idea. You wrote for that military paper, didn’t you?”

“Yes, but that was only a few times for fun.”

Griffin said, “What we do is fun, isn’t it, Casey?”

"Maybe for you. It's work for me." I fooled no one.

"I know," Griffin said. "We change the name from Double Header to Triple Play. Then Nick and I can divvy up your criticism and wisecracks."

"We'll talk," I said, contemplating how it would feel working with two brothers.

The menu was my favorite, a good old-fashioned New England clam bake, starting with homemade clam chowder. After the cups were cleared away, Jillian dropped off bowls of steamers while Mom distributed platters of potatoes, sausage, and corn on the cob. Everyone got their own lobster.

Settled in the place of honor with my utensils and plastic bib, I watched Nick field-stripping his lobster and Griffin dipping steamers in broth and butter then dropping them into his mouth. Since Mike's arm was still in a sling, Tess alternated between cutting up his food and taking bites of her own. Tommy deserted Nick for a seat near Elena. With one arm around her, he helped her crack a claw. Darin chatted with Vanessa and Bryson. About what—baseball, family, or God?—I didn't know.

Mom sat down beside me. "Having fun?"

"I am."

She looked over at Nick. "Dad would be pleased and proud."

"Think so?"

She saluted me with her decaf coffee. "I know so."

"Mom, I haven't had a chance to tell you. Remember when you told me to ask God for a sign?"

Her face brightened. "Yes?"

"I did. He gave me one I didn't expect."

"He's like that," she said. "Was it Nick?"

"Not Nick exactly. More what I sensed when we met. Peace and an inexplicable connection. Took me long enough, huh?"

She ran her hand down my cheek and under my chin, pausing there for a second. "God is love, Casey, and do you remember what love is? Love is patient, love is kind."

"I'm beginning to believe."

Keep believing, Casey.

About the Author

Clarice G. James loves to read and write contemporary and historical women's fiction. After many years of writing and editing for business and ministry, she now enjoys the freedom and fun of fiction. Clarice has been a follower of Jesus Christ for 35 years. She and her husband David live in Southern New Hampshire. Together they have five married children and ten grandchildren. *Double Header* is her first published novel. It won second place in the 2014 Jerry Jenkins Writers Guild Operation First Novel contest. Visit her website: www.claricejames.com

Discussion Questions
(Includes spoilers!)

1. Casey and her brother Griffin are close, yet they are so different. In what ways? Does one deal with life in a better way?

2. Why do you think the news that she has a half brother hit Casey harder than Griffin?

3. Casey's mother, Annie, forgave her husband, Ned, for the affair a long time ago. To what or to whom does she give the credit?

4. Do you think it's possible to mend a marriage after infidelity? Is it possible to make a marriage even better?

5. The theme running through this book is forgiveness. Is forgiveness something you struggle with?

6. What do you think of Casey and Griffin's literary agent, Roberta Herzog? Does she really care about them as clients or is she just using them?

7. Are you a planner like Casey? How do you react when something happens outside of your master plan?

8. Before she finds out about her half brother, Casey feels like her life is going just as she expected. Besides this revelation, what other changes happen in her life? What eventually draws her to God?

9. Are there times in your life when you have felt God's presence? Have you ever heard his voice? If not audibly, but in your mind or spirit? How did you react? If not, what do you think you'd do if you did?

10. Both Casey and her mother, Annie, sought a more personal relationship with God. They believed in God, but felt he was distant and unapproachable. Why do you think that is?

11. What would you have done differently if you'd been Casey? Would you have stayed at your job? Kept writing the column? Put writing the book aside?

12. Have you ever wondered if you could have a more personal, less religious, relationship with Jesus? Do you know how to go about that? Here are a few steps.

    - Confess that you've missed the mark (sinned) in your life. Everyone has.
    - Admit you need His Spirit to change you from the inside out.
    - Thank God for sending His son Jesus to die on the cross to pay the full price for all your sins—past, present and future.
    - Ask Jesus to be Lord over your life.

READY TO SHARE YOUR MESSAGE WITH THE WORLD?

Discover the secrets of powerful writing from Jerry B. Jenkins, author of the mega-bestselling *Left Behind* series, and learn to write a story with the potential to impact millions of lives.

If you'd like Jerry to be your virtual writing mentor starting today, just enter this link into your web browser:

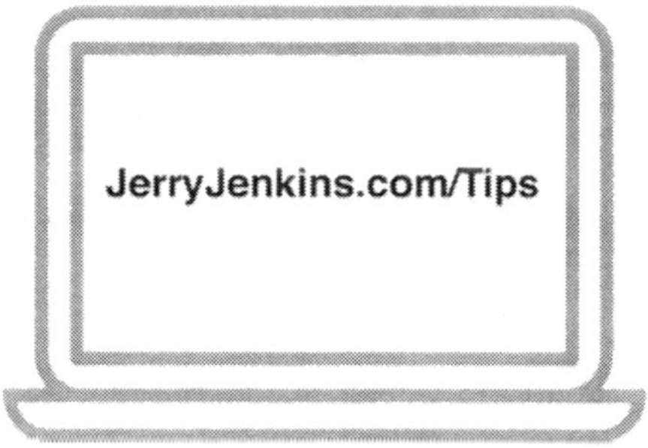

You'll instantly gain free access to Jerry's five things you *must* know if you want to write a book—as well as plenty more tips for aspiring authors.

Read the First Place winner of the Jerry Jenkins Writers Guild Operation First Novel contest

The Calling of Ella McFarland
By Linda Brooks Davis

Ella McFarland's dream is a teaching position at Worthington School for Girls. But scandal clouds her family name and may limit her to a life of grueling farm labor in the Indian Territory. Her fate lies in the hands of the Worthington board, and there happens to be one strikingly handsome man with a vote. Will they overlook the illegitimate son recently borne by her sister, Viola?

1905 brings hope of Oklahoma statehood and the woman's suffrage debate is raging, forcing Ella to make decisions about her faith, family, and aspirations. When she comes to the rescue of a young, abused sharecropper's daughter, her calling begins to take shape in ways she never imagined. Education is Ella's passion, but a new love is budding in her heart. Can she find God's will amidst the tumultuous storm that surrounds her?

Read the Third Place winner of the Jerry Jenkins Writers Guild Operation First Novel contest

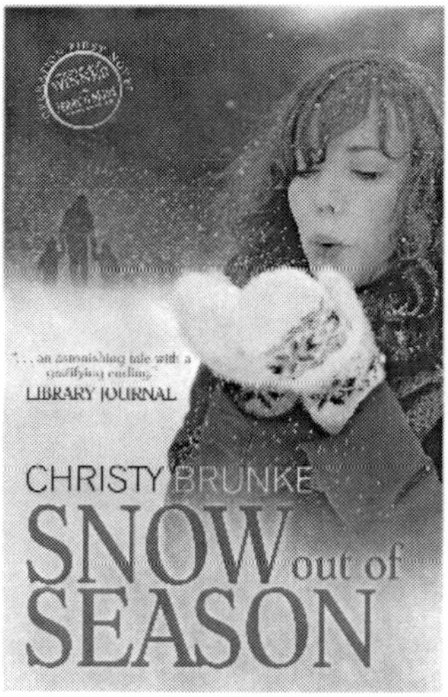

Snow Out of Season

By Christy Brunke

Two pregnant women separated by time . . . Are they more connected than they know?

Shannon Henry is just starting to put her life back together after the death of her infant daughter when she discovers she's pregnant again. Afraid of losing another child, at first she hides the news from her husband Wade. When her doctor presents her with the choice of either raising a child with Down Syndrome or terminating the pregnancy, Shannon is torn. Then things strangely start going missing—their wedding picture, a bracelet with charms for their three children, Wade's clothes on the floor which she's always complained about. And why is she having nightmares about losing her husband?

Leslie Gardner is a high-school senior in 1979 who dreams of becoming a professional ballerina, but she discovers she is pregnant too. If she has the child, her chances of a dancing career and college are over, but her friend shows her another option. If she secretly has an abortion like her boyfriend wants, her problems will be over and her life can go on as planned.

CPSIA information can be obtained
at www.ICGtesting.com
Printed in the USA
LVOW12s2010210316
480108LV00004B/211/P

9 781941 291245